1011531599
LP FOR
Ford, Leslie.
Double exposure / Leslie
Ford.
CACHE CREEK

D1791375

SPECIAL MESSAGE TO READERS

This book is published under the auspices of
THE ULVERSCROFT FOUNDATION
(registered charity No. 264873 UK)

Established in 1972 to provide funds for research, diagnosis and treatment of eye diseases. Examples of contributions made are: —

A new Children's Assessment Unit at Moorfield's Hospital, London.

•

Twin operating theatres at the Western Ophthalmic Hospital, London.

•

A Chair of Ophthalmology at the University of Leicester.

•

The establishment of a Royal Australian College of Ophthalmologists "Fellowship".

You can help further the work of the Foundation by making a donation or leaving a legacy. Every contribution, no matter how small, is received with gratitude. Please write for details to:

THE ULVERSCROFT FOUNDATION,
The Green, Bradgate Road, Anstey,
Leicester LE7 7FU, England.
Telephone: (0116) 236 4325

In Australia write to:
THE ULVERSCROFT FOUNDATION,
c/o The Royal Australian College of Ophthalmologists,
27, Commonwealth Street, Sydney,
N.S.W. 2010.

I've travelled the world twice over,
Met the famous: saints and sinners,
Poets and artists, kings and queens,
Old stars and hopeful beginners,
I've been where no-one's been before,
Learned secrets from writers and cooks
All with one library ticket
To the wonderful world of books.

© Janice James.

The wisdom of the ages
Is there for you and me,
The wisdom of the ages,
In your local library.

There's large print books
And talking books,
For those who cannot see,
The wisdom of the ages,
It's fantastic, and it's free.

Written by Sam Wood, aged 92

DOUBLE EXPOSURE

Identical twins Saskia and Anna Freeling have one great common ritual: their annual holiday together. One day, on the Caribbean island of Saint Theresa, Anna leaves Saskia sunbathing, wanders into the surf — and disappears. Two days later, Anna's business partner, Jilly, is found dead, and on her return to England Saskia determines to fathom the reasons behind both tragedies. Braving threats to her life, she begins to unpick a fabric of violence and deception. Startling truths come to light and, finally, she must confront the ultimate, unimaginable betrayal.

Books by Leslie Ford
Published by The House of Ulverscroft:

DIMINISHED RESPONSIBILITY

LESLIE FORD

DOUBLE EXPOSURE

Complete and Unabridged

ULVERSCROFT
Leicester
THOMPSON — NICOLA REGIONAL DISTRICT
LIBRARY SYSTEM
906 Laval Crescent
Kamloops, B.C.   V2C 5P5

First published in Great Britain in 1996 by
Headline Book Publishing
London

First Large Print Edition
published 1997
by arrangement with
Headline Book Publishing
a division of
Hodder Headline Plc
London

The right of Leslie Ford to be identified
as the author of this work has been asserted
by him in accordance with the
Copyright, Designs and Patents Act, 1988

Copyright © 1996 by Leslie Ford
All rights reserved

British Library CIP Data

Ford, Leslie
   Double exposure.—Large print ed.—
   Ulverscroft large print series: mystery
   1. Twins—Fiction 2. Drug traffic—Fiction
   3. Large type books 4. Thrillers
   I. Title
   823.9'14 [F]

ISBN 0-7089-3846-9

Published by
F. A. Thorpe (Publishing) Ltd.
Anstey, Leicestershire

Set by Words & Graphics Ltd.
Anstey, Leicestershire
Printed and bound in Great Britain by
T. J. International Ltd., Padstow, Cornwall

This book is printed on acid-free paper

1

THE tragedy happened so casually, so completely without warning.

My sister Anna lay next to me on the sand. I was immersed in my holiday paperback. The Caribbean sun caressed my bare shoulders as in the chilly, fictional Cotswold village, the heroine's husband announced that he was running off with the vicar's teenage daughter. When my sister murmured, "Off for a dip, Sassie," I have to confess I didn't even look up from my book. I remember a sense of her picking up her flippers and snorkel, hearing the slither of her feet in the soft sand. A short while later, there was a splash as Anna eased herself into the water.

Those sounds are still unbearably clear to me, years later. The scents remain vivid, too: sun-cream, sea-salt, the sweet smell of the half-drunk plastic cup of Coke Anna had lodged upright in the sand in her habitual neat way.

I dozed off very shortly afterwards. The chain-saw roar of a noisy speedboat brought me round after a few minutes. I opened my eyes, frowned, and glanced towards the vista of empty sea in time to see the offending boy-racer disappear round Emerald Point.

I got slowly to my feet, looked around.

There was hardly anyone there. Just two American kids who had needled Anna and me at breakfast. Typically, they were arguing in the surf. Barrages and counter-barrages of "No way!" and "Fuck you!" drifted up the beach towards me. Those teenagers were rich, good-looking, spoiled. They had nothing to be angry about, by most of the world's standards, but they were furious beyond belief. At nothing! I eased my Pentax from its bag and took a few shots of them, grotesquely squaring up to each other. Perfect for the 'Real Life' exhibition I had pencilled in at the Photographer's Gallery for the following winter.

Once I put my camera away again, my nerves started to go taut. At that point I was still merely irritated. Not frightened, just a little annoyed at Anna for changing her plan without telling me. Everyone else had gone up to the resort for lunch or a nap. It was, after all, terribly hot.

A few more minutes passed before the first wave of fear hit me, unexpectedly, like a sudden symptom of illness.

What I'm trying to describe — it's still difficult for me and painful even after all this time and with so much hard-won knowledge — is the realisation that there was absolutely no sign of the human being who had remained the one fixed point in my life since I tumbled out of our mother's womb thirty years ago, just minutes ahead of her.

Suddenly I knew I had lost Anna. My sister. My mirror-image. My identical twin.

In a panic I ran down to the surf and interrogated the brats. Sure, they'd seen Anna go into the water. Shortly after, they'd gone up to the refreshments shack to get a Coke, so what happened next — hey, who fucking knew?

My heart beating fast, I jogged quickly back up the beach, past our towels and belongings, to the resort office. There I sought out James Howell, the manager. An overweight public-school dropout, he was in the middle of his siesta, and he was not pleased to see me.

I blurted out something like: "My sister Anna's missing — that's Anna Freeling. I'm Saskia. She went for a swim . . . "

To do Howell justice, once he realised how upset I was, he became helpfulness and kindness itself. Within minutes, he had ordered the resort's outboard-powered dinghy to be launched. Even before it had started scouring the Bay, he was on the phone to the small coastguard-station ten miles away at Port-Choiseul, the island's capital.

I paced up and down the terrace, staring out over the blue, deceptively benign-looking waters. I was fast beginning to hate this place and everything about it. The sun, too. I resented that even more for making me so drowsy, so very careless.

The men in the outboard — locals familiar with this coast since childhood — did a wide circuit, then did it again. They found nothing and no one. By four, I could see from the way people were murmuring to each other and smiling at me with a chin-up, be-brave falseness that they had given up hope of finding Anna before nightfall, before the tide washed her in — if it ever did. I overheard someone discussing an American who had disappeared in a similar way a couple of seasons ago. They had found no identifiable remains.

By this time, oddly, my panic had given way to a sort of numbed efficiency. Like the sea, I was outwardly calm, despite my inner turmoil. With hindsight, I think I just couldn't accept that Anna might be dead. Maybe this accounted for my appearance of self-control which even then I knew some people found strange, or distasteful.

Certainly the immaculately uniformed Police Sergeant at Pitonville, the sleepy village next to the resort, squinted at me more than once to check my reactions as he took down the particulars later that afternoon. The way he did it, this was a very lengthy process.

"Please, the name of the disappeared

person?" he asked in his singsong creole accent. His voice was so soft that I strained to hear it above the hum of the cooler fan overhead.

"Anna Freeling."

"Date of birth?"

"Twentieth January, 1965."

He glanced at my passport, which he had demanded at the beginning of the interview.

"Same date of birth."

"We're twin sisters. Identical, actually."

The Sergeant nodded coldly. Caribbeans can be the friendliest people on earth, and they can — if they so choose — be magnificent in their hostility. This cop was definitely of the second school.

"So she go out for a swim here at Emerald Key, right?"

"Yes, Sergeant."

"You see her?"

I shook my head. "I was reading a book."

"So you didn't see her go in the water?" he pressed me, his eyes narrowing. "Not in the actual flesh."

"No, but other people did. She put on her flippers and she swam out quite a long way, they say. This would be nothing unusual — Anna's a very strong swimmer. At school she won — "

"I definitely speak to these people," the Sergeant cut in. "Where are they?"

"James Howell is outside — he's the manager from the resort," I said. "He talked to them. He'll be able to give you a list."

The Sergeant stared at me with one of those critical, searching looks I mentioned earlier. His phone rang. He picked it up in a stately, serious fashion, then launched into an animated stream of the creole *patois* that the locals speak when they are amongst themselves. He even laughed.

"Coastguard," he said simply after he had hung up, still with the tiniest remnant of a smile on his lips. My heart beat faster, although I tried not to get excited. "Found nothing still." Stony-faced again. "Now, you here on vacation, right?"

I put my head in my hands. My hopes had been raised, then dashed, with cold skill. I was starting to dislike this man, but as a photojournalist I had enough experience of the police's activities in picturesque little countries like this to know that you never, ever, let your irritation show. Especially if you had a white skin and they didn't.

"Vacation?" the Sergeant repeated with grim relish.

"Yes. Anna and I go away every year together, just the two of us. This year we chose Saint Theresa."

He seemed unimpressed by our preference. "She gotta husband?"

"No."

Big sigh. A note to that effect in the Sergeant's book.

"You gotta husband, madam?"

I hesitated. "Well, we're not actually married . . . "

He wrote something down. "OK, now we wait." He closed his notebook. "And all pray."

I could hold back no longer. "Do you think my sister has been drowned, Sergeant?"

"Madam, I a policeman, not a clairvoyant."

★ ★ ★

8

"You know, this happens maybe three times every tourist season, something like this," James Howell said afterwards, as he drove me back along the heavily pot-holed road that led to the resort. "Not that the Sergeant there, or any other government official, is going to admit it. And of course," he added hastily, "there have been cases where someone's been picked up safely by a fishing boat, or been carried along the coast by a current and found their way to an isolated — "

"But not many."

"I said, there have been cases."

"They certainly don't put any warnings about the dangers in the brochures!" I retorted, finding refuge in aggression as I fought back tears.

"They don't mention the muggings either," Howell murmured. He cursed under his breath, swerved slightly to avoid a chicken that had decided to hop off its roost atop one of the many rusting cars by the roadside. "Anyway, enough of this: a stiff rum for you when we get back. Then I'll fix you up with a folding bed in my office and we'll wait for a call from the searchers."

"The Sergeant advised us all to pray."

It was hard to keep the sarcasm out of my voice, but Howell didn't react as I expected.

"Seems about the most useful activity we could indulge in, actually," he said, his tanned, fat-schoolboy face set in solemn acceptance. Then he smiled nervously. "On the other hand, perhaps I've been on Saint Theresa too long."

We were bumping through the last village before the resort. The place was lush and beautiful, its brightly painted shacks almost swamped by torrents of bougainvillaea, but it was also obviously poor. That its inhabitants seemed more or less untouched by the tourist mini-boom of the past ten years was surprising only to those who don't understand the economics of Third-World tourism. Most of the visitors who came to this remote Cape were on 'all-inclusive' vacations, prepaid at the country of origin. A couple of restaurants had tried to make a go of it, but the package deals had killed them. Now even the resort staff were bussed in; Howell could take his pick from the sophisticated, educated citizens of Port-Choiseul, who knew how to make nervous First-Worlders feel unthreatened, and above all knew how to part them smoothly from their money. The locals who watched with listless resentment as Howell's ageing Range Rover passed them, grew and ate their own food. What little cash they had came either from fishing or from remittances sent by relatives in Brooklyn and Brixton.

A few minutes later, in the gathering dusk, we arrived at the entrance to the Emerald Key Estate. The two security men pulled up the barrier and waved us through. They both grinned; one even tipped his hat. We passed a few of the cheaper holiday cabins — just that little bit further from the beach — and then drew up outside the 'administrative centre'. This consisted of a neat bungalow where Howell lived, and a flat-roofed office annexe. He marched me in, sat me down on the sofa in the waiting room, poured me a neat rum, then went straight into his inner sanctum and picked up the phone.

When he emerged five minutes later, I

could tell immediately that the news was not good.

"No sign of your sister, I'm afraid," he said grimly. He looked outside; my eyes followed his. Darkness was descending in that sudden, final way it does in the tropics. "Not good," Howell added. "I mean, the loss of the light. Let's see, it's seven hours since you realised she was missing . . ."

Maybe it was the rum, but I was still feeling unnaturally calm. "I understand," I said. "There's not much hope."

Howell nodded reluctantly. "There's some — but as you say, not much." He rubbed his hands together, as if it were cold. "Listen, you've got the run of the phone. Anyone you want to ring?"

"I . . . I'll wait until the morning," I said. "I . . . can't . . ."

Suddenly, my self-possession disintegrated at last and the tears came. I put down my half-full glass and wept in great, aching sobs, for the cruelty of chance and for the sister who, for all our problems and fights, all our crises and betrayals, still felt like the closest human being in the world to me.

Oh God, I remember repeating to the wretched, embarrassed Howell. *Oh please God, I know I was only a few minutes older than her, but she was my little sister. I was responsible for her . . .*

2

NIGHTS such as the one that followed are conventionally described as 'the longest of one's life'. Well, mine passed quite quickly, in a blur of helpless pain and anxiety. I couldn't bear to go back to our bungalow, so I slept in the waiting room, with Howell asleep on the other side of the door that connected his residence with the office.

Shortly after midnight, the wind started to get up. The creepers covering the building shook and rustled, then began to claw at the waiting-room window like importunate ghosts. I lay on the folding bed in a state of terror. The few times I managed to fall asleep, I woke with a jerk, to imagine the telephone ringing with news. But it stayed silent the whole night. Then came another blank period, and finally a hand on my shoulder, shaking me . . .

It was Howell, barefooted, in shorts

and T-shirt, smiling blearily at me.

"I phoned the coastguard again. Still nothing, I'm afraid," he said. "I'll go and make some coffee."

I waited, shivering although the morning was already warm. There were birds screeching outside.

"Here you go," Howell said a few minutes later, handing me a mug of Nescafé. "As I said, please feel free to use the phone to call home — on the resort's tab, of course. Might be a good idea to alert your parents, whoever . . ."

"They're both dead," I said quickly, "but there is someone I should call — the man I live with."

James left me alone with the phone while he went off to check around the resort for wind-damage.

The international line was crackly, like in an old film. We've got so used to calling California or Australia or Tokyo from the UK, and people sounding as if they're in the next street. Phoning from Saint Theresa restored that feeling of a fragile physical link to the outside world — in this case an undersea cable dating from the 1930s.

At first I got Tony's recorded voice, honed by three years at RADA and a decade of more-or-less regular acting work: *Neither Anthony Patterson nor Saskia Freeling can come to the phone at the moment, but if —*

Then the receiver was picked up, and I heard the real voice of the man I loved.

"Hello? Tony here."

"Darling," I said, my heart beating fast. "It's me, Sass."

"Are you all right?" he asked quickly, before I could continue. "You sound . . . not yourself."

"I'm . . . I'm afraid something terrible's happened. To Anna."

"Oh Christ! What?"

"She went out for a swim yesterday afternoon and, well — she hasn't come back. Yet." My voice quivered.

"They've searched for her?" he asked concernedly.

"Yes. Coastguard. Local people."

"Are you all right?" he repeated.

I leaned forward onto my elbows on Howell's battered desk, easing the pressure in my tightening chest. "I'm coping." A beat. "Can you . . . I mean, do you think — "

"I'll be on the first plane out of Heathrow."

"Oh, if you can."

"Natch. I'll call the airline as soon as I get off the phone."

"Darling, if there's a problem about the money — "

"Don't worry. I got called in for a voice-over yesterday. John Hurt came down with 'flu. Big car ad."

"My travel agent can put it on my account."

"No, I'll charge it to Visa. By the time the bill comes in, I'll have been paid for yesterday's job."

"OK. Whatever," I said, then hesitated for a moment before continuing. "Listen, darling, before you leave, please ring Jilly Mattheson and warn her. Tell her that obviously we're still hoping."

Jilly was Anna's best friend and business partner. Together they ran a small accountancy practice concentrating on international and offshore business.

"Yes, of course. You're so brave, love." Tony paused. "Jesus, this is only just starting to sink in. *Anna . . .* "

"I need you here with me, darling. The manager is being marvellous, but he's not you. He doesn't really understand."

"No — how could he? Listen, I'll be on the first flight out," Tony repeated. "Just hold on till tomorrow. I love you, all right?"

I nodded, the foolish way you do on the phone, even though the other person can't see.

"Still there, Sass?"

"Yes. Oh Tony, I love you too."

Afterwards I sat with the cold remains of the coffee Howell had brought me earlier and stared out at the patch of lawn beyond the window. It was still breezy out there. Beds of exotic flowers rippled in the wind as if turned to water.

I have never felt more terribly alone. My only comfort was the knowledge that Tony would be here tomorrow. He possessed the sort of resourcefulness and physical courage I can't help wanting in a man, even while my liberated feminist side tells me I shouldn't. Oh, and he was very handy around the house; nothing Tony couldn't fix or build.

I've often tried to analyse this attachment to men like him, who can take such effortless care of the practical side of things. Perhaps it's because from an early age I've felt besieged by emotional responsibility.

Our mother, you see, died when Anna and I were six. One of those hidden, congenital heart defects that can kill suddenly in early middle age. I remember her in my mind's eye as a blur of fair hair, and I can still hear the distant echo of a voice, a clear, young woman's laugh. Old photographs show that we took after her in looks: fair, athletic, the sort of girls men like, even if they find them somewhat intimidating. Our father, an accountant, seemed to withdraw from us after her death in a way that pushed us back on each other even more than our accident of birth. We didn't understand it at the time. Of course, Daddy was simply paralysed by grief and loss, too weak from his emotional wounds to have anything left to give us. Every time he saw his blonde, blue-eyed daughters, he glimpsed our lost mother, the tennis-club queen who had to his surprise and delight consented to love him. I think that to Daddy, until the day of his death, we felt like nothing so much as a pair of noisy, all-too-concrete and demanding ghosts.

So, between the ages of seven and eleven, Anna and I were sent off to board at Hippley Hall, a perfectly nice and very traditional little boarding school in Buckinghamshire, where the teachers were stuffy but kind, and the other girls mostly as bewildered as we were.

All the same, it ended up being us against the world. At Hippley we were known as the 'Fiendish Freelings'. With me as the leader and Anna my helpmeet, we ruled the dormitory, largely through psychological terror. We were, I now realise, making others suffer for what we had to suffer. We were not physically cruel, but both of us, and me in particular, could be horribly, annihilatingly sarcastic. Girls would flinch even before I opened my mouth.

But school was a sideshow; it wasn't really important to us. During those years we really only came into our own — I almost said 'came alive' — in the holidays. Daddy, alone in the house in

Surrey, tried once to have us home when school was over. Even with a housekeeper it didn't work. We were simply too much for him, practically and emotionally. So, every holiday after that, we were packed off to his mother's place in south-west Cornwall, to Trerose, overlooking the Helford River.

To paradise. For two little orphans, a temporary Eden between school terms. A time of such closeness, such intensity, and such pleasure that I can still scarcely think about it without a lump coming to my throat.

To look at, Grandma Freeling's place was nothing particularly grand. Built to a simple timber-framed design in the 1920s, it looked more like a vacation home on Cape Cod than a classic Cornish house. Trerose's real glory consisted of its grounds — four acres of subtropical gardens luxuriating in a shallow, rocky chasm that sheltered its lush vegetation from the prevailing winds and enabled plants to thrive there that could rarely be grown in England, even in the mild climate of Cornwall. There were high Chusan palms, rare ferns, strange, pungent lilies, and great ten-foot-high clumps of Gunnerah, which they call Cornish rhubarb. At its heart in summer grew those huge, sinister-looking seed pods that resemble the mouths of some carnivorous plant on an alien planet.

This was our world. Mostly Grandma Freeling and Mrs Williams, her young housekeeper, looked after us. It was a place where Daddy felt able to visit while keeping his grief within sufficient bounds, which was as much as he could manage. Perhaps this was why, as a woman, I always depended on Tony so much. Where my father had been helplessly weak, Tony seemed to be effortlessly strong.

So at Trerose we were alone together, Anna and I — except for mealtimes with Grandma, and Daddy when he was there, plus little outings from time to time, usually to Grandma's elderly friends. Occasionally we would be invited to play with these people's own visiting grandchildren. We did our best to avoid this, but when forced to 'socialise' we terrorised and dominated much as we did at Hippley Hall, until the invitations dried up and we could be alone together again. Then we would return to building camps among the Gunnerah, scaring ourselves deliciously and telling long, long stories about mythical gods and goddesses; tall and strong mothers and fathers who would never weaken or sicken or die.

Looking back on those years, I can see now that the relationship that had developed between Anna and me was unhealthily exclusive. As identical twins, when one of us looked at the other, she seemed to see herself, even though we each of us knew that our sister must be another person. We played hide-and-seek among the hydrangeas, and when I found her or she found me, it was like discovering a moving, living mirror. We felt safe with that. We were not consciously happy or unhappy. The only clear thing was that we wanted nothing else but each other.

Then suddenly, our father married again. Paradise was not so much lost as changed; changed until only its appearance remained, while its heart had been sucked slowly out and devoured.

These were the memories that coursed

through my mind the night before Tony arrived.

Oh God, I thought, why had Anna and I kept up this stupid annual tradition of taking an exotic beach holiday together? I don't even like lazing around in the sun. Climbing in Nepal, travelling across America in an old Chevy pickup — those were the kind of things Tony and I enjoyed. Perhaps it was down to guilt. I had a man, and was acutely aware that my sister had no one. Ten days a year of lotus-eating boredom seemed a small sacrifice. But on the other hand, there was the possibility that Anna and I were driven to recreate in some temporary way those delicious summers at Trerose, to seek echoes of long-ago Cornwall in Bali, Skyros, Goa, and now — fatally — Saint Theresa.

That night as I lay sleepless again, longing for and yet dreading the dawn, I fancied that I found new understandings.

I was wrong. Absolutely, terrifyingly wrong.

3

LATE the following afternoon, near the end of another fruitless day of waiting, a phone enquiry to Miami confirmed that Tony had changed from a Jumbo onto the BWIA Saint Theresa shuttle. James Howell drove me to the airport near Port-Choiseul to meet him.

After checking that the hire-car he had booked for us was ready, Howell and I sat on a bench in the little terminal building, he chain-smoking cheroots, I sipping coffee from a flask I had brought with me. I still felt empty, hollow.

Soon came the grumble of aircraft engines, distant at first. We walked out into the open air and watched the ageing turbo-prop drop slowly from the sky, clear the tall palms at the seaward side of the airfield, and bump in to land.

The plane took another five minutes to taxi over to the passenger terminal. Tony was first out of the door and down the steps, clutching a fat carry-on bag, moving with his usual easy, athletic purpose. His clear blue eyes were already searching the tarmac, his square, even features set in a look of calm determination. Tony was always close to the top of the list when a casting-director needed someone who could do 'quiet man of action'.

Those parts of my heart that were functioning gave a tiny, hopeful leap. On impulse I ran forward, ignoring the waiting immigration officials, and hurled myself into Tony's arms.

"Oh darling," I kept repeating, looking up into the face I adored, scarcely able to believe the reality of his presence. "Thank God you've come!"

"Any news?"

I shook my head slowly.

"My poor love," Tony murmured, and held me even closer.

After a while we turned and walked slowly, hand-in-hand, to the terminal building. Tony passed quickly through the immigration formalities, and within minutes we were in the crowded, neon-bright arrivals lounge.

Howell made his way over, held out his hand. "Hi," he acknowledged Tony's presence. "Awful business. I'm James Howell."

"James has been marvellous," I murmured.

"Yes." Tony shook Howell's hand firmly. "Thanks so much for looking after Sass."

Even in my confused state I recognised that some obscure male ownership ritual was being enacted here in the sweltering arrivals area. In my usual state I would have been irritated. At that moment I felt grateful. Independence was the last thing on my mind.

So then I went into a kind of trance, led here and there while Howell and Tony sorted out the hire-car, stashed Tony's bag and made arrangements for driving in convoy back to the resort, since Tony didn't know the road.

I suddenly came to about halfway there, when I remember Tony saying, "How did Anna seem? Did she give any indication of . . . you know, depression?"

I shook my head.

"It doesn't make any sense," Tony

persisted. "Calm waters. And she was a really good swimmer, Sass."

"I know, I know. That's why I was still hoping . . . "

Tony drove on in silence, concentrating on keeping Howell's taillights in view. In repose his face was quite fierce; it revealed a dissatisfaction that chafed with his easygoing conversational manner. I liked that. It stopped him, I thought, from being bland, gave him a hidden emotional range. I suspect it was this sense of strange, inexplicable conflict that had drawn me to Tony so strongly from the first. Ninety-nine per cent safe, but with that little edge of danger. Perhaps that's what all women want from their men. I certainly did.

"To tell the truth, I think she was a bit down lately," Tony remarked after we had driven another couple of miles.

"Anna, you mean?"

"Yes. Just a feeling I had."

"All I can say is, while we've been here, she didn't seem in the slightest bit depressed." I shrugged. "She was flirting with some guy a few nights back at a barbecue."

"Yes?"

"I really thought she might take the plunge for once and have an affair. She didn't, but she seemed to be having a wonderful time."

I bit my lip at the memory of my sister's laughing face. Tony took one hand off the wheel and briefly touched my cheek.

"Right," he said, "forget it. Maybe it was just pressure. She'd been working hard, hadn't she?"

The next thing I remember is quite a bit later, when we were safely arrived and in my bungalow. Tony had unpacked and we had got into bed together. He was holding me, just holding me. We were both suddenly exhausted beyond all imagining.

"I spoke to Jilly Mattheson before I left," Tony mumbled. I could see he was dying to go to sleep, but it was just like him to want to cover everything first.

"Did you go and see her?"

"No time. I phoned."

"How did she take it?"

"Not too well. I mean, why should she? She and Anna were about as close as people can get without being family. I know I'd be gutted if someone rang me up and told me my best friend was missing, possibly . . . you know . . . "

"I'll ring Jilly myself tomorrow."

"Leave it for a few days, love."

"But I ought to!"

"Listen to me, Sass." Tony stroked my hair. "Forget 'ought' or 'should'. You've got to conserve your strength. Jilly said she planned to go to her parents' place in Somerset at the weekend. They'll look after her; she'll be OK."

I thought about it, then nodded. "I know you're right. George and Pam are real stalwarts."

"Salt of the earth," Tony yawned drowsily.

I lay for a while, watching the floating three-quarter moon through the window of the bungalow.

"I'm so glad I've got you, Tony," I said. "Otherwise I don't know how I could go on."

Tony didn't answer. From the slow rise and fall in his breathing, I realised he was well on his way to sleep. He had been in the air for almost twenty-four hours, and the twelve before that must have been tense and hectic. I stroked the cool skin of his chest.

Then the moon drifted behind a cloud, and the room went dark.

★ ★ ★

Tony got up before me. When I awoke I could hear him talking on the phone in the next room. He reappeared a couple of minutes later, already dressed in a Lacoste shirt and jeans and looking totally recharged.

"I've hired a boat," he announced. "A guy's going to take me along the coast a bit."

"What guy?" I said blearily.

Tony sat down on the bed. "There's a good boat-hire place in Port-Choiseul, apparently. It's important to *do* something," he told me. "I can't just sit here drinking rum-punches and waiting."

"I'm hearing a lot of first-person singular," I objected, beginning to wake up. "Let me come with you."

He leaned over, kissed me on the forehead. "You've had enough stress already, Sass."

"But I want to come."

"Sweetheart, I don't know what we'll find," he said gently.

"I still want to be there, whatever happens."

I hated the implications of what Tony had said, but knew he was doing the right thing by facing up to the worst.

"OK, love," Tony murmured. "If Anna was unlucky with the tide, that's tragic but fair enough. If some bastard . . . well . . ."

"At least we'll know the truth," I said, hoping I sounded more courageous than I felt. I had seen some bad things in my career, but they hadn't involved my own sister.

For answer Tony looked at his watch. "I ordered the boat for ten-thirty. Can you be ready by then?"

I nodded. "I think I'll bring my camera."

"That's the spirit," Tony said.

I didn't reply. I knew it wasn't. I was reaching for the device that was my emotional crutch of preference — and Anna's most hated enemy.

The capturer of the pinned-down moment. The all-seeing, all-recording lens.

4

OH yes, the camera. In our Garden of Eden, the camera was the apple. And, if that's true, then my stepmother must have been the serpent. Not that she was evil, or stupid, or even careless. She was ... well, just Maggie. The exact opposite of our natural mother, and to us a very unexpected choice by Daddy as his second wife and carer for his daughters.

The deputy headmistress of a local primary school, Maggie had met my father through a 'professional people's' dating service. We were just turned twelve and locked completely into the rituals and perspectives that made up our tight, close worlds of school and our holiday home at Trerose. To us, Daddy was like one of those minor figures in Ancient Greek mythology — flawed, even a little ridiculous, and very fallible, but a god nevertheless. He always seemed solemn, stiff, a little sad. Anna and I had never conceived of our father as a person with emotional and sexual needs; in short, as a fairly standard-issue sort of man. But he was. For years, I suspect, he had been in need of a good cheering up. And that is exactly what Maggie supplied.

The first intimation of the new order came at the start of the summer holidays that year. We had installed ourselves at Trerose but hadn't yet had time to settle in to our routine. Perhaps that was why Daddy and Grandma Freeling conspired to spring the surprise precisely then. Daddy, who had arrived a couple of days earlier and been if anything even more silent than usual, suddenly announced over breakfast that this afternoon he would be picking up someone from Truro Station, "Someone who has become precious to me, and whom I very much want you to meet."

I looked at Anna and she looked at me. We burst out laughing. Of course, this was actually more an expression of tension, even horror, than of hilarity. Whatever: it didn't amount to the right response, not by any stretch of the imagination. Daddy looked hurt, and a bit angry, and Grandma Freeling gave us a very beady look.

"I met your father's friend last month in London," she said. "She's very nice. Please remember that."

An unfortunate choice of words, but they summed up Grandma Freeling's mixed feelings about certain aspects of Maggie's personality. However, she had decided that Maggie would be good for her widowed son, and that was that. When it came to people, Grandma was an all-or-nothing sort of person. A hundred per cent or nought. No second prizes.

Everything then seemed to go normally until lunchtime. We had an hour outside after the meal, and then Mrs Williams came seeking us out among the undergrowth. We were to come inside, take showers, and change into something respectable. After some argument, this turned out to be clean shorts and T-shirts, with proper buckle-up sandals. Father inspected us before he drove off to Truro to meet the train. The next couple of hours, while we waited, were spent hanging around in the house. No garden, in case we got dirty again. Then we heard the car coming up the steep drive from the lane.

A couple of minutes later, the front door opened and my father ushered in a casually dressed bottle-blonde. Maggie must have been about forty then; six or seven years younger than Daddy. Attractive, with a warm smile. A great asset, that smile of hers.

"Hello, you two girls," she said, betraying a slight Scottish accent. "My name is Maggie Dobson and I'm very pleased to meet you. David's told me all about you — or all the bits he feels I should know!"

Again Anna and I exchanged looks, but this time we didn't giggle. Suddenly it was like school. We were the 'Fiendish Freelings' again.

Daddy glared at us, so we mumbled something which he seemed to find acceptable. Then he carried her bags through into the hall, including one large, canvas shoulder-bag with lots of zips and pockets, which he put down very carefully, as if he had been trained to do so.

"Thanks, darling," Maggie murmured. There was something about the way she used the word that was like a brand, an indelible claim. "It's great light this afternoon. Maybe I'll go out and take some pictures after tea."

"Of course," Daddy said without notable enthusiasm.

She turned back to us. "Photography is a passion of mine," she explained. "I have had exhibitions locally, in Hertfordshire." She pointed to the bag. "This is my camera bag. I go nowhere without it."

Despite ourselves, Anna and I crowded in on our father's new friend as she unzipped the shoulder-bag and took out an exquisite-looking little black device with a huge lens attached. I had never seen anything like it before.

"This is a Leica camera and it's extremely precious," she said. "I have others you can borrow, though. Do you girls like taking pictures?"

Anna solemnly shook her head. Maggie fixed her gaze on me. It was like a test, though of what I couldn't know. Taking my cue from Anna — rare that I did such a thing — I shook my head too.

But from the way Maggie smiled I could tell she knew I was lying to her and to myself out of loyalty to my sister.

"You can show me the garden while I snap," Maggie said, indicating both of us but looking at me.

Anna said nothing, but I found myself coming out with the words: "The garden's very pretty. Grandma always said someone should take pictures of it."

"Well, I will. So can you, if you like," Maggie suggested with a little trilling giggle. She patted the camera lovingly.

I laughed. And I nodded. It was my first, tiny betrayal of Anna. The beginning of adulthood.

★ ★ ★

I still had Maggie's shoulder-bag with me, the day Tony and I hired the boat to look for Anna. At the end of those school holidays, when I had already shot half-a-dozen rolls of film and was nagging Grandma to let me use the potting shed as a darkroom, Maggie gave the bag to me, along with her second-best Pentax. The Pentax got stolen on a photojournalist assignment in Rio five years ago, but the bag, very battered and somewhat torn, still went with me everywhere, like a talisman. It had carried on even as its original contents had disappeared. Considering some of the places I took it, I sometimes suspected it might outlive me. Even in my wildest fantasies, I never suspected it might outlive my sister . . .

Tony and I were puttering along, about a hundred yards offshore, heading south from Emerald Key towards the twin peaks above Port-Choiseul. The boatman, squaffing at the helm in front of the Yamaha outboard, was a laconic Saint Theresan by the name of Roland, which he pronounced in the local way as 'Roh-lon'. Saint Theresa had been settled for a century by the French, then became a British possession after the Napoleonic Wars. As a result, many of the locals had French names, often quite grand-sounding ones, borrowed from aristocratic slave-owners of centuries past. They communicated amongst themselves in a colourful dialect of creole. Fishermen like Roland tended to speak poor English, though I soon learned that they understood it well enough.

"Where does the current go?" Tony was asking him now.

Roland indicated north-to-south.

As I listened to their conversation, I was surveying the shore through the long-lens I had fitted to my new all-singing, all-dancing Ricoh. Tony had commandeered my binoculars, so the lens had to do, and it did quite well. I could make out steep cliffs rising from shore-level, a couple of small beaches.

"There are places she could have come ashore," I said, without taking my eye from the viewfinder. "There must be dozens, though I suppose the closer to Emerald Key, the more likely."

"Can you go in there?" Tony asked Roland, indicating the shore. "Could we land?"

"Risk," Roland answered simply.

"How much risk?"

Roland shrugged expressively, but without another word began to steer his modest craft in closer to the shore.

We ended up going all the way in, to a little beach about fifty or sixty feet long. Behind it was impenetrable vegetation, and behind that a steep, rocky cliff. I reckoned that the resort must be about a mile to the north-east of us, but it could have been a hundred, the place felt so remote.

The boat sat in the gently lapping surf, rocking with the waves. Roland, impassive as ever, peered around with some curiosity. It looked as if he had never been here before. We left him in the boat and waded the last few yards ashore.

Once we reached the dry sand, Tony looked at me intently. "There's always funny stuff going on in these little island paradises," he said, "with someone high up taking a cut. What if Anna stumbled on a smuggling operation?"

I looked at the innocent white sand, the virgin forest, and shivered a little. A couple of minutes later we got back on the boat.

We didn't get out at the next little cove. Or the next. Or the one after that. But we worked our way along, and at the fifth, Tony grabbed my arm.

"Look!"

I looked. "What?"

"Something on the sand."

Once more Roland took us into shore. We padded up the beach. There, up against the rocks, something big and plasticky-red was wedged. Tony headed for it. I followed him.

"Was Anna wearing flippers when she went off for that swim?" Tony asked quietly. He picked up the item of jetsam and held it out to me.

I nodded. "Yes," I said shakily. "She'd really got into snorkelling this holiday." I took a deep breath. "That looks like one of the pair she bought in Goa two years ago."

I examined the flipper more closely. Its rubber was a little worn, and the branding was faint, but I could still make out the sea-horse stamp that the Indian manufacturer had printed on the ankle-strap.

"Pretty sure," I whispered. "Certain, in fact."

We embraced there, me still holding the flipper in one hand, and I wept with mingled anguish and relief.

★ ★ ★

When we got back to Pitonville a couple of hours later, we made another visit to the po-faced Police Sergeant. Of course, as we realised after our initial wave of hope, the recovery of Anna's flipper meant very little. She might have been on the beach at some point, or she might have lost it at sea — which was perhaps why she had got into difficulties. However, the Sergeant wrote it all down in his file, and in his dour way, he also checked up on Tony.

"You say you an actor in London?"

"Yes."

"On television, right?"

"Yes."

"Never heard of you."

"I suppose I'm not that famous." Tony was keeping pleasant and polite.

"No," the policeman agreed with a faint smile. "So, you went round the coast a bit, right?"

"I wanted to see where Anna had been." Tony corrected himself. "*We* wanted to see — Miss Freeling and myself, that is." He paused. "Sergeant, will you be informing your superiors of this incident?"

The policeman shuffled the papers on his desk. "I send a report to Port-Choiseul," he said stonily. "Drownings happen everywhere people swim in the sea — specially where they don't know the waters."

"If it *was* a drowning," Tony said.

"And what do you think, Mr Patterson?"

"I don't know. But we want to be sure that Anna's disappearance is properly investigated."

I noticed how carefully Tony kept referring to 'the incident' and 'the disappearance', avoiding the word 'death'. I knew it was silly; every hour that passed made it more likely that we would never see Anna alive again. All the same, I was touched by his efforts to let me down gently.

"You think there were suspicious circumstances?" the Sergeant queried, reopening his notebook.

"Anna was a strong swimmer."

"Strong swimmers take more risks," the Sergeant commented shrewdly. He was no fool. "Plus, what's this got to do with suspicion? Please tell me what you think happened."

"What if she stumbled on some drug-smugglers?" Tony said.

The Sergeant's eyes narrowed. "No drug problem on this island. Try Jamaica. Try Bahamas." He closed his notebook firmly. "Thank you, Mr Patterson and Miss Freeling. We contact you if we find out anything. How long you intend to stay here on Saint Theresa?"

"I — I . . . until we find out what happened to Anna," I stammered.

"Could take time, madam. But of course, is up to you."

Outside in the street, we found that someone had stolen the windscreen wipers from the car.

"Rainy season can't be far off," I said in a pathetic attempt at humour.

Tony gave me a ghost of a smile, unlocked the door and started up the engine.

He drove back to the resort, dodging the pot-holes, chickens and children expertly. As we approached the bungalows, we saw Howell standing talking to two Saint Theresans in expensive leisurewear and shades. Government officials? He looked strained. We slowed down. Howell glanced away from his conversation for long enough to acknowledge us with a wan little wave. As he did so, he shook his head meaningfully. *No news*, that gesture clearly said. We carried on and parked by the bungalow that I still thought of as mine and Anna's.

"I'm starving — going over to the bar to get a sandwich," Tony announced. "How about you?"

I shook my head. "I'll just have a lie-down for ten minutes. You could bring me something back."

I must have fallen asleep, for I had no idea how much later it was when Tony came back.

"Got talking to this American," he told me. "Plenty of drugs coming in and out, the guy reckoned. Apparently the government and the police here are hand-in-glove with the cocaine barons. He'd read an article somewhere about it. Plus there's some cigarette and booze-running from the French islands, where taxes are lower, but that's not the kind of big-money operation you'd kill to protect, is it?"

For the first time Tony had mentioned death and Anna in the same context. I was still lying on the bed. Tony came over and sat down heavily beside me. He looked miserable, defeated.

"Hard to know where to go from here, isn't it? I mean, really hard."

"Yes."

"Want to know what I think?" Tony continued. "I think it was an accident. But if something shady really did happen to Anna, the powers-that-be here will make bloody sure we never find out what it was."

"Perhaps you're right, but I can't go yet while there's still hope." I paused. "Would you hold me, Tony?"

We cuddled and lay entwined for some while. The room was silent except for our breathing. It was like a meditation of closeness and warmth.

"Go or stay, we're doing it together, right?" Tony murmured at last. "If you want to stick around, Sass, I'll stick around too. I can't leave you alone."

He took my head between his hands

and kissed me on the forehead. Then on the lips.

At that precise moment there was a loud knock on the door.

Tony ruffled my hair affectionately, then headed through to the lounge and opened the door. Thinking it might be someone with news, I quickly got up and followed. In fact, our visitors were the two well-dressed Saint Theresans we had seen talking to Howell earlier that afternoon. I had assumed they were long gone back to Port-Choiseul or wherever they came from.

"Mr Howell told us you were taking a lie-down, while Mr Patterson was chatting in the bar," said the taller one of the two. He had a neat little goatee beard and gorgeous teeth. The look was Marvin Gaye on a good day, circa 1979. "So . . . we thought we take a look round first, then drop by and see you."

"Excuse me, who are you?" Tony asked.

The man smiled and flashed an ID card, complete with photo and official-looking stamp.

"My colleague and I, we're from the

CID," he said, all the time looking past Tony towards me. "Checking out the circumstances concerning the death of Miss Anna Freeling, this lady's sister."

"No body's been found," I said angrily. "How do we know she's dead?"

The man shrugged. "Mind if we come in?" he said politely, but the message from his body-language was, *Lady, we're coming in anyway, so why not be easy on yourself?*

I nodded to Tony, who moved aside. They were scrupulously polite in their dealings once they were inside the bungalow. The trouble was, their dealings consisted of searching all of our belongings, Anna's included, plus the mattresses and spare cupboards.

"Been talk of drugs, I hear from our colleague in Pitonville," the junior CID man explained earnestly as he squeezed the toothpaste out of the tube in Anna's vanity bag. "Gotta check, make sure absolutely no question of that kind of thing."

"I never said *Anna* had drugs," Tony muttered.

"Ah, you can never tell with people,

no matter how well you think you know them." The CID man tasted the pad in Anna's powder compact just to be sure. "Good island people go off to New York or Miami, they come back with crack, heroin, stuff like that. They changed. You can never tell."

And when the farce was over — for farce I knew it to be — we got down to business.

"Place looks clean," goatee announced finally.

I relaxed a little. If Tony's suspicions about cooperation between police and drug-smugglers were justified, I wouldn't have put it past them to plant something illicit on us. No, I decided, these guys weren't here to persecute us, just to speed us on our way. Goatee's next statement acted as confirmation.

"Well, as you know these things happen," he said, exactly echoing the Station Sergeant at Pitonville. It was the island line on beach casualties, evidently. "Even on dry land, tragedies occur." He shrugged. "In the midst of life . . . You set out to drive to town, then — " He smacked his right fist gently against his left palm, "Accident! You are gone, and your family must grieve."

"They might also want an explanation," Tony put in drily. "Your family, that is."

"Of course — only natural. You know, I really am sorry, but maybe we never find a body. Strong tides, sea creatures . . . Best to accept things as they are."

"So this is where your investigation ends?" I said.

"Investigation? Ma'am, this is not an investigation. As I said, we are checking, is all, as a result of statements you made to the Station Sergeant at Pitonville. To make sure there's no funny stuff about drugs. You see, we care about the people who come as guests to our island. We don't want any misunderstandings." He fixed me with a guilelessly appealing look. "So, when they go home, visitors can't say we didn't do the right thing or give them sufficient attention."

"OK, so you've checked," Tony said. "Do you propose to do any more *checking*?"

Goatee shook his head. "Case closed, I would say, Mr Patterson. You and Miss

Freeling go home and do your mourning. Among your family and friends, like we all need to do when tragedy strikes."

★ ★ ★

I'm not sure what time during the night the phone rang. I remember sitting bolt upright in bed and realising that Tony was no longer beside me. Then the ringing stopped. He had gone through into the living room and picked up the receiver.

I had drunk a couple of stiff rum-and-Cokes before turning in the previous night, so my head was still a little muzzy. All the same, I switched on the bedside light, did my best to concentrate, and found I could pick up most of Tony's end of the conversation. I felt like a little girl eavesdropping on the grown-ups when she was supposed to be asleep.

Tony said: "Oh Christ. No . . . this morning? I . . . I don't know what to say. Well, yes, Jilly did seem extremely upset when I told her about Anna's disappearance, but she always struck me as being so strong . . . "

The rest of the call was quiet, monosyllabic answers and only one question, which came right at the end.

"How's Mrs Mattheson taking it? Right. I understand. We'll be thinking of you both." He sighed. I heard the phone click back into its cradle.

Tony padded slowly back into the bedroom. Framed in the doorway, his shoulders were hunched. He looked crushed, distraught. For the first time since his arrival here he seemed helpless, truly at a loss as to what to say or do.

"What is it?" I asked fearfully. "I heard you mention Mrs Mattheson. Did you mean Jilly's mother? Was that Jilly's father on the phone?"

He came over to me, sat down hard on the bed as if he'd been hit, then held my hand for a while in silence.

"What's wrong, Tony?" I murmured eventually.

"She . . . " He struggled to get the words out. "Jilly was due to arrive at her parents' yesterday evening. She was very late. Some time after midnight a policeman appeared at the door. Apparently Jilly set off to drive down to Somerset in mid-afternoon, via the motorway. We know this because she rang her father immediately before leaving. But then she obviously made a detour, because . . . "

"Yes?"

Tony's voice became a whisper. "Jilly's body was found at the bottom of the Avon Gorge. Seems like sometime after dark, she'd parked on the Downs at Clifton, took a walk . . . and jumped off the Suspension Bridge."

5

USUALLY, in the past, I was always glad to come home to London. No matter what was happening in my life there, no matter the weather. To experience that long, controlled drop from 35,000 feet in cloudless weather, following the Thames westwards, spotting the bridges and buildings, trying to make out the different districts, gave me almost childlike pleasure.

This November day, though, the unseasonal sunshine, lending pin-sharp clarity to the London panorama below me, did nothing to lift my leaden spirits. Ten days had passed since Anna had disappeared, a week since Jilly's death. The worst time of my life, which only Tony's unflagging support had enabled me to survive with my emotional health halfway intact. I was returning from Saint Theresa with my sister not even found, let alone mourned. My heart weighed heavy with sadness and unfinished business.

I nudged Tony in the ribs. He stirred, rubbed his eyes.

"We'll be landing in ten minutes or so," I said.

"What's the time?" he mumbled.

"Eight-ten."

We had taken the villa-owners' charter special, flying overnight. It was all we could get at such short notice, after we had decided to try to make it to Jilly's funeral. We had just about enough time to nip back to Kensington, drop off our stuff, then drive down to Somerset for the service. Whether we had enough energy was another matter, but I just knew we had to be there. We owed it to Jilly's family. And there was my own urge to make some sense of this tragic mess.

"Looks like a nice day," Tony said, without enthusiasm.

"Yes."

"Bet it'll be cold, though . . ."

Now we were over the terraced rooftops of Staines, scudding in. The airport perimeter fence came up fast. As Tony spoke, the undercarriage of the 737 touched the ground, we bounced very gently and then the brakes went on. His following words were lost in their comforting squeal.

"I didn't hear you!" I had to say loudly.

Tony shook his head. "It's OK. I was just bitching. I won't bore you by repeating myself."

I took his hand and gave it a squeeze. "Oh darling, bitch all you like. God knows, you've put yourself out for me this last week. I'll never forget it."

"Nah. After what's happened to Anna and Jilly, it all seems trivial, doesn't it?"

Yes, I suppose it did.

We got through immigration on schedule, picked up my Jeep from the long-term parking lot where Anna and I had left it at the beginning of our holiday, and were in Kensington by just after ten. As usual, finding a parking space within walking distance of the flat seemed to take longer than the drive from the airport.

I had owned the pretty basement flat in Kensington Church Street for eight years; Daddy died when I was twenty-two and just a year out of art college. My part of his estate — which I shared with Anna and Maggie — was just enough to put down a decent deposit and minimise my mortgage commitments, so that I ended up paying about the same as I would have for a rented place in a much less nice part of town. This was just before the Lawson property bonanza really got going. Within a couple of years, two things had taken off — my career as a photographer and the price of property in London. By the end of the 1980s, I was earning six figures, and my humble flat was worth three times what I had paid for it.

Even when the boom went bust at the beginning of the 1990s it didn't affect me. In fact, I benefited from the recession: the flat upstairs, unaffordable just a short time earlier, became available at a bargain price. I bought it, knocked through the ceiling and put in an ornate spiral staircase, turning my little burrow into a somewhat posher and roomier duplex maisonette. Of course, meeting Tony on a commercial shoot had a lot to do with the expansion. Once we started living together, we needed the space. I put up the finances, and he did the conversion. Our deal. And that's pretty much how we had been living for the last three years. Me earning most of the money, Tony being a sweet, sexy, talented man who when he wasn't working seemed more than happy to support me in my career.

When we arrived back from Saint Theresa, Tony and I dumped our stuff in the bedroom, then he rang through and booked a room at the pub near Jilly's parents' place. We showered, changed into our sober suits, and were out of there again inside an hour. It was a Wednesday. Fortunately, the motorway was clear and it took us just a couple of hours to reach the village on the edge of Exmoor where the funeral was due to take place. I knew the church; we had all been here for Jilly's sister's wedding the year before.

We made it to the service with a few minutes to spare, slipping in at the back. Obviously, a funeral is very different from a wedding, particularly one that takes place under circumstances such as these. Luckily the village had a nice New Age vicar who didn't think of suicide as a sin (he didn't consider marriage a particular virtue either, I seem to recall). There were merely a couple of references to 'very difficult burdens' and the fact that 'we all make choices; and sometimes we make the biggest one of all — the one only God really understands'. Then it was out to the churchyard for the burial in the family plot.

The weather in Somerset was altogether fresher than London's. In fact, as we trooped out it felt downright threatening. The wind seemed to be picking up towards gale force. At the graveside most people were concentrating on keeping hold of their hats.

I, however, took in two things as I stood there. First, up on the wooded hillside above the church, the sunlight was reflecting off some kind of small, polished surface — a mirror or a lens. Second, before I even had time to think about that properly, I found my attention drawn to a very tall, striking young woman in a black leather jacket and jeans who had emerged from the church just behind us.

The leather-clad girl was crop-headed, like a penitent. She walked proudly, looking to neither side of her. And her skin was black too.

"I wonder who she is?" I whispered to Tony.

He shrugged. "A client?"

"I'd like to know."

"Shush."

As the vicar tossed back his long fair hair and began an enthusiastic rendering of the 'Dust to dust, ashes to ashes' speech, I caught the eye of the black girl, who was holding back slightly from the crowd. She was absolutely impassive, but all the more obviously sad for that. She looked at me for a long moment, shook her head briefly, then returned her attention to the burial.

After the coffin had been lowered, flowers thrown into the grave, and commiserations exchanged with Jilly's parents and family, people started to drift away. The young woman in the leather jacket didn't budge. She neither came closer nor made any attempt to leave. I wanted to say something to her, but Tony was nudging me.

"Come on. We'd better go and have a word with George and Pam," he said.

I nodded. "Just a quick one. I'm sure we'll be going back to the house."

With one final glance in the black girl's direction, I allowed myself to be guided over to where the parents were standing. I thought that George, Jilly's father, looked in dreadful shape — puffy and sallow-faced, as if sickening for some terrible illness. His wife's well-bred features were gaunt and pale, but in some subtle way she exuded a kind of strength, a raw dignity. Perhaps she had already done the worst of her grieving, had fallen apart so thoroughly over the previous few days that she could start to put herself together again, for the sake of Jilly's sister, and their baby grandson. The four of us stood there awkwardly, the women holding on to their hats in the wind.

"Hello, Saskia," Pam murmured. We embraced. "So good of you to come back for Jilly." She paused. "No definite news?"

"None, but . . . things don't look good."

"Our thoughts will be with you," Pam said, and I didn't doubt that they would.

George and I had a hug then. He said he didn't understand, just didn't understand. Then he patted my arm, braced his shoulders, and asked us back to the house for a drink.

I accepted the invitation, knowing they would be horribly offended if we didn't. I looked around. No glint on the hillside any more. And the black girl had gone.

She wasn't at the house either, as it turned out. I spoke to Jilly's brother, Peter, who worked in the city, but felt it would be inappropriate to ask about her — gossipy, sort of, a piece of trivial exotica-spotting, though I ached to do so. Instead I made a mental note to contact him when we all got back to London, to find out if he knew who she was.

During the post-funeral drinks, my exhaustion from the last few days and the long flight began to catch up with me. I recall a lot of quiet talk and some tears; everyone sort of skirting around the issue of Jilly's death. It was as if she had been carried off by some sudden illness, which I suppose is one way of viewing suicide. In fact, most of the time people commiserated with me about Anna. Again, what nobody mentioned was the fact that the two things might be connected — that the news about Anna might well have tipped Jilly over the emotional edge.

Englishness. Intolerable a lot of the time, but under certain circumstances a mercy. Tony and I left at about seven and headed for the pub, which was a couple of miles away.

The place was charming without being too tarted-up. We parked among ancient Landrovers, rusting Metros, a Skoda or two. The only car that came close to matching my two-year-old Suzuki 4X4 was a nearly-new blue Ford saloon next to the entrance, with car-phone aerials and a big road atlas on the back parcel-shelf.

"At least we won't be alone among the yokels," Tony muttered.

We announced ourselves to the landlord, changed our clothes in a chilly little room under the eaves and went back down to the bar. As the car park had indicated, it was full of locals, this being neither the weekend nor the holidays, when the urban middle classes come down to take occupation of their nice little country cottages. The exceptions were a couple of youngish men in city casuals at a corner table. They stuck out like sore thumbs. I guessed the gleaming, executive-model Ford belonged to them.

The only free seats were at the bar, so that was where we installed ourselves. Tony ordered a pint of real ale for himself and a gin and tonic for me. We glanced at the bar snacks menu. I also glanced at the two men in the corner, deep in conversation. One of them was actually rather good-looking, fair-haired with intelligent, humorous features and a tiny dimple in his chin. I love dimpled chins. Tony and I had this long-running joke: the first starring part he got in Hollywood, he'd be off to the best plastic surgeon in Beverly Hills to 'get a dent'.

"You're doing a lot of staring," Tony said.

"I'm curious."

"Well, get curious about this menu, because they stop serving hot nosh at half-past eight."

"Half-past *eight*?"

Tony snorted. "Where do you think

you are? Le Caprice? This is the country, darling."

"All right. I wonder what the soup of the day is?"

"Minestrone."

"Where does it say that?"

"It's always minestrone in these places."

"You're feeling militantly urban tonight, right?"

"I always do."

It was true. London born and bred, Tony had studied drama there, always lived there. To him the country was not so much a place as a location. A film location.

I enquired about the soup and found out Tony was dead right. I ordered a Cumberland sausage and a hunk of garlic bread.

We had our bite to eat and finished our drinks. Out of the corner of my eye I saw the good-looking man with the dimple come to the bar with two empty beer-mugs and clunk them expectantly down on the counter.

"Same again," he said in a gentle but very definite London accent.

"Fish biting today, were they?" the

landlord asked cheerfully as he pulled the pints.

"So-so."

The man's voice was guarded, even slightly hostile. He might be nice-looking, I thought, but he definitely wasn't my type.

"Chilly, sitting by that river bank all day."

"Too true." Getting him to talk must have been like pulling teeth. "That'll be three pounds seventy," said Mine Host with a sigh.

All this I heard rather than saw; I was sat with my back half-turned. But at that moment I decided to go to the ladies' and got to my feet. The man had his wallet on the counter and was looking for folding money. As he flicked it open, just for a second I saw, clear as day, a Police ID card. Metropolitan Force. I'd spent a couple of days on patrol with the Met boys once, for a colour supplement assignment, so I knew what one looked like. Then the moment was gone; the fisherman had found his ten-pound note and was handing it over to the landlord. He didn't look at me at any point. I hope

I don't sound vain if I say that was in itself a bit suspicious. I'm blonde, five-ten, and generally considered attractive. I almost always get at least a sidelong glance. Even gay men usually sneak a look, because of my height, perhaps to check if I'm a particularly convincing transvestite.

When I got back after visiting the loo I said to Tony: "See those guys in the corner?"

"Yes."

"They're police. Met, I think. Or at least the nice-looking one is."

"Even cops go fishing, darling."

"For what?"

"Fish. Sometimes, anyway." Tony yawned. "I'm totally wiped, my love. Come on, let's turn in."

★ ★ ★

It was the first night for over a week that I slept soundly and didn't dream about either Anna or Jilly. The cathartic power of the funeral ritual? It was as if I had buried the two women together.

We had a quick breakfast the next

morning, took the most direct route to Taunton and got onto the M4 around ten. Feeling refreshed, I had decided to do the drive. Tony, by contrast, still seemed tired, and grateful in a very un-male fashion to leave the wheel to me.

I was cruising in the nearside lane of the motorway, preparing to overtake a slow truck, when I glanced in the rearview mirror and felt a tiny bell ring. Shiny-blue saloon, aerials . . . It had to be the Ford from outside the pub. The car had been gone this morning when we left — I presumed the fishermen had made an early start at their river — but now here it was behind us.

I put my foot down and pulled out to pass the truck. A minute after I had swung back into the nearside lane, the Ford tucked itself in behind me once again.

This happened a couple of times more. Then I decided to play a little game. I slowed right down to fifty. Initially the Ford kept behind me; then it pulled out and passed. It drew level for a moment. The good-looking one was in the passenger seat, his friend driving.

All else was exactly as it had been the previous evening. Except that now something else had been tossed onto the back parcel-shelf with the atlas. A camera, still with a long telephoto lens mounted, pointing upwards. Most people wouldn't have spotted it, but I did. What a way to treat a delicate instrument! To me it was like seeing an animal being abused.

The Ford pulled quickly away, and soon it was a dot in the outside lane, vanishing into the distance at close to ninety miles an hour. No chance of *them* getting booked, I thought.

Tony stirred.

"The policeman from the pub just went past us," I said.

"I daresay he's going back to the Smoke too."

"He had a big long-lens camera in the back of his car."

"Maybe he's been doing a little wildlife photography on the side."

I mentioned my suspicions that someone had been taking pictures up on the hill behind the cemetery during the burial.

"Mr Plod?"

"It's possible."

Tony looked alarmed. "That kind of thing gives me the creeps. Reminds me of *1984*. Makes me want to just . . . bugger off somewhere relaxing and forget everything. I know we can't yet," he added hastily. "We've got to sort out this business with Anna, but long-term . . ."

"I can't think long-term yet, darling."

"Fair enough." Tony stared gloomily out over the wintry landscape beside the motorway: England at its most unappealing. "But I mean, even before this happened, remember how we occasionally fantasised about going to Australia for a really long visit, maybe even to live?"

I nodded, trying to keep an eye on the road. It had started to rain, and most of the other drivers were going too fast for the greasy conditions. Australia was where we had met, curiously enough. Me shooting a series of ads for a Japanese off-road vehicle, Tony playing the campaign's rugged driver hero.

"You could get tons of fashion and advertising work in Sydney. I remember you had plenty of offers just in the few weeks we were working out there."

"And you? What would you do eleven thousand miles from all the people who know you and your work?"

"Yeah, well, there's always the Grundy soaps," Tony said with a sardonic smile. "Every time I catch an episode of *Prisoner Cell-Block H.*, this or that old chum of mine from RADA pops up, playing the evil boyfriend or some chain-rattling psycho of a warder."

"Come on. I just won't let you scrape the bottom of the barrel. You're far too good."

"*You* won't let me?"

"Oh God. Didn't mean it that way."

"Well then, don't put it that way!" Tony said sharply. He folded his arms and frowned.

"I meant it when I said you're far too good, though," I coaxed him. "I'm sorry I put my foot in it."

He sighed. "And I'm sorry I blew up. Thank you for the compliment, anyway." He leaned over and ruffled my hair in that way he had. "We luvvies are sensitive souls. Touchy."

6

I KNEW I had to visit Maggie, sooner rather than later. The morning I arrived back from Jilly's funeral, we spoke at length and got the initial wave of sad news out of the way. We arranged to have lunch in two days' time at the club off Sloane Square where she stayed on trips up from Cornwall. She had been living alone at Trerose since Daddy died, seeing her friends, gardening, painting a little, but she came to London quite often, so the lunch was not an unusual thing. Only the circumstances were tragically different. At that stage I was still telephoning James Howell almost every day, so I knew there had been no progress in the search for Anna.

Maggie and I embraced long and closely in the shiny little lobby of the club. She carried a scent of the things mothers traditionally are supposed to smell of: lipstick, face-powder, and good, well-washed wool. She said nothing for quite some time. She didn't need to.

"Our table won't be ready for twenty minutes or so, darling," Maggie said gently, drawing back but with one hand still on my arm. "There's no one in the sitting room. Let's go through there."

We sat together on a chintzy sofa. Maggie asked after Tony in her usual slightly concerned way. It had always been obvious to me that she fancied I deserved better than a jobbing actor, no matter how handsome and charming. She enjoyed Tony's charm, laughed at his jokes, but as she told me meaningfully after one liqueur too many: "There are girls of whom it is said, 'have your fun with them, but whatever you do, don't marry them'. Well, there are men like that, too!"

But we soon returned to the subject of my sister.

"Age shall not wither them . . ." Maggie said with a sigh. "Anna will be one of those people. She'll always be thirty-one. Always the blonde, blue-eyed angel." She dabbed a tear away from her eye and sniffed.

The sadness in Maggie's voice held an

element of self-pity, though I was hardly going to tell her that. Age had, after all, done its work on her. She was still a very presentable woman, hair neatly rinsed and permed, skin still flawless, but she had lost the earthy, confident sexuality that had so impressed me when she first came into our lives. Maggie had bloomed late, but the bloom had now definitely gone. Until recently, I had always thought that in the exchange between herself and my father, in which she had garnered his social position and financial security, and he had received her life-giving qualities, her sexy zest, Maggie had the better deal. As a wife and a widow, she had no financial or practical problems. But Maggie's energy, her most precious and irreplaceable commodity, had slowly been sucked out of her over the years. I knew she drank too much.

"You were my favourite, Saskia darling," Maggie continued. "But you know I did grow to love Anna, no matter how hard she tried to push me away."

"Yes, I know," I said. "She could be a tough proposition when she took against somebody."

"Strange that you could accept me, and she couldn't. That two girls so close in every way should take such a very different attitude."

Maggie in Miss Jean Brodie mode was absurd, but also genuinely unsettling, because Anna's alienation — and not just from her stepmother — remained a mystery.

"How's Trerose?" I asked, changing the subject.

"Fine. The garden's still a riot of colour. That's Cornwall for you." She sighed deeply. "The old house will be yours now when I go. Yours alone."

Maggie saw me wince. She never did miss much.

"I'm sorry, darling," she said. "Clumsy of me. But the place was so much yours *and* Anna's. And in a way it always will be. Once you're over this trauma, perhaps it will serve as a reminder of happy childhood days."

It occurred to me that I might never be able to go back and live there, not even with Tony and perhaps a family of our own. Time would tell. But at that moment such an idea seemed impossible.

The waitress came through to call us into lunch. God alone knew what she thought of these two glum women, one biting back tears. Maybe Maggie had explained why she was meeting me. Anyway, the waitress was impeccably kind and considerate, almost nurse-like.

Then, shortly after we had finished the tinned-asparagus starter, Maggie dropped her little bombshell.

"Of course, darling, we'll both have to look for a new accountant, won't we?"

I was taking a sip of chilled Chablis. At this, I spluttered "I . . . I didn't know you were a client of Freeling, Mattheson," I choked.

"After your father died, I wasn't happy with the firm he had been using. One wonders whether the big expensive offices these city companies insist on might have a bearing on the size of their bills, doesn't one?"

"Oh yes," I muttered, still stunned.

"When Anna set up on her own with Jilly, she suggested she deal with my affairs, and I thought, why not keep it in the family?" Maggie took a sip of wine. "I suppose, in a way, I was reaching out a bit."

"Why didn't you tell me?"

"She instructed me not to, in no uncertain terms."

"Anna did that?"

"Yes. Anna."

The main course arrived — chicken in some kind of thick, creamy sauce, but I wasn't feeling anywhere near as hungry as I had first thought.

"Well," I said, "why not? They're . . . were very competent, I think. But why did she insist you keep it a secret from me?"

Maggie pursed her lips. "One-upmanship," she said definitely. "She wanted to have something with me that you didn't know about. Sibling rivalry, my dear. It seemed trivial, almost comic at the time. Why, does it matter?"

I swallowed a bitter rejoinder. I couldn't see Anna's behaviour as unimportant or amusing. We had always been completely honest with each other — or so it had seemed. As Maggie looked at me quizzically, all I could think was, what other things had my sister kept from me?

"Why are you revealing this to me now, Maggie?" I asked. My hurt made the words come out more harshly than I had intended.

"Because you're bound to be involved in winding up her estate, Saskia darling," Maggie said gently. "You, me, and Mr Mulcahy the solicitor."

"But Anna hasn't been declared dead yet! Nobody's even sure she is."

"It's hard for you to accept, isn't it, Saskia?"

"For God's sake, please don't patronise me!" I hissed, causing the heads of some diners to turn. "I love my sister and I don't think the pain of losing her will ever go away — but I can still function. You managed to keep going after Daddy died, didn't you?"

Maggie looked away for a moment. Her readiness to care for my father was one thing; whether she ever loved him in the conventional sense was another. When she met my gaze again, she was quite collected. A mask had been imposed.

"One does carry on somehow, it's true," she said. "I admire you very much indeed for the way you're coping."

I felt sick inside. Partly because this conversation had torn the bandage from the wound left by Anna's disappearance, but partly also because at this lunch-table I was learning things about myself that I would rather not have acknowledged. Like the fact that the childhood jealousy between us, which I thought had died along with our childhood closeness, was still powerfully present in my adult self. The push of jealousy, the pull of love . . . poison and antidote present in the same relationship. And now that Anna was gone, it would never be reconciled — which was part of the agony of loss.

I took a mouthful of the chicken, but it tasted like puréed ash. I lowered my fork once more.

"She was a very secretive girl, was Anna," Maggie confided. I went to pour myself a small, second glass of wine, but the bottle of Chablis was nearly empty. "A keeper of secrets," my stepmother said tipsily. "In a world of her own."

★ ★ ★

When I got back to the flat late that afternoon, I felt depressed and confused. I had one of those awful afternoon hangovers. Maggie had ordered a second bottle of wine, and I, who rarely drink even a glass at lunchtime, had foolishly helped her get through it. Tony was still in the bedroom, clearing away his tools.

"Hi," I said, tossing my bag on the bed. "How's it going?"

"Finished the rewiring," he answered in discreet triumph, then eyed me keenly. "You look a little rough, if I may say so."

"Well, I had several glasses of wine. You know I can't drink at lunchtimes. I needed the support of booze, I confess."

"Maggie being difficult?"

"Not really. She tried her best, but perhaps I'm in a weaker state than I thought. She told me something strange and a bit disturbing, actually."

I relayed to Tony the story about Maggie's becoming a client of Anna, and how my sister had so strangely sworn her to silence.

Tony laughed. "Come on, get a sense of proportion, Sass. Everyone tells lies sometimes. Little white ones . . . "

"Never! Not Anna and I!" I snapped angrily. "We argued, fought, sulked and made up, but we were always completely honest with each other."

Tony looked quite shocked at what he had unleashed. "Sass," he said gently, "does it occur to you that this reaction might be a little excessive?"

"You don't understand!"

"Understand what?"

"What it's like to love someone so much they're almost indistinguishable from yourself, but also to hate them so much you wish they'd just die! I thought you did, but you don't!"

Those dreadful words had just tumbled out before I could censor them. Afterwards I just stood there, trembling. Fear had replaced anger, self-righteousness given way to self-disgust.

"I think we both need a cup of tea," was Tony's wry response. As he walked down the hall towards the kitchen, he called to me over his shoulder: "When people die, lots of stuff comes up, you know. Psychological stuff."

I stood there for a while, digesting what

he had said, then followed him into the kitchen. He was plugging in the kettle.

"You're going to find serious anxieties and even nightmares jumping out on you when you least expect them," Tony continued. "This will carry on for some time."

"Have you made a study of this?" I demanded. "I mean, are you an expert or something?"

Tony calmly retrieved a couple of mugs from the cupboard and shot a tea-bag into each.

"No," he said, "but I do remember this friend of mine from RADA, who was very close to his mother. She died, he seemed completely in control, organised the funeral, sorted out the estate, ploughed stalwartly on. Then — *poom!* — a few months later he had a sudden crack-up. Just like that. Found in his mum's bedroom, curled up like a baby, sobbing his heart out. He was like that for days. Couldn't work for a year."

"Oh, thanks," I grumbled. "So I've got that to look forward to, have I?"

"I'm just saying. All your unresolved

issues with Anna are going to surface."

"Maybe. So?"

"Be prepared."

The kettle didn't seem to be boiling. I pointed this out to Tony. He smacked his forehead.

"Christ. While you were away I moved the bedside power point. Forgot to switch that circuit back on!"

While he disappeared hastily to the fuse-cupboard under the stairs, I pondered Tony's words with gloomy resentment but a growing awareness that, of course, he was right. I'd come to pretty much the same conclusions about my emotional condition — minus the amateur psychobabble — just before Maggie had ordered that problematic second bottle of Chablis. I just didn't enjoy hearing stuff like this from an outsider, even if that person was Tony.

The fact remained, this was between me and the sister I loved. I missed her. I wanted to talk to her about it.

Every love lost is Paradise Lost. And paradise is essentially a private place, isn't it?

7

OUR family solicitor rang the next morning. Mr Mulcahy was genuine in his sympathy — he had known Anna and me since we were children but also clear that there were practical matters to be dealt with. Twenty-four hours later I drove down to Surrey to see him.

"Your sister did make a will, and in it she left everything to you," said Mr Mulcahy. "Not that this makes any difference until Anna is formally declared deceased."

Patrick Mulcahy was my father's solicitor and golfing-companion for more than twenty years, and had been executor of his estate. Anna and I had brought our own bits and pieces to 'Paddy' as a matter of course — conveyancing, notary work, that kind of thing. A bald, bloodhound-eyed man of about sixty, whose lugubrious appearance belied an irreverent sense of humour, the senior partner of Derris, Liedtke, Jackson & Mulcahy claimed that he only kept going 'to stop the young shits taking over and trebling all your fees'.

I knew what he meant. The youngsters — male and female — weren't like rumpled, shrewd-but-sympathetic Paddy. To me they resembled suited sharks, hurrying from office to office, swimming on and on to keep death at bay, as the predators of the sea so famously do. They had only one diet, and that was clients.

"Since Anna and Miss Mattheson were joint owners and operators of the actual accountancy partnership," he said, "I'll be talking with her family's lawyer about winding up the practice, arranging for clients to be cared for elsewhere, and realising any assets — technical stuff, though straightforward enough under normal circumstances." Mulcahy looked at me sternly over his half-moon glasses. "But Saskia, there's something else I need to tell you. It could be important, or not. There has been official interest in the affairs of Freeling, Mattheson."

"What?"

"I learned yesterday that a warrant has

been issued, allowing the police to search the premises and suborn any documents considered relevant to legal proceedings, should such be undertaken."

"So I'm not the only one who thinks the coincidence is a bit odd! You know, Anna disappearing and then Jilly killing herself."

"I suppose not." Mulcahy looked up at the ceiling as if for inspiration. "I've been wrestling with my own conscience the past few days. You see, Anna instructed me . . . " He hesitated, searched for a form of words. "And while she's not officially dead . . . "

"Just tell me what this is about, please."

Mulcahy nodded. He reached into the drawer of his impressive Victorian partner's desk and took out a white A5 envelope. "I'm giving this to you now; it's up to you what you choose to do with it. That was Anna's stipulation in the event of her death, from whatever cause. She came in and gave it to me less than a month ago."

"Just before we left to go on holiday together?"

"Precisely."

I gingerly picked up the envelope. There was something small and hard inside it. I looked enquiringly at Mulcahy.

"I believe it is a computer disk," he supplied.

"I can't believe . . ."

"Oh, I'm certain it's what Anna intended, though I suppose the Law Society might take a dim view if it ever came to that."

"Yes, but are you sure this is all right?"

The look in Mr Mulcahy's knowing eyes told me that he understood my difficulty. Not so much anxiety on his behalf but an ominous sense that what lay in this letter might be difficult.

"Of course," he said, choosing carefully to misinterpret the signals. "If they were to disbar me now, it'd just mean my getting into my golf and my wine cellar a year or two earlier than intended. Frankly? Saskia, I've got pension plans coming out of my ears. What do I care?"

"That's a very incautious, unlawyerlike thing to say."

"I've been practising for thirty-five

years. Almost enough is almost enough." Mulcahy looked at his watch. "And now, my dear, if you'll excuse me, I have a pressing appointment with a curved stick and some holes in the ground." He offered me his hand. "Take care, whatever you do. Especially if the police pay you a visit. Any doubts on the legal front, just get me on the telephone."

I left, found a deserted café nearby and ordered a double espresso to steady my nerves. The envelope Mulcahy had given me lay untouched on the table in front of me for some minutes, until I had already drunk half my coffee. After all, I thought wildly, what's the point? I've got no computer with me . . .

In the end I had to look inside. Around the disk was a rubber band; and tucked inside that was a folded note. My heart beat fast as I smoothed the paper flat and saw the message in Anna's neat, ornate hand. These lines had been written, the note said, in the car park outside Mulcahy's office before her appointment with him.

Funny things are going on, was the key sentence. *Dangerous things. Maybe everything will tee fine, but if not, please get to your computer as soon as possible and read this, darling Sassie. Afterwards do what you think fit.*

I stared dumbly at the disk. Then, as if in a dream, I got to my feet, paid, and headed for the multi-storey car park where I had left the Jeep. By the time I reached it, I was running. You would have thought the Hounds of Hell were after me.

★ ★ ★

There was no one at the flat when I got back to London. Tony had left a note to say that he had gone to help some actor friends look at a house they were thinking of buying. He probably wouldn't be back until late.

I went straight up to my study and switched on the computer. It had occurred to me that the disk might not be compatible with my system. With a grim little smile, I decided to load it and see. Anna was nothing if not thorough. It would be surprising if she hadn't thought of that.

I wasn't disappointed. Word for Windows: Anna gets it right again.

The file was dated six weeks ago — just over two weeks before we had gone on holiday to Saint Theresa. So she had prepared this disk just in case, then delivered it to Mulcahy and scribbled the note to prepare me for what it contained. Which was . . .

Darling Sassie,

I hate to be melodramatic, but the fact is that if you ever read this, it will be because I am dead.

I want you to know that something strange and probably dishonest has been going on in the practice. Jilly has acquired some very peculiar friends. I think she's been using a couple of her clients' accounts for illegal purposes, moving money and valuables offshore — whether with their permission or not, I don't know.

I talked to her about these irregularities, you see, and all she did was to tell me to mind my own business. When I said this was my business — as well as hers — she just repeated it. The second time, it was obviously meant as a threat!

Since then, I haven't mentioned the matter again, but I can tell that Jilly isn't happy. Also, she seems very up and down, one minute excited, the next gloomy and, withdrawn. I wonder if she's on drugs.

Darling, this is all I know. But things have a very dangerous feel to them. I intend to make my mind up about this while we're on holiday together. Maybe I'll discuss it with you, maybe I won't. But I'm depositing this message with Paddy Mulcahy just in case something should happen to me before I can resolve this problem.

I hope you never read this, for both our sakes. But if you do, my love to you and Tony. Do look after him (and let him look after you). He's a wonderful man.

Lots of love,
Your sister, Anna

I don't know how long I sat there, occasionally glancing back at the flickering screen as if to check I had read this terrifying message from the grave correctly. Now I *knew* Anna had been murdered; there was no doubt in my mind. And the key lay not on Saint Theresa, as I had fleetingly thought, but here in London. Unless ... I remembered now that it was Jilly who had recommended Saint Theresa earlier in the summer, when we had discussed where to take an early winter holiday. Some friend of hers knew it well, apparently, and thought the island wonderful. That was why we had ordered the brochures for Emerald Key Estate and decided to book a holiday there.

On Jilly's advice. Manipulated by Jilly.

But then why had Jilly seemed so upset when Tony contacted her after Anna's disappearance? Was she just a consummate actress? If so, why had she then gone and killed herself?

My mind was spinning. And into that lurching, frightening world that was my imagination came a rude intimation of reality.

The downstairs doorbell rang.

I looked out of my study window. It was already dark. How long had I been sitting here at the computer?

When the doorbell rang again, I tiptoed down the spiral staircase and made my way quietly up to the front door. I hadn't yet switched on the carriage lamp at the bottom of the basement steps, but the street-lamps shed enough light for me to peep through the spyhole and see who was ringing.

It was a figure in a leather jacket and jeans: the good-looking man from the pub in Somerset. The 'fisherman' I had thought carried police ID.

At that moment all I wanted to do was fling open the door, invite him up to my study and let him take over the quest for the truth about Anna and Jilly.

But could I be absolutely sure he was really a policeman? Did I want to let him into my house without Tony or anyone around to monitor the situation?

Paralysed by indecision, I watched as he frowned, then rang the bell once more.

My hand reached for the chain, then recoiled. Not now: I couldn't do it. I would wait for him to come again, I thought, when Tony was here. I needed

Tony's protection. Surely he would be back soon.

I froze, held my breath. Finally the fisherman rocked once more on his heels, gave one more intent stare at the unreceptive door. He knew I was in there, or that someone must be. But then he turned quickly and bolted back up the steps, his feet in trainers making scarcely a sound.

Relieved that he had gone and yet somehow bereft, I slumped against the door, feeling like a weak, old-fashioned woman — the kind I have despised all my adult life.

* * *

Tony arrived back at close to midnight. I was lying on the bed, fully clothed, and didn't get up when I heard him come in.

Tony banged around for a bit in the kitchen and the living room, then sought me out.

"Hullo, love. Slump time?" he said with a tight smile.

I nodded mutely.

"Yeah, well, got a call from Di Winstone just after you left this morning. Remember my old mate Di?"

"Didn't you have an affair with her a long time ago?"

"Er . . . yeah, that's the one. Anyway, first she tells me she's shacked up with Cal Osterly. He was in *The Regiment* with me, remember? Anyway, Di's got this terrific job — playing Hilary, the sexy blonde heart surgeon in *Intensive Care* . . ."

I lay there, struggling with faint feelings of jealousy, not wanting yet to bother him with my problems, wondering if I should wait until the morning. And Tony chatted on . . .

"Di's pushing me for a guest role, actually."

"Really? So you'll be up for a part in *Intensive Care*, working with Di?"

"Yeah . . . not jealous, are you?"

"Of course not," I said, sweetly and far from truthfully.

"Great. Anyway, if it happens, it'll be pretty soon." Tony shrugged and pressed on. "Then comes the down side. She and Cal have bought this cottage in the wilds of East Sussex, I think — all these places look the same to me — and they wanted me to give it a quick survey. Under the circumstances, how could I refuse?" Tony looked sheepish. "Plus Cal and Di offered to buy me supper at a country pub on the way back, as a thanks for my help. I was famished. You're not pissed off, are you?"

"It's not that," I murmured. "I'm glad you had a nice time. It's just that my day was weird, that's all."

"Jesus, you sound really spooked, Sassie." Tony sat down on the bed. "Tell your good friend Tony," he coaxed. "Reveal all. He will understand."

So I did tell him what had happened. The trip to Guildford to see the solicitor, the envelope, the note and the contents of the computer disk, and finally the evening visit from the 'fisherman'. By the time I had finished, Tony was looking a whole lot more sober than he had when he came home.

"Right," he said very deliberately. "I see what you mean. And there was me gallivanting round the South Downs with a couple of unreliable luvvies. Please forgive me."

I stroked his cheek. "People use you, because you're so obliging. How could you know what would happen, love?"

There was a silence. We lay there very still.

"What are you — what are *we* — going to do about this?" Tony murmured.

"You can start by holding me close," I said.

Suddenly I wanted him. I wanted to do something for life, something to cheat death.

And so we did hold each other close, and a little later we made love for the first time since Anna had disappeared.

The experience seemed poignant, beautiful, like renewing a vow. I felt closer to Tony than ever before. Closer, more trusting, more vulnerable.

He was my lover, my friend, my protector. Apart from Maggie, the only family I had left.

8

OF course, that first summer I didn't use Maggie's old Pentax all the time, especially after Anna 'accidentally' knocked it off a wall. It wasn't damaged, but I took the hint.

At a jumble sale I bought an old box Brownie which turned out little train-ticket-sized images in black and white. Not the professional look of the Pentax pictures, but it did for a while. It was cheap and disposable. Then, for my next birthday — Anna and I would have been twelve — I was given a simple but effective little automatic snapper that took 135-colour film. I was really in business then.

In an attempt to placate my sister, I used to make her the 'star' of all my photographs — posing as an actress in tablecloth priestess's robes, or a fashion-model in an old frock of our mother's that had been saved in that apparently heartless middle-class English way for the dressing-up box. I even rigged up a remote-control shutter-system that I worked from a thumb-operated button concealed in my pocket, facing the camera as it stared at us from where I had propped it on a rock or a wall. These were the occasions Anna seemed to like the best — or hate the least . . .

This approach worked during term-time at Hippley, then again during the Easter holidays that followed. Until one day the little snapper simply disappeared from the shelf in my bedroom at Trerose.

Anna denied having anything to do with it. She said I had probably left it out in the garden after a photo-session the previous day. Holidaymakers walked past the bottom of the garden all the time, she pointed out primly; the public footpath was separated from Grandma Freeling's property by just a low, picket fence. And some trippers *steal*, Anna added darkly.

Of course, I was sure I hadn't mislaid the camera, but two days later we found it lying smashed against a boulder, almost exactly where Anna had announced last seeing me with it. She was triumphant. She even managed to feign a little sympathy. But I wasn't fooled.

Shortly after the beginning of the next term, we each received a letter from our aunt in Canada — my mother's sister whom we hardly ever saw. The letter apologised profusely for having forgotten our birthdays and enclosed an international money order. Mine was enough to buy another camera, this time with a case and carrying-strap.

I had really learned my lesson. For the next two or three years I never let that little camera out of my sight at Trerose. I carried it to church, on outings, even took it with me to meals. I slept with it under my pillow.

At the price of intense vigilance, this camera was kept safe and my photographic career assured. Nothing was ever actually said between myself and my sister. We continued on the surface to be just as close and exclusive of others as before. There were no more 'accidents'. But the strange thing was, until she finished her A-levels and left school, Anna never again let me take her photograph, not together nor alone.

Only when Anna met Jilly, her first-ever 'best friend' who was not also her sister, did she relax this rule. Jilly could take pictures of Anna and me together. And Jilly did.

It was the weirdest thing. Inexplicable. Or so it seemed.

★ ★ ★

Tony served coffee in bed the morning after I had returned home with Anna's computer disk. He also brought croissants from the patisserie up the road. And the day's newspaper.

"There you go." He put down the tray. "Service with a whatnot. Sleep well?"

I smiled weakly, nodded.

"That's the thing. Got to keep your strength up." Tony ruffled my sleep-tangled blonde hair. "I warned you a while back that there'd be delayed reactions, didn't I?"

Yes, he had. But this wasn't an irrational reaction, I thought. Bad things had happened yesterday.

"Well, I was doing all right until I got my sister's note explaining that she was probably murdered," I said. "I hope you're not implying that my response to that was hysterical."

"Course not," he denied hastily. "Absolutely not."

"I — we — have to decide whether to go to the police," I said.

Tony had brought his own mug of coffee with him. Now he took a thoughtful sip. "Well, if the fisherman who came knocking yesterday really was a cop, that indicates they're already trying to come to us," he pointed out. "Mulcahy said the police have a warrant to go through Anna and Jilly's stuff, right?"

"Yes."

"In that case, if they really want to talk to you, he, or someone else from the Met will be back. Otherwise what do we do? Put on your best jeans and troll round to the local nick with one little computer disk and a bunch of half-formed ideas about your sister's disappearance?"

I nodded. Where did one start when it came to reporting something so extraordinary and horrific? And did I want to take the initiative in something way beyond my experience?

"Perhaps we should wait for the fisherman to come back," I conceded. "But I want you to be here when he does."

"Goes without saying."

"What are you doing today, darling?" I asked.

Tony shrugged. "Waiting for a phone call from my agent, as per normal."

"Yes, well, let's *be* as normal as we can, shall we?" I said. "Let's catch the new show at the Royal Academy. You can beep in for messages."

So that was my decision. To clutch at the normal, the everyday. Not to rush to judgment. But before we went out I put Anna's computer disk in the little mini-safe in my study and locked it. If anyone wanted to see the disk, they would have to ask me, her sister, and tell me why — and give me some idea of what was going on.

9

"I'M still unsure what to do about that computer disk," I said to Tony. "If something funny *was* going on, and Jilly was involved, perhaps it would count as evidence. It also occurs to me that if Anna knew something and was — oh God — murdered because of it, then I too am in danger now that I have got involved."

Twenty-four hours had passed. We were walking through Hyde Park. As part of my campaign to return to 'normality', I was on my way to lunch with Daisy Tyler, an art director at the ad agency JWT who had become a friend. Tony was heading towards an audition for a nasal-decongestant commercial, It wasn't exactly a career-boosting job, miming blissful relief as those sinuses miraculously cleared, but if you don't go up for everything, pretty soon your agent stops calling you. Or so Tony claimed.

Tony nodded. He seemed to be

watching the riders on Rotten Row with more than his usual intensity.

"That had occurred to me," he said. "Though since nobody knows you have the disk, apart from Mulcahy, it shouldn't be a problem. Then you'll give it to the police for safekeeping? Fine. Mind you, you — or we, rather — are still taking a risk."

"Yes." I paused. "I feel bad about involving you, darling. But do you think there's a physical risk?"

Tony took my arm tenderly. "Not really. But you know what I said about your emotional health."

"I'm stronger than anyone could have expected, don't you think?"

That tentative tone gave the game away. My confidence was tissue-thin. Tony held my arm like a mincer until Green Park, where our ways parted.

Daisy was a California-born exile, a petite blonde whose nervous energy tended to erupt into laughter on the slightest pretext. Some made the mistake of thinking that this signified amusement or enjoyment; in fact, it was an indication of unease and usually preceded an explosion. Nevertheless, she was loyal, hard-working and witty — a paragon in a notoriously tough and demanding business.

We usually ate round the corner from her agency in Berkeley Square, but today Daisy dragged me through the western approaches of Soho to the cavernous and remorselessly fashionable bedlam of the Atlantic Grill in Glasshouse Street. She was wonderfully sweet about Anna's disappearance, which I still couldn't bring myself to call a 'death', but she soft-pedalled on the curious enquiry front, for which I was grateful. I'm cynical enough, even about people I like, to know that she must have been bursting to get the inside track from me.

Daisy picked up the tab for lunch, then suggested I come back to the office with her. She'd been asked to choose a photographer for the launch of their new cosmetics account. Top secret, very different. She was convinced I was perfect. I protested. Pressure was the last thing I wanted.

"Wrong, honey. Best you stay busy," Daisy insisted in her curious anglicised

LA accent. "Take my advice."

"Honestly, I'm not up for jobs again yet."

"Keep your mind off the dark stuff, Sassie."

"No need. I'm fine," I insisted, but I was weakening.

Daisy stood up to her full five feet three, fixed me with her direct gaze and snorted with laughter.

So there we were, twenty minutes later, sipping cappuccinos in her office at the agency and sifting through the images presented by the competition.

"The other brands will be running big campaigns next year too," Daisy said. She searched through her cluttered desk, picked up the latest edition of *Harper's & Queen* and opened it at a marked page featuring a rival product. "They're currently running old ads — typically cheap — but the word is they may originate some fresh stuff soon."

We studied the material. I made a few comments and asked if she had examples of the ads the new client had run before hiring her agency.

"Sure," Daisy said. She fished out a

copy of *Vogue* from a couple of months before. "In this issue, I think. I forgot to mark it . . ."

She flipped quickly through. Suddenly, without even consciously knowing why, I said: "Stop! What was that?"

Daisy looked at me. "What?"

"A fashion spread. There's somebody I know . . . Could I just take a look?"

Daisy shrugged. "Go ahead."

I found what I had wanted. A tall black model with a cropped head, standing in an alleyway, dressed in leathers. Smouldering, but somehow not truly threatening. Grace Jones with vulnerability. We had seen her in Somerset. This couldn't be mere coincidence, I was sure of it. If I were a religious person, I would have said this was the hand of God.

"Who's she?" I asked breathlessly.

Daisy peered at the spread. "Search me. The credit says Tom Zuckerman shot this, here in London by the looks of it. He likes to use unknowns. She's quite something, isn't she?"

"Oh yes, she certainly is."

The rest of the conversation went

completely flat. Daisy quickly realised I had gone cold on the job. "*Please* think about it," she repeated. I nodded, though of course I had no intention now of taking it. I was out of there in ten minutes and waiting on the pavement for a cab to pass. The sun had come out; it was like a fine April day instead of early November.

Not that I cared for such trivial considerations. My heart was racing, my throat bone-dry. Now all the fear and uncertainty of the previous day were banished. My body might still be fragile, but my mind was working with crystalline clarity.

A black cab stopped in response to my frantic signals. I leapt in.

"Beak Street, please," I croaked from the back seat.

The cabby gave me a quizzical look.

"You're a bit pale, love," he said. "Seen a ghost?" He chuckled. "Or maybe you heard the nightingale. You know, Berkeley Square? Nightingale . . . "

"Please — I'm in a hurry."

"Oh, pardon me for breathing."

The man's sarcasm just rolled off me.

I felt strangely invulnerable.

The pictures of the black model in the magazine. The camera again. Coming to my rescue in its troubling, double-faced way, as always.

* * *

Tom Zuckerman's studio was near Beak Street in Soho, on the top floor of one of those eighteenth-century tenements. The building seemed so ancient and untouched that no one would suspect a spacious studio could exist within its rickety warren of rooms and hallways.

I climbed bare stairs towards the fourth floor, I had only visited Tom here once, years ago, though occasionally we met socially, so when I stopped in front of the unmarked entrance that I thought must be his, I felt a moment of panic. What if there was some weird S & M session going on behind the door? This was Soho, after all. I pressed the button and heard a buzzer sound inside.

The door was opened by an attractive red-haired girl whom I took to be Zuckerman's assistant. He was quite a ladies' man, notorious for picking up pretty young women. Whatever happened between him and them sexually, they got one of the best trainings in advertising photography anyone could wish for, and I gather most were satisfied with at least that part of the deal.

The girl looked at me. Her eyes narrowed slightly. "Yes?"

"I'm Saskia Freeling. I need to speak to Tom."

She paused. "I've heard of you. You're a photographer too, right?"

"Yes."

The girl relaxed, turned. "Tom, it's Saskia Freeling to see you."

I heard a set of cigarette-scarred North London vocal cords sing out a welcome from somewhere deep inside the studio. The girl let me in at last.

Zuckerman was poised at his camera, which was set up on a tripod. He was focusing on a bottle of lager and a full glass on a table. It was beautifully lit, I could see that. Without looking away from his viewfinder, Zuckerman growled, "Hi, Sass. Just a sec."

I stood very quietly and watched as he

shot a roll of film. Then he turned to me at last. "I'll make this bloody beer look so pretty everyone'll buy it. Once."

I laughed. "That's all the client can ask. After that . . ."

"You got it. I've tried the stuff, I want to tell you, and it tastes like hyena piss."

"When did you ever try *that*?"

"Lost on safari, my dear," he said, lighting a Marlboro full-strength. "And I strangled the beast afterwards with my bare hands."

Zuckerman grinned wolfishly. He was forty, drank like a fish and smoked like a forest of chimneys. His uncombed hair provided a rough frame to a battered, sallow face. Plenty of women go for that seedy charm. Not me. I liked him but had always resisted his half-hearted attempts to put the make on me.

He snapped his tobacco-stained fingers at the girl assistant. "Tea!" To me: "Or would you like some wine?"

"No."

"Tea for two, Suzie!" Zuckerman was suddenly serious. "Heard about your sister, love. Terrible breaks. Really really sorry."

"Life goes on."

"They still haven't found her?"

I shook my head.

"You were identical twins, right?"

"Yes."

His assistant brought in the tea, bags dunked into chipped mugs. Zuckerman told her to move the lights and reflector umbrellas around a bit while he talked to me.

"OK," he said. "Rush job, Sass. Just time for a quick cuppa, then Suzie and me'd better press on. So, what can I do for you?"

"You did a fashion shoot a little while ago, for *Vogue*. Moody shots in alleyways. Lots of leather. You used a tall black girl with cropped hair."

"Oh yeah. We had to do that really fast, too," he recalled. "They pulled the previous work just before the issue was due to go to press. Soup to nuts in forty-eight hours, the resulting shoot. Up in Camden Town, back of the Regent Canal. Very iffy light conditions, had to push that new fast film right to its limit; turned out the graininess was just what we needed, though . . ."

"When was this?" I interrupted.

"Couple of months ago. New girl from the Tina King Agency. I wanted someone without much experience so's to get that raw, real look. Worked well. So?"

"What was the black girl's name?"

"Zena. That's all I know. Never got her surname. She came from the West Indies, bit of an accent."

"It wasn't Saint Theresa, was it?" I suggested.

"Could be, can't remember. Don't really know the Caribbean. Terrific looker, anyway, but too much of a challenge even for me."

"You're not getting past it, Tom, are you?" I couldn't resist the jibe.

"Oh no." He looked genuinely offended. "I was just being diplomatic. What I meant you to understand is that if Zena stood around by the sea in Holland for long enough, little Dutch boys would put their fingers in her. And they'd get karate-chopped for their pains. She's a dyke, Miss Freeling."

My heart went into freefall. Over the years, like most people in the media, I had worked with gays and straights and all the varieties in between, so much that I scarcely registered that kind of thing any more. But it's different when it's so close to home. All at once, I saw the possible implications about my quiet, shy sister, who always seemed to go so long between boyfriends. This was yet another detail of her life that Anna had kept from me. I desperately wanted to talk to Zena. I *had* to know.

"Tina King, you said?" I asked quickly. "The agency you got the model from."

"Yeah. Want to use Zena? Remember, I discovered her. Nice-enough girl, but no sense of humour."

"That's OK. I'm looking for a model, not a stand-up comedian."

"Touché!" Zuckerman tossed the dregs of his tea down the sink in the corner. He flashed one of his rare smiles, and it lit up his well-used features, made him almost handsome for an instant. "Suzie will get Tina King's details for you," he barked. "WON'T YOU, SUZIE?"

And she did. She was still in the adoring phase, I decided. Definitely.

★ ★ ★

I called Tina King from a payphone on the corner of Soho Square. Tina was pretty well-known in the business. I mean, she wasn't the absolute top, but she had had a steady stream of successful models on her books since the 1970s. I had seen her at the odd party over the years. When I heard her voice on the other end of the line, I started to remember what she looked like: fiftyish, with sharp features framed by suspiciously jet-black hair that she wore in cascades of tight ringlets, giving her a resemblance to an intelligent, chain-smoking, unclipped poodle.

I made up some story. Dropped Daisy Tyler's name, mentioned Zena's work for Tom Zuckerman, hinted at plans for a long shoot on Saint Theresa. Big new launch. Cosmetics. Secret. Couldn't reveal more than that at the moment. All this got Tina talking.

"You know Zena's from Saint Theresa, do you?" she said in her husky voice. I heard the flick of a lighter on the other end of the line, a relieved intake of breath as she took her first hit of nicotine. "In fact, her family are very prominent there, darling."

"Goodness, is that right?" I said innocently. "*What* a coincidence. Could help us in getting local cooperation."

"Yes, true." A pause. "One thing, Saskia my dear. Zena's terribly upset at the moment. About some girls she knew . . . I mean, one in particular. She did away with herself." Second pause. "You know that Zena . . . "

"Is gay, yes," I finished for her. "Why — is it a problem?"

"Oh no, she can do the Hackney bad-girl thing — I mean, that's her milieu, sort of — but underneath it she's nice as pie," Tina assured me.

"I'm sure she is," I said breezily, and filed that piece of information away. I couldn't ask her point-blank for the model's private address, but that kind of detail would help me narrow the options if I needed to.

"Anyway," Tina continued, relishing her story, "she was very close to the woman who committed suicide. I spoke to her a few days ago, when something came up that would have suited her, but Zena said she couldn't cope with any jobs at the moment. She also mentioned another mutual friend, a girl who was drowned while on holiday on Saint Theresa. Zena said she felt awfully guilty, because apparently she provided this woman with all the info she needed to go there."

"Oh," I said, suddenly feeling dizzy, as if my blood had thinned on the spot with the vertiginous coincidence of it all. "Is that right?" I trailed off lamely.

Of course, why should Tina King connect me with the drowned woman she had been told about? She had never met Anna, so far as I knew, and obviously hadn't yet heard through the grapevine that my sister had disappeared. The thing was, Zena had suggested Saint Theresa in the first place. I found it all very chilling . . .

"So what I'm saying," Tina pressed on, perhaps taking my silence for professional impatience, "is that, given these two tragedies so close together, Zena may not feel like jumping around in front of a camera for quite some time to come. Especially, I have to say, on Saint Theresa."

"On the other hand, she may want to work. To divert herself."

"You could be right, I suppose — but darling, why take a chance? If it's a tall, somewhat butch black girl you're looking for, I've got Roberta. She's Barbadian. *Stunning*. And rather easier to get along with than Zena, if the truth be told . . ."

So I had to listen to Tina singing the praises of Roberta until I could decently ring off, with a promise to bear her girl in mind when Daisy definitely decided on the shoot, and so on and so on and blah blah.

I put the phone down, wondering if Tony would be back from his audition yet. Then I noticed that someone was waiting outside on the pavement. With a murmured apology, I made to leave the booth. Then the blood chilled in my veins.

There, in the fading autumn sunshine, I saw the fisherman from the pub, the man who had knocked on my door the previous night. He was dressed in the same casual jacket, jeans and trainers, and looking straight at me. He also wore the same arrogant air that had irritated me then. I was damned if I'd show any weakness.

"Yes?" I asked in what I knew was an unnaturally high voice. "Can I help you?"

He smiled fleetingly. His teeth were perfect, just as I remembered.

"I certainly hope so," the fisherman said. He reached for his wallet and flicked it open, revealing the warrant card I had glimpsed on the pub counter. "Inspector Harry Allardyce. Can we go somewhere and talk?"

"I was just going to phone my boyfriend," I said, expanding the truth a little. "I want him to be present if you're going to ask questions about Anna."

"Miss Freeling, let's go and sit down somewhere and I'll buy you a nice cup of real coffee. This is purely informal. We'll want you to make a statement at some stage, I think, but not yet. When we do, Mr Patterson is welcome, as is your lawyer, and whoever you darned well like." He smiled. "Please?"

Inspector Harry Allardyce was no

amateur when it came to persuasion. Five minutes later he had me sat down in a quiet corner of a smart brasserie off Old Compton Street. He ordered two double espressos.

"First," he said carefully, "let me say I'm really sorry to have to bother you in the first place. I know you must be going through a hell of a time."

"Thanks," I murmured. "Most of me's just very sad, but the bits that aren't are angry. So I'd be glad if you'd get on with explaining yourself."

"Yes, of course. Well, I'm a policeman as you know. I was down in Somerset at Jill Mattheson's funeral, checking out who was there. Since then, I've been following you about a bit."

"Yes. I got that."

"You were there the other night, weren't you — at your flat, when I rang the doorbell?"

I nodded. No point in denying it, however foolish it made me look.

"We weren't that bothered at the time," he told me, "thought we'd leave you to spend another couple of days getting yourself together!"

"Who is *we*, Inspector?"

"A team of CID officers," Allardyce said quietly. "I suppose you would call us part of the anti-drugs effort, although our official title doesn't mention drugs. Our speciality is not the stuff itself, you see, but what the suppliers do with the proceeds from its distribution and sale."

Allardyce had a way of imparting unsettling information in that flat London voice of his as if he was just commenting on the weather. I struggled to take on board what he was saying.

"Very well . . . " I stuttered, "but what would your interest be in Jilly and Anna — and in me?"

"Offshore money — millions of pounds' worth," Allardyce said. "Money which seems to have disappeared into some untraceable black hole, via Miss Mattheson and Miss Freeling's accountancy practice." He looked at me very steadily. "Our enquiries involve massive sums earned from the illegal drugs trade. Money-laundering. And, almost certainly, murder," he added with careful emphasis.

A wave of fear passed over me, but not far behind it was relief. Confirmation at last. And someone on my side who might be able to actually *do* something about this crime, this cruel waste of life."

"You're . . . you're talking about Anna? My sister, that is?"

Allardyce nodded. "We have reason to believe that there are suspicious circumstances surrounding her disappearance. And possibly Miss Mattheson's death too."

For a moment at least, I trusted his steady blue eyes.

"I have a note from Anna," I said. "And a computer disk. She left it with our solicitor, to be given to me if anything happened to her. I picked it up from him a couple of days ago and was wondering what to do with it."

Nothing changed in Allardyce's relaxed expression. "And what's stored on this computer disk, Miss Freeling?"

"A letter telling me she was worried that Jilly was up to no good. Drugs. And that Anna felt her life to be in danger."

"This is just a computer print-out though — right?" Allardyce asked quite sharply. "No handwriting, no signature?"

"You're implying someone else might have written it?"

"We have to think what would stand up in court."

"In that case you should talk to Mr Mulcahy, our solicitor," I said. "He'll testify that Anna brought the disk in and lodged it with him." I thought for a moment. "Oh, and there was a little handwritten note with it. Nothing specific, but it confirms Anna was worried."

"OK. We'd like to see the disk and the handwritten note. Just in case."

"It confirms that she suspected Jilly was doing something illegal which proves that Anna herself was innocent, doesn't it?"

Allardyce nodded, but a crooked little smile gave the gesture a strange ambiguity.

"Are you saying Anna was involved?" I asked hotly.

"If it's any comfort, I can tell you that all the potentially incriminating documents in our possession carry Jilly Matteson's signature." Allardyce paused. "However, it was a two-woman practice, and we're not sure Miss Mattheson could have transacted such business without your sister's cooperation."

"If so, why would Anna write me this letter about her suspicions?"

Allardyce shrugged. "We don't know. We're still piecing together the jigsaw, Miss Freeling."

"My solicitor said you had applied for a warrant to search the premises. Is that right?"

"Yes. We have taken away the documents we require. We found nothing in either of the women's flats. However, we have requested that the office remain sealed until further notice, and permission has been granted."

I nodded dumbly, shivered. The thought of strangers rummaging around Anna's private space was unsettling, almost obscene, like grave-robbing.

"Not a particularly nice neighbourhood, actually," Allardyce observed. "Couldn't your sister have afforded somewhere nicer?"

"Anna needed a big house," I said mechanically. "Plenty of space for offices as well as living accommodation. She planned to run a practice from there, you see, even before she and Jilly became self-employed. The compromise was, the house was in a borderline sort of area."

"Makes sense," Allardyce agreed. He paused. "How was your sister during your holiday together?" he asked, unexpectedly shifting his emphasis.

I looked towards the window facing onto the street. A scruffy young man lurched into view. He was drunk, or on drugs. His gaunt face was pale, his eyes red-rimmed. He stopped for a moment and looked inside. My gaze and his locked. He put his hands up, palms forward, and seemed to push against the glass of the picture-window, and made a grotesque, tongue-lolling face.

I tore myself away. Allardyce had seen the street-crazy too. But he just kept waiting patiently.

"You asked me about how Anna was on holiday," I began. "Normal, I would say. Shy, thoughtful. She loved to swim and poke around. While I took pictures, she would either go snorkelling or just mooch around, sight-seeing — the usual routine when we went on holiday together."

"Right. You're a photographer, a professional."

"Yes." I remembered the camera on the back seat of Allardyce's car, with its telephoto lens. "How about you?"

He didn't miss a beat. "I dabble, you might say." Pause. "Now, about Jill Mattheson. Had she and your sister known each other a long time?"

I nodded. "They were at college together, both got jobs with the same international accountancy firm, then went into business together, serving a few clients who needed to juggle a US tax return with a UK one, especially those who held property and interests offshore. But surely you've got all that on file?"

"Yes. What I really want to know is, how close they actually were."

"Jilly was like family to Anna."

"Would you say that as adults Anna was closer to her than to you? I mean, we've already discussed that big house your sister bought. Miss Mattheson lived with her there."

I was just finishing my espresso. The remains at the bottom of the cup were cold and bitter, and so, I realised at that moment, was my heart.

"It depends what you mean," I managed to answer. "They were friends. As you grow up, friends replace family, don't they? It is quite natural."

I hadn't fooled Allardyce for a second. He let me hang for a moment, almost savouring — so it seemed to me — my moment of self-betrayal.

"Yes. You can choose your friends, can't you?" he said then, with an understanding smile. He downed his coffee and raised a hand to ask for the bill. "Well, thanks a lot, Miss Freeling."

"I have one more question to ask you, actually," I said.

He looked slightly surprised, but recovered quickly. "OK, fire away."

"Zena Dubois is a young black woman, a friend of Jilly's. I want to know if you've spoken to her."

Allardyce shrugged. "She was at the funeral. Did you talk to her?"

"No, but as you're probably aware, she's a model. Someone told me she comes from Saint Theresa, where my sister . . . disappeared. Have you interviewed her yet?"

"The answer to that is no, not yet."

"Do you intend to?"

"That will depend on how our enquiries proceed," Allardyce answered blandly. "So far, there's no indication that Miss Dubois is personally involved in illegal activities."

Allardyce looked at his watch. I could tell he wanted to get out of there before I asked any more questions. I felt a stab of irritation at being underestimated, dismissed. Then he was on his feet and heading for the door. Somewhat to my shame, I found myself following him.

"So what do I do now?" I asked as we emerged into the street. "I'll help in any way I can. So will Tony."

"I'd like you and Mr Patterson to come to my office at New Scotland Yard at eleven-thirty tomorrow, if that's all right," Allardyce said. "If not, we can work out another time. As I said, this meeting was completely informal. The next one will be strictly on the record."

"I have nothing to hide," I said steadily. "And neither had my sister."

"Which reminds me — bring that computer disk and the note, please,

Miss Freeling. The more we know, the surer we'll be."

"Yes."

Allardyce switched on his smile one last time. "Relax, give yourself a chance to heal, Miss Freeling," he said quietly. "You've done everything anyone could have expected of you. We'll take over now. That's our job."

I watched Allardyce stride athletically off down the street, heading for Shaftesbury Avenue, powerful shoulders braced against the world, his narrow hips moving easily in well-cut jeans.

I wasn't sure I liked him, but I remember thinking that if I hadn't already got Tony, I might have been tempted to get to know him better.

It didn't occur to me that this was already programmed into the situation — although not, perhaps, in quite the way I would have wished that bright Soho afternoon.

10

I'VE always been a ringleader. When Anna and I were little, I was invariably the one who wanted to do the very thing that was forbidden, to push against authority. And my sister just seemed to go along with it all, often nervously but always loyally.

So Allardyce's none-too-subtle hint for me to leave the matter alone only increased my desire to meet Zena Dubois, if only to find out whether Anna had been gay. And whether the model's connections with Saint Theresa were truly just a matter of chance. I wandered around the West End for half an hour, wrestling with my desire for knowledge, playing it off against my anxiety, watching the people hurrying around between the offices and shops and bars. I wondered, as they moved around so purposefully, how many of them had just lost someone they loved.

In the end the Hand of God

theory — the coincidence of seeing Zena Dubois in *Vogue* just days after she had appeared at Jilly's funeral tipped the balance. I dropped into the office of a production company I knew, and persuaded the receptionist to let me consult their phone book. Almost immediately I found *Z. Dubois*, with an address in E8.

Hackney, just as Tina had said.

★ ★ ★

I know I've mentioned that the defining moment in my relationship with Anna was when my father's second-wife-to-be gave me a camera. Well, that's with hindsight, of course. It's certainly from that time that I can now date Anna's little acts of sabotage, her sulking sessions. But it was still 'us against the world', the 'Fiendish Freelings' taking on allcomers.

At the time, the really big event was when we had just reached thirteen and my father formally married Maggie. Among other things, this meant the end of dividing our time between the prison of school and the freedom of Trerose.

I have indelible memories of the day they got married. Me sitting with Anna in our new frocks and white knee-socks, with sky-blue velvet Alice-bands forced onto our hair.

The wedding was in a register office, in Guildford. We giggled and sneered a lot. The registrar sounded like Sibyl in *Fawlty Towers*. Then there was a stiff little party at Daddy's house, at which he kept introducing us as 'Double Trouble' to friends and relations. Maggie got rather drunk, thereby establishing a long-term trend.

And suddenly Anna and I had a 'family home' again, just like other children. A suburban house with a little garden. Tame. Dull. It drove us back out into the world.

From then on, we went to a day school in Guildford and life became, superficially at least, pretty normal. No big dramas. No huge rows. I started to get quite social. I set up a camera club at the school and dominated it until I left. I worked hard, excelling in English and Art. Anna would follow me pretty much everywhere I went; everyone who was my friend, she wanted too. It was as if she had to feel what I felt, possess what I possessed.

I didn't mind. She was my twin. Despite the minor imbalances that had developed in adolescence, I never doubted our love for each other. Above all, I knew that she was subtly weaker than me. When she did things that annoyed or hurt me, her actions always seemed, I thought, to come from that weakness. I could always excuse her. Before long, my irritation would ebb and I would find myself consumed by a protective urge, a forgiving warmth that made me want to hold her, make whatever ailed her better.

When we went down to Trerose — first to see Grandma Freeling, and then, after she died, to spend holidays there with Daddy and Maggie we were encouraged to take friends. I usually did. Anna did not.

By and large, my sister didn't seem to have any interests of her own. Then came the next key moment: we were eighteen, and had our A-level exams. I did very well, got straight into Saint Martin's

College of Art, planning to specialise in photography. Anna wasn't quite so successful. She was offered a place at a provincial university to study Maths or Social Science, her strongest subjects, but instead insisted that she had to be in London with me. This was when she made the surprise decision to take an accountancy course at a Polytechnic. Just like Daddy. And it was there she met Jilly.

It was a really weird paradox. On the one hand, Anna stayed in London because she couldn't bear to go and study up north and be separated from me. On the other, within a few months of starting at the Poly, she suddenly discovered someone who was not just a best friend but a 'new sister'. Jilly. County family. Dark, big-boned, with a ready smile but, like Anna, a secret side to her that was hard to fathom. At first I thought the whole thing was a phase, but I was wrong. For the next few years, except at Trerose family Christmases, I always seemed to see Anna and Jilly together. In fact, one year Jilly even came down to Cornwall too. Maggie liked her but presciently wondered if she and Anna were good for each other.

Anyway, there we were. I graduated; Daddy died shortly afterwards, as I've already said, of a heart attack. The poor man had only just taken early retirement from his partnership; perhaps he simply had no idea what to do next. Meanwhile, Anna and Jilly had taken their intermediate exams and, in the boom atmosphere of the late 1980s, managed to get jobs in the same international accountancy firm, providing an income while they prepared for their charter finals.

When our inheritance came through, Anna, like me, bought property: in her case a sizeable house in a fairly unfashionable part of Islington. This she shared with Jilly for a couple of years, commuting every day together to the City offices of their international employer. Then, when they had decided to launch their own accountancy practice, Anna converted it into an office-with-two-flats complex.

Funny. When Anna used to come to parties with me, acquaintances, titillated by the fact that we were identical sisters, would ask me what she did. I would say, with a smile, "She's an accountant." Everyone, being creative types, would be suitably amused. Anna didn't seem bothered, though, that the laugh was at her expense. In fact, she seemed to relish going all 'mousey and quiet' to contrast with me. I swear she and Jilly would dress the part too, in their sensible suits and shoes. Even then, it occurred to me that it was the mockers who were really on the receiving end of some subtle private joke of Anna and Jilly's. Now I was certain of it, and I didn't find the idea amusing. If dirty money had been going through the books at Freeling Mattheson, was it another joint secret, another private game, or was only one of the two partners involved — Jilly, according to the evidence Allardyce had mentioned? I liked to think so. But then, I was the protecting twin, always finding excuses for my sister.

It wasn't that neither Anna nor Jilly had ever been out with men; just that none of the relationships seemed to last for long. Except one, in Anna's case — with a nice older man who worked in publishing. The trouble was, he turned out to be married. That went on for a year, until he decided, "I just can't do this to my wife." There was no pressure from Anna for him to leave the marriage, I seem to recall; in fact, she told me she rather liked not having to make decisions about cohabitation or nuptials. She and Jilly got on very well, she always said. Having a man around all the time would just have been a nuisance.

What to make of all that now? We never really discussed these problems, even when we were alone together for long periods. Anna would just laugh, or make some remark about liking her freedom. So many things I should have pressed Anna on, during the holidays we had taken together every autumn of our adult lives but didn't, because I didn't want to make her feel bad, or because I thought in my wet, modern-miss sort of way that her love-life was her own affair.

Perhaps I always suspected, deep down, that if I pushed too hard I would find out something I didn't really want to know.

Well, now I wanted that knowledge desperately, for my own peace of mind and to help me understand my sister's actions. After all, there was the bitter, aching certainty that I would never hear it from Anna's own lips. Never.

★ ★ ★

It was almost dark by the time my cab dropped me at the top of the street where Zena Dubois lived. This was Dalston, but the smartish end, towards London Fields. Junkies and muggers, yes, but also RSC actors and stockbrokers who were prepared to take risks to live near the shop.

The address given in the phone book was a mid-Victorian terrace. A door painted cherry-red, with a brass knocker. Quite *bijou*. I had asked the cab-driver to take me via Jilly's place in Islington, and if his route was any guide, it was about ten or twelve minutes, door-to-door. Fairly convenient if Jilly and Zena had actually been lovers; especially if one or both of them had wanted a bit of space.

There was a bell, also brass, set into the doorframe, and an entryphone — unusual for a terraced house. I took a deep breath and pushed it. I waited. And waited. Then rang the bell again.

Finally a voice emerged from the grill of the entryphone. I started. I had already begun to withdraw from this place, sure that no one was home, or at least that no one was prepared to admit they were.

"What can I do for you?" crackled the voice. It was soft-spoken but unmistakably male, educated yet touched with Creole inflections. *She lived with a man*. This was getting complicated.

"I . . . dropped round to see Zena."

"You're a friend, are you?"

"A friend of a friend."

Pause.

"Well, she's down the Duke."

"The Duke?"

"You don't know it? Maybe you should stay out. Your friend can't know Zena so well."

"It's a pub?"

"What's your name? I'll tell her you came round."

The voice was jealous, possessive. It

saw you off like a fierce dog.

"Are you a friend? Or family?" I asked.

"Give me your name. I'll tell her."

Some instinct made me glance up. An upstairs curtain twitched shut again. This was spooking me. I didn't want to give my name. Not the way I felt.

"I'll drop round later, OK?" I said.

The entryphone wasn't answering any more.

It wasn't until I rounded the corner and found myself out of sight of that unnerving upstairs window that I started to think clearly again.

Down the Duke. OK. When you said something like 'down the shops' or 'down the pub', you usually meant somewhere local that you expected would be easy to find. With this in mind, I began to pace the grid of nearby streets, checking the names of any pubs or clubs or cafés.

I must have done this for about five minutes when it started to rain. The weather had been springlike when I had come out that morning, planning to meet Daisy and then head home. Seven, eight hours later I was still wearing a camelhair coat over a skirt and a light sweater, my informal ladies-who-lunch outfit. Not even an umbrella.

Within a couple of minutes I was starting to get thoroughly soaked, so I ducked under the awning of a newsagent's shop.

There was a pub opposite. I peered hopefully at the sign through the now-heavy downpour, but it was one of those tarted-up places, all fake palm trees and Somerset Maugham shutters. It was called, bizarrely, TROPICALE.

It occurred to me that the shopkeeper might be able to help.

"Excuse me," I said, paying for a copy of *Time Out*, "but do you know a pub round here called the Duke of Something-or-Other? I arranged to meet a friend there, but I must have got the name wrong."

"Sorry, I haven't lived here very long," said the newsagent, a scholarly-looking Bangladeshi. "And also I do not drink."

I turned to go and there stood a short, wizened old man in a mac and flat cap, hunched as if against a permanent wind. He must have entered the shop after me and overheard our conversation.

"'E don't know — 'ow could 'e?" the old man said in pure Dalston cockney, jerking a thumb in the direction of the shopkeeper.

"Know what?" I said.

The old chap smiled the sly but sad smile of someone who is trying to prolong an encounter, because when they get home they'll have no one to talk to except the cat.

"Abaht the pub," he said. "The old pub."

"You mean there is a Duke-of-Something?"

"Not any more. I used to take the missus there years ago, God rest her soul."

"Right. So could you tell me where it is?"

"Just across the bloody road, innit? Used to be the Dook of Cymbridge. Now it's the wadjummacallit . . . y'know, jungle . . . Tropical."

As I fled I heard the old man declaring loudly to the shopkeeper: "Wouldn't believe it, would you? She looked like a nice respectable girl."

I had no time to wonder what he meant. I was already dashing across the street with the magazine held over my head to protect me from the rain.

A glance inside the bar told me little, because the lighting was very low. I dimly made out a few people in suits at the bar, others in dresses. Nothing particularly odd in that; certainly not to justify the cockney pensioner's objections — unless, like the shopkeeper, he had become a devout teetotaller.

When I pushed open the door and walked into the air-conditioned bar of TROPICALE, my rain-soaked shoes squelched gently on the carpet. One or two suited types turned and looked at me curiously, then a few more, but I kept going. By the time I reached the bar, the back of my neck was prickling. I felt as if I was entering some kind of exclusive club, though I couldn't work out what the qualifications were for membership.

The person serving drinks was beefy, short-haired, clad in a waistcoat and bow tie.

"Can I get you a drink?" asked one of the suits to my left.

I ignored the invitation. "I'd like a glass of dry white wine, please," I murmured to the person behind the bar, putting a five-pound note on the counter.

This was served quietly and impassively. I collected my change.

"What do you think?" said the suit who had wanted to buy me a drink. "Out of ten, I mean."

Of course, I realised I was the one being talked about. I half-turned and frowned.

Both suits were smiling at me.

"Seven," said one, in a light contralto.

"What did I say when she walked in? A hundred-per-cent femme, or what?"

The first suit's friend took a sip of beer. "Different between the sheets, I'd guess."

I've been round the block enough times to know the jargon. They were butch lesbians, and they thought I was some lipstick-and-curls cruiser, come here to be picked up. TROPICALE — still known by an abbreviation of its old name, The Duke of Cambridge — was a gay bar. Everything fell into place, and I felt a complete fool.

For a couple of seconds at least.

"I'm taken, I'm afraid," I said then, tossing my hair and pouting slightly. I wasn't wearing the regulation high heels and drop-dead frock, but never mind. "Looking for Zena Dubois."

"Playing pool." The first suit gestured over her shoulder.

"Thanks." I picked up my wine and headed for the back of the bar.

"See you later!" I heard them chorus.

It was even gloomier out the back except for the light over the pool-table. A couple of ultra-femme girls in frilly skirts were waiting obediently in the shadows while their butch companions nudged balls across the green baize, drifting in and out of the intense lamp-beam as they positioned their shots.

I lingered on the threshold. One of the players turned and glanced at me. She wasn't Zena. Nor was the other player. And neither of them looked friendly. I stood tongue-tied, fearing I had made a terrible mistake — until I noticed a movement to my right, by a door marked *Toilets. Telephone.* It eased open and in walked a statuesque crop-haired figure in black leather. Even in the half-darkness she was unmistakable.

"Zena," I said.

Zena Dubois stopped, looked at me, her eyes wide with fear and surprise, and then she turned quickly and bolted back in the direction from which she had come.

I went after her like a hare. Already the pool-players were moving in my direction, but I was at the door before they could block my way, and through it before they could drop their cues and grab me.

On the other side there were toilets to the left, a payphone, and another door. It slammed shut just as I arrived in the corridor, so I kept going.

I careered through, not knowing where I was about to end up, and realised I was back in the main bar of TROPICALE. I could see Zena Dubois already on the far side of the bar and heading for the street. She moved like a sprinter — but then I have long, runner's legs too.

I pushed my way through, not bothering with apologies (it really wasn't that kind of a place). No one stepped aside, but on the other hand no one seemed to mind. I heard laughter.

"Go for it!" someone called after me. "Don't let her get away!"

A general whoop went up. Then I was out of the door, panting like a greyhound, frantically scanning the street for my quarry. The rain had eased off. I saw Zena loping in great easy strides towards the next corner. She glanced behind. I glimpsed her face only for a moment, but even at that distance I could see there was real terror in her hunted-gazelle eyes and in the rictus of her mouth.

"Zena!" I yelled. "I'm Anna's sister! I just want to talk!"

But she kept going.

I pursued her for another three or four hundred yards as we moved from prosperous streets into an area that looked rundown. She seemed to be flagging; it occurred to me that she might have been drinking before I arrived in the pub. I was right. Suddenly Zena stopped, then staggered off the pavement towards an abandoned petrol station. She leaned against one of the pillars that held up the peeling canopy, half-panting, half-gagging. I slowed down too. By the time I reached the edge of the garage's darkened forecourt, I was moving at walking-pace, holding my aching ribs and trying to get my breath back so I could form words, ask some questions.

"Zena," I wheezed, "don't be scared. I told you, I just want to — "

At that moment I heard the squeal of tyres on wet tarmac. A spanking-new red Mercedes had come to a dramatic halt just yards behind me, and already figures were piling out of the back.

I knew I was in terrible trouble. This was someone else's territory, not mine. These were no longer busy, well-lit streets. I should never have come here without Tony . . .

The arrival of the car seemed to act as some kind of signal to Zena too. A stricken goddess one moment, she found a new lease of life and bolted again, limping slightly but moving with a desperate purpose. I tried to follow her, but already two bulky characters were cutting off my route. I stopped.

There was no way I could run Zena to earth now.

There were three of them. Wearing suits. I recognised them from the pub. They were all women. But then, just getting out of the car was a tall, willowy man, wearing a raincoat. Zena ran through the menacing cordon and over to him. They embraced. This was confusing.

The man said something to Zena. She hesitated, then moved over to stand by the car. The three women in suits were almost at me now. One cracked her knuckles. I took a step back. They kept coming.

"Wonder what she wants with Zena," one hissed. "Little Miss Seven out of Ten."

She was the first of the butch 'suits' I had encountered at the bar in the TROPICALE.

"I just wanted to — "

"Talk to her," the woman finished for me. She stepped forward and gave me a vicious shove. I stumbled, almost fell. "Well . . . " another push, "she . . . " push, "doesn't . . . want to . . . talk to . . . " big shove, "You!"

I was almost at the shell of the service-station building, with its empty-shelved mini-mart. The world of civilised London seemed not hundreds of yards away but hundreds of miles. At that moment I was sure someone was going to produce a knife or a gun, and that would be the end of Saskia Freeling.

But the suits held back. My chief tormentor stayed her hand, looked around for some kind of instruction. The man was walking forward.

The trio of suits moved to let him through. The man approached me. He had a handsome, arrogant face. He was a shade paler than Zena but still obviously of Afro-Caribbean birth.

He stopped. "OK," he said softly. "What do you want with Zena?"

I had heard the voice before — over the entryphone just half an hour or so ago, back at Zena's house.

Double-confused.

"Zena was a friend of Jilly Mattheson," I began falteringly. He looked at me keenly but far from encouragingly. "She also knew my sister Anna," I pressed on.

"Anna disappeared on Saint Theresa. I wanted to talk to Zena about it . . ."

"I told you to come back later," he said, wagging a finger at me. It was almost ridiculous. Almost, but not quite. His eyes were very hard, and the suits behind him weren't smiling either. "Zena is entitled not to be pursued about this. Absolutely entitled."

"I'm . . . I'm sorry," I stuttered.

"I could get the police on you," he said. "I done nothing wrong. My sister done nothing wrong!"

"You're Zena's brother?" I asked in a rush of astonished understanding.

He said nothing. In fact, he half-turned and seemed to be looking at a cluster of rock-concert posters that had been roughly pasted to the garage wall. Ignoring me, like a deliberate insult.

"Listen. Jilly's dead!" I snapped, outrage conquering fear. "My sister Anna went for a swim and hasn't come back. I'm entitled too — entitled to ask their friends about them."

Still he ignored me.

"Will you talk to me?" I said angrily. Suddenly the man swung forward with his whole upper body. The flat of his hand struck the side of my face. The force of the slap snapped my head back. Not hard, but enough to make me gasp with pain. My own hand went automatically up to my smarting cheek.

"What the hell d'you think you're doing?" I said. The words were brave and defiant; I suspect the shocked expression on my face gave a more accurate account of the fear I was experiencing.

His finger wagged again. The man's cold eyes were narrowing all the time, just slits now. "I told you," he chided.

The world had shrunk to just me and this tall, elegant and obviously violent man. I have never felt more alone in my life.

"Johnny!" I heard a voice say then, anxious but imperious. "Please leave her alone."

It was Zena.

He turned to her, frowning. "Girl," he snapped, "*you* get yourself into trouble; *I* try to get you out of it. What do you really want?"

Zena didn't respond. Her eyes were on me.

"You spooked me, OK, Saskia?" she said. Her voice, like his, was educated Caribbean.

"I'm sorry," I said.

Zena shrugged. She seemed to be relaxing a little, for what it was worth. "You were the spitting image of Anna, standing there in the bar. All wet, with wild blonde hair like you just walked back out of the surf, you know what I mean? I freaked."

I swallowed hard, nodded. "You told Anna . . . I mean, *us* . . . to go to Saint Theresa," I said.

Zena looked around warily. The suits and Johnny were waiting.

"You go back to the car," Zena said. "I just want to talk with Anna's sister for a bit."

"Zena — "

"I'll be fine! Just a minute, right?" she pleaded with her brother. To the suits she said: "Thanks, girls. Owe you a beer."

Three bulky shrugs. "Any time."

The three women walked away without looking back. To my relief, Johnny retreated too, though only as far as the car. There he lit a cigarette with eloquent contempt.

Zena turned back to me. "Sorry. Johnny overreacted. He's very protective. You know . . . the family thing."

I didn't want to hear about precious families, hers or anyone else's. After all, I didn't have one, not since Anna disappeared.

"So why did you tell Anna to take me to Saint Theresa?" I demanded.

"I did not tell Anna or anyone else to visit Saint Theresa," Zena shot back. "Listen, I hate the place. Or rather, I hate what it has become!"

I could sense no evasion in her words, no dissimulation. This was an authentically messy response to a difficult question.

"OK," I said. "Are you saying you never discussed it with Anna before she and I went on holiday there together?"

"Anna called me up, asked for advice on places and problems, you know, the stuff only a local would know. Seemed to me she had already decided to go to Saint Theresa, so I thought, may as well put her right."

I nodded. Over by the car, Johnny had

tossed away his half-smoked cigarette and was looking pointedly at his watch. "You suggested the Emerald Key Resort?" I asked.

"Sure. A decently run place, right?"

"Yes." I thought for a moment. "You say you hate what Saint Theresa has become. What do you mean?"

Zena rubbed her thumb and forefinger together in the universal sign for money.

"What kind of money? Drugs?"

Zena glanced in Johnny's direction, shrugged.

"You see, I suspect Anna may have been murdered. And . . . and Jilly too," I blurted out.

At the mention of Jilly Mattheson's name, Zena took a sharp intake of breath and flinched as if she had been struck a blow.

"I just don't know," she murmured anxiously. "I'm still getting over that. Jilly was . . my friend."

"And your lover too?"

I don't know where I got the courage to say that. Maybe from a sense that soon brother Johnny would be snatching Zena away from me, and it would be a lot harder to get hold of her a second time.

Zena looked at me with eyes of fire, then nodded slowly.

"Zena!" Johnny called over. "We going to stand around here all night? What you got to discuss with this person?"

"He knew Jilly and Anna," Zena said. "They did his accounts as well as mine. He spent a lot of time talking business with them." She looked at me almost beseechingly. "Just business. What's it to do with me or you?"

Though I liked Zena, I couldn't afford to support her self-delusion. "I've got evidence that this business was crooked. Something Anna left behind."

Zena looked nervous. She was getting ready to bolt again, I could tell.

"One more thing," I said quickly. "Anna . . . was she gay?"

"She wasn't part of our crowd," Zena said matter-of-factly. "Jilly and me, we reckoned there was someone, but who, or how her taste really went, we never knew."

"Johnny?" I asked softly.

Zena let out a weary little laugh.

"Saskia, I think you should go back to taking pictures."

Johnny Dubois had got into the Mercedes, and was revving the engine noisily. Looking at the car properly for the first time, I was startled to see that it bore a 'CD' badge — Johnny Dubois had diplomatic status. Tina, I remembered, had mentioned that the Dubois family were 'prominent' on the island. Well, those simple little letters were ample confirmation, I thought.

"Got to go," Zena said. She looked at me levelly. "I'm so sorry. About Anna as well as Jilly. So sorry."

"Can we talk again?"

"Maybe I'll ring you."

"I'm in the book. S. J. Freeling. Kensington Church Street."

Zena Dubois' voice dropped to a whisper. "I need time to think. Maybe in a while. Take care, Saskia — I mean that."

She ran over to the car and got in, without looking back. Zena Dubois was no longer a proud Amazon but a child obeying her brother, because his job was to look after her. That was the deal they had worked out, somewhere a long way away and a long time ago.

★ ★ ★

After Johnny Dubois had driven his sister away, I walked slowly back towards the lights and the people. I considered flagging down a cab to take me home. Then, from nowhere I recalled my conversation with Allardyce and thought, I'm just a mile or so from Anna's house. I could get Tony to meet me there and we could look it over together — make sure everything's all right. And then Tony could drive us back to Kensington.

I rang home on my mobile. Tony snatched up the phone in the flat as if he had been expecting news from a disaster.

"Darling," I said, "will you meet me at the veggie café down the road from Anna's?"

"Sass, where the hell have you been? And what is going on?"

His voice was too cool, too controlled. I could tell there was a volcano seething under there.

"No time to explain. Just meet me there, will you? Get in the car and come straight away. I really need you."

I killed the phone and set off for Islington.

11

I SETTLED down to wait in the café, nursing a cup of camomile tea and a sore face that brought sympathetic glances from the South-American woman who ran the place. I had only been there for about twenty minutes when Tony burst in. He must have driven like the wind up from Kensington. He had thrown a raincoat over the sweatpants and shirt he wore at home, and he looked enraged. Angrier than I had ever seen him.

"Where in the Christly fucking hell have you been?" he demanded, slumping into the chair opposite me.

"Just let me explain," I mumbled.

"Yeah, I'd say so!"

The little South-American woman at the counter had been joined by a friend, several inches taller and at least thirty pounds heavier. They looked as though they were planning to raise a lynch-mob to deal with the presumed partner-batterer sitting opposite me. Tony certainly looked crazed enough to have done me an injury. I seized his hand, pulled him in close.

"Listen to me!" I hissed. "Before we get thrown out of here."

My cheek had swollen since Johnny Dubois hit me, giving my diction a soggy, lisping quality; the way you sound when you're still shaking off a dental anaesthetic.

Suddenly Tony peered at me hard. "Dear God, what happened to your face?" he said. "It looks really sore."

"Someone hit me. The brother of the black girl who was at Jilly's funeral. Her name's Zena Dubois. He's called Johnny and he got very cross with me, OK?"

Tony's mouth opened and shut wordlessly. His expression crumpled from furious lover to worried parent.

"Sorry to fly off the handle," he apologised. "I was just so bloody worried. Why didn't you phone earlier?"

"I thought you'd still be at your audition, and then — "

"OK. OK. But where have you been?"

"It's a long story." I looked at the

woman behind the counter and gave her a slightly twisted but, I hoped, soothing smile. "Could I have another cup of camomile tea? Same for my friend here," I said. I looked back at Tony, "He needs something to calm him down."

I filled in the outline of what I had done with myself. The coincidence of seeing Zena in that back number of *Vogue*. The visit to Tom Zuckerman. My close encounter with Inspector Allardyce and what he had told me. Tony seemed all right with that stuff. His expression started to darken again as he dunked his tea-bag morosely in its mug and I got to the crucial, dangerous bit. The trip to Dalston. The lesbian pub. Zena. Johnny . . .

"Jesus, Sass," he said, finally taking a sip of the herb tea. It must have been almost cold by now. "I really don't think I ought to let you go outside alone. You get yourself into trouble, don't you?"

All I could do was nod miserably. "But I believe Zena Dubois when she said she didn't tell Anna to go to Saint Theresa."

"Yes, well, maybe. But her brother

sounds like a psycho."

"I expect he was worried about her," I said. "You know how it is with family." I paused. "Listen, I know it's not really relevant to anything, but I think there's a strong possibility that . . . well, that Anna might have been gay."

Tony was lifting his mug to his lips. He paused, then pulled a face. "What do you base this on?" he asked eventually.

"I'm not certain. But . . . well, there was Zena Dubois and Jilly. And now I come to think of it, Anna never showed that much interest in men. Not these last few years."

"She was a quiet sort of girl, I'll grant you that," Tony agreed.

"If it's true, I think I can handle it," I said. "I just wish she'd told me, that's all. I could have got used to it. Plenty of people's brothers and sisters come out, and in the end things are fine."

"Yeah. You're just hurt, right? Because she didn't confide in you."

I nodded. Tony's anger seemed to have completely subsided. This was the old Tony, the man I loved.

All at once I remembered his business

of the day. "I'm so selfish!" I exclaimed, changing the subject. "I haven't asked you about the audition."

Tony sighed. "Many are called, but only one is chosen. Not me, in this case."

I gave his hand a squeeze. "Never mind, darling. There's always next time. Look — I've got the duplicate key Anna always left with us. Why don't we go round to her house — just take a look and make sure everything's all right? For my own peace of mind. Then we can go home and call it a day."

He pushed away his mug, got to his feet. "OK let's do it," he said. "Bags I drive."

Five minutes later we pulled up outside the tall, narrow Victorian building where Anna lived. The street was very dark.

I rummaged for Anna's key — we had both exchanged duplicates when we bought our places — and reached for the door-handle on my side of the Jeep. Tony gently restrained me.

"Are you sure you want to do this?" he asked. "You still seem a bit fragile to me."

"We have to face up to what's happened."

"Well, I hope you know what you're doing. And I hope that bloody policeman knows what he's up to, as well."

"We have to trust him. Oh, come on," I said impatiently, and got out of the car.

I could hear the dull thud of rap music from along the street. In the context, it sounded menacing. Tony carefully set the anti-theft alarm and locked the doors before he joined me on the pavement.

I took the lead, quickly climbing the steps at the front of the house. When I reached the door, I went to insert my duplicate key, then caught my breath as the door gave and swung open on its hinges.

"Careless. I'll give Allardyce trouble about this."

"Don't bother," Tony said quietly. "I don't think this has anything to do with the police."

I followed his gaze, saw the shattered glass panel to the left of the door.

"Shit. The vultures have arrived, Sassie," Tony said.

He insisted on going in first. I followed. The hall was dark. We cautiously crossed the rustling savannah of bills and junk mail that had grown up even in the few weeks since Anna's disappearance, found the light and switched it on.

"Better call an emergency locksmith service, or they'll be back to strip the wallpaper," he said.

I nodded. "First let's check out the full damage."

The house was a shambles. The usual things had been taken: video, television, computer. The rooms had been systematically trashed, too. One of the intruders had even defecated on the floor in Anna's living room. A used syringe had been left on the coffee table.

Tony stood bleakly on the threshold of the living room, shaking his head. I moved rubble around with my foot, gently, almost idly, fixated on the mess. I suppose I was in shock.

"Bastards," Tony kept repeating, his voice thick with disgust. "Complete bastards . . . " He took my arm. "C'mon, love. You don't need to see this."

I shook him off, went down into

a crouch. Something had caught my attention. It was a colour photograph in a sterling-silver frame. The glass was broken, but I could see it clearly. It looked like me and Tony, in some pub somewhere.

"I don't recognise this picture. Don't remember where it was taken, either," I murmured.

Tony squinted at the image. "By the look of the short-back-and-sides, it must have been when I did that stint in *The Regiment*."

I nodded. "Anna was thrilled. Loved bragging about her sister's TV-star boyfriend. Must have been why she kept the picture."

"Yeah," Tony said with a sad laugh. "Anthony Patterson's fifteen minutes of fame, poncing around for twelve million punters, pretending to be a gunnery captain." He bit his lip, looked away. "Sorry to go on," he whispered. "I'm very moved, actually. I didn't know Anna cared."

I reached out and touched his shoulder. "She was very fond of you. She always said you were right for me."

Tony nodded, looked away. "Let's get out of here."

I handed him my mobile. "No way, mate," I said briskly. "There's a phone book on the table in the hall. You call a twenty-four-hour locksmith and get someone over to fix the door, and I'll get stuck in here. I can't leave things like this. I just can't. Not my sister's place. Not Anna's."

We duly cleared up. The locksmith came and installed the best protection he could supply. I paid him with a large cheque.

And finally, very late, we de-alarmed our fortress car, climbed in, and Tony drove us home. We took with us the picture of Tony in his television-army-officer haircut with the me I couldn't remember. It all seemed somehow appropriate.

★ ★ ★

It was that night I first heard the voice.

It seemed to be in the room with us. At first, when I woke, I thought it was a radio in a car out in the street, something like that. Then I remembered that I'd had the windows on the street side double-glazed last year. In any case, it was three in the morning.

A low, sibilant whisper: "*Sassie. Sassie. Sassie . . .*"

Then there was silence before it started again.

It happened three times in all; I was sweating, though the room wasn't especially warm. Even in the last week of November, I didn't like to overheat the place.

I nudged Tony. He grunted, rolled away from me. Eventually I managed to goad him into wakefulness. He lay squinting blearily in the moonlight, propped up on one elbow.

"*Sassie. Sassie. Sassie . . .*" I heard.

"That's it!" I said excitedly.

"What?"

"Anna's voice."

He smiled in that humourless way people do when they're worried. "I don't hear anything, lovey."

"You're sure?"

"Course I'm sure," Tony said, looking at me closely.

"Oh God."

"I'll go and take a look around," he said. "Maybe we've left something on."

Tony got up and padded to the door. He was away for a couple of minutes. I heard him wandering around the flat, checking things. He reappeared looking even more concerned.

"Nothing," he confirmed, climbing back into bed. He thought for a moment. "Maybe you should see the sainted Dr Wiseman, get something to bridge you over the next week or two."

I stared at the ceiling. "Are you saying I'm off my head?"

"I think we're still talking about the after-effects of Anna's disappearance. And I think we're now talking really seriously, OK? Can I say that?"

I stared hard at Tony's face. He seemed in dead earnest.

"We're going to Scotland Yard first thing," I said firmly. "We can't cancel — particularly after everything that's happened."

"Dr Wiseman has an evening surgery as well. Do it, will you? For me."

I lay back on the pillows and listened.

Nothing. It was as if Tony's search of the flat had exorcised whatever ghostly static I had been picking up.

"He'll only put me on drugs," I resisted stubbornly. "Let's give it a day or two first, shall we?"

Tony stroked my arm. "OK," he conceded. "I'm sure it's just a passing phase, Sass. Symptom of overload."

I nodded, tensed. I was waiting. But still I heard nothing. Soon there was only the gentle sound of Tony's sleeping breath. A little later I must have fallen asleep myself, because the next thing I recall is struggling back to consciousness with grey morning light leaking in through the window and the other half of the bed empty.

I panicked. I scrambled out of bed, grabbed a short silk robe, and walked around the whole flat half-naked, room by room, calling: "Tony! Tony!" He was nowhere to be seen.

I told myself to calm down. I remembered I had to take the computer disk to Scotland Yard, so went upstairs to my study.

To find the mini-safe on my desk

wide open, and the disk and the note both gone. Someone had expertly cut out a square of glass from the study window, then simply opened it from the inside. Cold November air coursed into the room. This was no casual, opportunistic burglar. This was a very professional-looking, targeted burglary.

I stifled a scream and bolted downstairs, ending up locking myself in the bathroom, still just in that flimsy robe, shivering in the early-morning chill.

A few minutes later I heard the street-door open. My relief when I recognised Tony's voice calling my name was beyond describing. I unbolted the door and edged out onto the landing.

"Tony!" I called out. "Darling?"

He came briskly trotting up the stairs, in his winter jacket and jeans, carrying the paper and a carton of milk. He stopped dead when he saw me.

"You're practically starkers, sweetheart," he said. He sounded almost disapproving. "And . . . please don't smile that weird smile."

"I'm smiling?" I shook my head like an embarrassed child. "It's fear, not smiling.

Someone broke into my study last night and took Anna's things out of the safe. I can't stay here, Tony. We have to get out!"

Tony flinched slightly at the flood of words that poured out of me. As I babbled on, he put his shopping carefully on the floor. Then he came to me gently, took me by the arm and kissed me on the lips. The words stopped.

"Let's get you dressed before you freeze yourself blue," Tony said. "Then talk me through the whole thing, Sass. From the top."

12

IT wasn't that Allardyce looked especially different when we saw him in his official context. More, I suppose, that I found myself looking at him in a new way. There were lots of smartly dressed men and women around with a similar efficient, intelligent air. An élite unit. And you had a sense of where Allardyce's quiet authority came from: a hundred years of tradition at Scotland Yard, and a sense of knowing whose side he was on.

Yes, of course I've heard all the stories and seen all the cop shows, and know in my head that it's not that easy, identifying where a policeman's real moral centre lies. But Allardyce really did seem straight, a man who knew right from wrong.

We were treated with kid gloves. Honoured guests. Offers of coffee, comfy chairs. Everyone took their cue from Allardyce. I was glad for the Armani suit

I was wearing and the extra make-up I had forced myself to put on. You wanted to look good in this company.

I told Allardyce straight away about both the burglaries, first the one at Anna's and then the break-in at my flat.

He glanced at his assistant, an attractive fair-haired woman in her late twenties with rather wild green eyes who had been introduced as 'Gwen Carver'. She raised an eyebrow just for an instant.

There was an unmistakable hint of intimacy in that little exchange. I wondered about their relationship outside the Yard. Then wondered why I wondered.

"How would any intruder have got up to the rear window?" he asked.

"Extendable ladder," Tony put in. I was grateful for his intervention. "Glass-cutter to score out the hole, sucker-pad to remove it. Do you think there's any connection between the two burglaries?"

Allardyce shrugged but didn't comment. "Now, Miss Freeling, I know this might sound like a foolish question, but do you have any idea who it might have been?

The person who broke into your flat, I mean."

"No."

"Did you mention the disk to anyone except me?" Allardyce said.

"Mr Mulcahy. And Tony, of course."

Gwen Carver was making notes, looking hard at both me and Tony between jots. It was unnerving.

"No one else?" Allardyce pressed me. "You're sure?"

"I . . . actually I did see Zena Dubois. And I said something to her. Not specifically about a disk, but . . ."

Allardyce's sudden interest was electric. He had me take him through the entire encounter in detail, especially my brush with Johnny.

"You seem very interested suddenly," I pointed out. "Yesterday you insisted Zena wasn't part of your enquiries."

"What I actually said was, I had no evidence she was personally involved in criminal activities," Allardyce corrected me.

"Her brother's car has CD plates too."

Allardyce thought for a moment. "You might as well know," he said. "You're dealing with class. Johnny and Zena's uncle is Deputy Prime Minister of Saint Theresa. Johnny's got a diplomatic passport too, for that matter."

I shook my head in disbelief. "If last night's behaviour was typical of his negotiating style, I'm glad I don't work for the Foreign Office."

"Wait a sec," said Tony, who had been very quiet so far. "Dubois or not, let's suppose whoever broke in was looking for evidence that might incriminate them — the disk, whatever — maybe something else that we don't even know about. They broke into Anna's flat, found nothing there. Afterwards, they came and did Saskia's place — and got the disk."

Allardyce looked doubtful. "From Miss Freeling's description, the burglary at her sister's house sounds like a particularly nasty grudge-job."

"Maybe that's what they *wanted* it to look like!" Tony suggested.

Allardyce made a little nod of concession, while Gwen Carver pursed her rosy lips and wrote down Tony's contribution.

"OK," I said, to fill the silence, "what

do Tony and I do now? Apart from installing a burglar alarm?"

"That's probably advisable, actually."

I nodded. Tony folded his arms and looked at the ceiling. I could see he didn't like Inspector Allardyce at all.

"And we'll be keeping an eye on your flat," Allardyce continued. "Any problem with that?"

"After what happened last night, hardly."

"Right. The thing is, we're pursuing various lines of enquiry. All I ask from you and Mr Patterson is that if, over the next days or weeks, any suspicious persons approach you, or if anything you consider odd or unsettling happens, just ring my direct line."

"Is there any chance Saskia's personal safety is at risk?" Tony demanded.

"I don't think so. I'd say that whoever broke into her flat probably got what they wanted, don't you, Mr Patterson?"

Tony took my hand in his. "Saskia's got healing to do," he said.

"Of course," Allardyce nodded. "We all understand that completely."

He wrote a number down on a neat

little sheet from his desk pad. I could see Tony's hand move out to take it, but Allardyce deftly circumvented his grasp and directed the note quite deliberately to me. All politely and unobtrusively done, but it left Tony flushed with embarrassment and me feeling oddly privileged.

* * *

Afterwards, Tony and I went out into Victoria Street and headed for a nearby pub. The place was full of neat civil-servant types from the nearby Board of Trade, sneaking an early lunch.

Tony had gone very quiet. He got himself a pint of lager and a not-bad-looking sandwich; I, having no appetite, opted for a mineral water as my liquid lunch.

We sat in a corner, surrounded by the Ministry's finest, and for a while there was silence between us.

"I don't like it," Tony announced eventually.

"What?"

"I don't like Inspector Allardyce. Nor

do I like his plan — mainly because I don't trust him. He's going to use us as bait, I reckon." Tony paused, took a sip of lager. "And I don't think all this stuff is good for you."

"I want to find out what happened to my sister," I said. "The police want exactly the same thing. Sounds good to me."

"You're still upset."

"I'd be crazy if I wasn't! You said you'd support me. And the fact remains, all I've agreed to do is to report anything odd to Inspector Allardyce."

Tony could see I was annoyed. For a moment he looked like a nervous little boy. Then he got his chin up, quite literally, like the actor he was, deciding to play the part a different way.

"Yeah, fine," he said. "Well, just leave things to him and don't you go running around London talking to dodgy people and getting yourself slapped, agreed? Deal?"

He held out his hand.

"Deal," I said, and we shook on it, though I was puzzled by his attitude. Was Tony really anxious on my behalf, or was it something else. Jealousy of the smooth-talking Inspector Allardyce, perhaps?

Tony was obviously anticipating my suspicions. He took another swallow of his lager. "I'm sorry to be such a pain. It's just that I'm worried about you. About us."

"Oh, you don't need to worry about our relationship," I responded hastily, as I'm sure he had hoped I would.

"I meant our safety, actually." Tony smiled almost shyly. "But it's very sweet of you to reassure me on the other score." He put down his pint and took my hand. "Presuming that was what you're doing."

"I was."

He looked at me in a level, direct kind of way. "Two things. One, let's ask about visas for Australia. If you moved your photographic work and your capital there, you'd qualify as a business emigrant. I meant what I said on the plane about wanting to get away from the past, and to go somewhere warm."

I nodded noncommittally. "OK. But there were two things you wanted to bring up."

"Oh yeah. And let's get married."

There was a silence. I laughed.

"Marriage!" I said. "We've never even talked about it before!"

"We never talked about Australia either."

Somewhere a clutch of men from the Ministry started to sing a rude song about the Germans.

"I'll answer your question in two parts," I said softly "Australia: maybe. Marriage . . . " I inhaled deeply. "Yes. Absolutely."

So that was Tony's proposal. Quirky. Irresistible. Very cleverly done.

By the time we got back to Kensington, I had started to get used to the idea of becoming Mrs Saskia Patterson. Soon I was walking on air. I started doing wifely things. While Tony worked in a desultory fashion on a script, I did a quick shop for basics down at the Italian deli — even though we were going out to celebrate that evening.

"*Ciao, bella!*" the fat proprietor greeted me. I beamed. I felt loved and approved of. Safe, in a profound way.

Of course it was crazy. Even then,

not just in retrospect. But despite the fact that my sister was missing, believed drowned, and that my flat had been broken into, and although I had the knowledge at the back of my mind that I'd started hearing voices — and never mind the beating-up I'd earned myself the previous evening in the East End — that afternoon after accepting Tony's proposal I would have classified myself as one of the happiest women on earth.

13

OF course, it's easy to misunderstand my relationship with Anna. People often did. I was more upfront, gregarious, pushy. It's why I chose the career I did. Anna was cautious, but she was also very practical. When she passed a judgment about a person or a situation, I tended to go along with her opinion.

Take Tony, for instance. As I said, I met him in Australia during an advertising shoot — a *big* advertising shoot, launching a new four-wheel drive. The ads, including my stills, had him bouncing across rugged terrain (near Broken Hill) or crashing through jungle (Queensland), but actually, like all these things, the vehicle was aimed at the Kensington Cowboy market. Twenty-five grand for a high-and-mighty off-roader that could take you anywhere but usually got its owners as far as Safeway and back.

Tony does have rugged, Marlboro-man good looks, which is why he got the job on the campaign. I watched him staring ahead in that steely way as the vehicle careened across the desert rocks for the umpteenth time, and I didn't so much fall in love with him as in lust. Even when he complained of feeling car-sick! We talked quite a bit, did a bit of exploring together, but we never even kissed, let alone slept together. We agreed that we were both, in our ways, orphans. I had lost my mother as a child and my father in early adulthood. Tony was an only child whose father, an East End bus-driver, had died when he was fourteen. His mother, a flighty beauty from Edinburgh, had remarried and gone back to Scotland. Tony and his stepfather didn't get on, and his mother sided with her new husband. I suspected it was her genes that had created Tony as such a mischievous, seductive, and occasionally angry man.

I didn't mind that he was a bit chippy, that he was complex. I liked those things about him. But then Tony let slip he had a steady girlfriend back in London. They had problems, he said, but they were working on them. It was a clear hint of 'maybe, but not yet'.

Well, just after we got back I heard that Tony and his lover had, in fact, split up. So the reunion barbecue I insisted on giving for the crew, the cast, and the agency people a week or two later was not entirely the self-sacrificing gesture it appeared to be. I wanted to lure Tony into a relaxed social situation, one where he could stay behind when everyone else had gone . . .

It was a Sunday in June, I remember. My little back lawn rippled with sparkly sunlight and my carefully tended clematis was in full bloom around its trellis. Anna and Jilly had come along after breakfast to help out and do their buttoned-up double-act in front of my so-called 'glitterati' friends.

People had been invited for one o'clock, and they piled in at a pace. Soon there must have been a couple of dozen guests there, but no Tony. Two o'clock came. Then half-past. Still no sign of the whole reason for my throwing the party in the first place.

A married account guy from the agency was trying to chat me up when Anna sidled up and said, "Got something to tell you." A sweet smile to the account guy. "In private, Sassie."

Relieved to have the pressure taken off, I made my way through into the living room of the flat with Anna.

"Yes, what?"

"Your nice actor hasn't come, has he?" she said. "The one you showed me the pictures of."

"No. Maybe he isn't so nice," I suggested grumpily.

"Rubbish, Sassie. I can tell about people. Trust me." Anna giggled. She was a little drunk. Maybe more than a little, come to think of it.

"Well, he said he was coming, and he hasn't. I call that nasty."

"Or shy." Anna frowned thoughtfully. "Who do actors most want to meet?"

"Casting-directors," I said cynically.

"You really like him, don't you?"

I shrugged.

"Now, Sassie, I need to know that you really want him. I'm your sibling. I need to feel that twinge of rivalry to get me going."

"Yes, I like him," I had to confess.

"OK. Give me his phone number," Anna continued, "and I'll ring him. I'm just an accountant, unthreatening and so on. I'll get him for you." Pause. "What's his name again?"

I told her. Gave her his number. Then I heard her on the phone, saying she was glad he hadn't left yet. She was organising this party on my behalf and had forgotten to get enough Pimm's. Could he pick some up on his way? Oh, he *must* come! Everyone would miss him so much if he didn't. And there was a casting-director here who was *dying* to meet him.

When Anna put the phone down, I expected to see a look of spluttering amusement on her face, a rush to share this wonderful joke with Jilly, but she was utterly serious.

"There you are," she said. "Your mousey sister fixed you up with the man of your dreams, and don't you forget it."

Tony arrived half an hour later — he

only lived in Shepherd's Bush — with the Pimm's. Anna met him at the door. The casting-director had left just a few minutes before, she lied surprisingly smoothly. But what the hell, the party had turned out to be a sensation.

True. And it got more sensational still.

Tony stayed afterwards, just as I had hoped. And he confessed that the real reason he hadn't responded to my invitation was because he hadn't felt ready for another serious relationship so soon. My lovely twin had pricked his conscience. And now he had changed his mind about the relationship, that was. Could I forgive him and start again?

I could. And we didn't have to go anywhere for the next two days, anywhere at all. Except my comfortable double bed.

★ ★ ★

Dinner on the night of our engagement was superb, the service at 'Tiberio' impeccable.

The night was cold but clear. We

decided to take an after-dinner stroll around Mayfair.

"Have you thought about Australia again?" Tony asked as we wandered down Jermyn Street. I think we were just at the corner of Simpson's and had paused, debating whether to go straight on towards the Haymarket or cut left and up through to Piccadilly.

I gave him a sideways look. "I'd forgotten. I sort of thought you were joking."

"No, I'm really serious, love. Couldn't you fancy a change? Sunshine, hedonism, no more crime?"

I knew people who had lived in Sydney for long enough to get over the initial knocked-out, gee-this-is-paradise impression. Most of them liked the place just the same, but they didn't exactly confirm the sun, fun and safety image. There were drugs and thievery and violence Down Under, just like anywhere else.

"Yes, maybe I could," I found myself answering all the same. That night I was the bride-to-be, putty in Tony's hands.

"We should make enquiries. It'll take time, of course."

"We're still making much more important enquiries — about my sister's death," I pointed out.

"As I said, it'll take time. The least we can do is drop by Australia House, check out the situation for business migrants."

"God, you're keen."

"I'm tired of London," Tony said with sudden passion. "I'm tired of pessimism, cynicism, constantly reducing expectations."

I looked at him in surprise. There wasn't a trace of his habitual irony in Tony's expression.

"But we don't have a bad life," I said.

"Not bad isn't good enough."

We walked in silence up to Piccadilly and Tony hailed a cab.

★ ★ ★

The voice did not come back that night, nor the next, nor the one after that. Tony suggested that now I was near-as-dammit a married woman, I had regained my sanity. The worst sense of jeopardy had certainly disappeared.

In fact, life returned to what passed for normal, except that the day after our engagement, temperatures dropped dramatically. Winter arrived. And Tony got a job.

Just as he had hoped, Di Winstone's efforts came up trumps. He was asked at very short notice to guest for a few weeks on *Intensive Care*, starting the coming weekend. He was to play Di Winstone's long-lost brother who, curiously enough, had been living in Australia for the past twenty-odd years. Tony was thrilled, anyway — or about as thrilled as an actor can be who's been reduced to bit-parts in TV soaps.

I know we had agreed to take time off to deal with Anna's death, but how could Tony pass up an appearance in one of the most successful shows on television?

Intensive Care was shot in an abandoned Victorian mental institution just outside Bristol, where the production company had built an entire mock-up of an operating theatre and a high-tech hospital ward. The canteen scenes were staged at the local Tech during the college holidays. Lots of jokes about all those actors being 'cared for in the community'. Even more jokes at the expense of the British Further Education system. But the show got fifteen million viewers every Tuesday and Thursday night, which meant few who were offered something turned it down, or complained about the weeks spent back-to-back filming, living in hotels or serviced flats, or struggling up and down the M4.

I said I didn't mind. But I did. It wasn't, at that stage, envy or possessiveness — though I knew Di Winstone and Tony had been involved years before I met him. After all, he had just proposed marriage to me, and it felt as if nothing could ever really go wrong between us. No, despite Allardyce's assurances, at that juncture I was just plain scared of being in the flat without Tony to protect me.

But I didn't tell Tony of my fears. I toasted the fact that he was working. I insisted everything was fine. And on the day before he was due to go down to Bristol we did, in fact, drop into

Australia House to pick up some stuff about business migration. On the face of it, things looked very good. When I totted up all my capital, potential and available, it actually came close to a million pounds. I — we — qualified.

But that was just a beginning, as Tony said. Something to dream about. And despite my apprehension about his going away, I was in the mood for dreams.

He started work first thing on Monday, and needed a day or two to read scripts and get organised. On the Saturday morning I saw Tony onto the Bristol train. Afterwards, reluctant to go home to an empty flat, I wandered into the big John Menzies at Paddington Station and browsed through the books and magazines. I turned away from the shelf after a while, guiltily clutching a schlocky bestseller to help while away the weekend, and there stood Detective Inspector Allardyce.

"It's good, that one," he said pleasantly. He had this capacity for behaving as if every situation, no matter how bizarre, was absolutely natural. It was one of the things that intrigued me about Allardyce. Still is.

"Have you been watching me long?" I asked.

"Not really." Still the trademark matter-of-fact good humour. "I saw you say goodbye to Mr Patterson. Then you came in here. I thought, why not join Miss Freeling in the literature section and improve my mind?"

I glanced at my paperback. "Perhaps *literature* isn't quite the appropriate word. Anyway, I thought I was supposed to be contacting you."

"Yes. Well, I thought you might like to be kept informed on how the case is going."

"How kind, Inspector." I sighed. "Should I get used to our meeting like this?"

"Probably. I could ring you up, but it's so much less interesting, don't you agree?"

Allardyce took me to a Greek-run place in Praed Street. Once we had sat down he didn't beat about the bush.

"Zena's left the country," he said, thoughtfully spooning froth off the top of his cappuccino, then plunging it down back into the cup once more.

"Oh yes?" I looked at the grey weather outside. The cold snap was lasting. "Don't blame her."

"Along with her brother."

"The diplomat who slaps people about? I see. Well, well. Where have they gone to?"

"They flew into Miami a couple of days ago," Allardyce told me. "After that we don't know, though we're sure they'll pop up somewhere pretty soon."

"She said she needed a holiday."

Allardyce snorted loudly. The Greeks stopped chattering and turned to stare at him.

"Sorry," he said. "Yeah, I'm sure that's what *Zena* wants. What Johnny wants might be something different. I wouldn't be surprised if they're heading for Saint Theresa, nor if they were travelling on a government ticket. Don't forget who their uncle is."

"Listen," I said, suddenly sick of it all, "why are you telling me this?"

I just wanted to go home now, solitary or not, and read a book. So far as my feelings for the handsome Inspector Allardyce were concerned, I had my peaks and my troughs, and I was definitely heading into a trough.

"I owe it to you, Saskia," he retorted, imperturbable as ever. "Why, don't you want to know what's going on?"

I had no idea how to reply. *Yes, I do. No, I don't.* Neither was true; both were true.

"Only if there's some point to that knowledge," I said finally. "You seem to be implying that Johnny and Zena are involved in this business, but then you leave me — and Tony especially, because I notice you choose to approach me when he's gone off to work in Bristol — in the dark as to the big picture."

"A long sentence, but perfectly sustained," Allardyce commented. "The big picture is, there's a lot of money disappeared and we don't know where it's gone. The small picture — the one we're trying to fill in — has to do with Zena, Jilly Mattheson, and Johnny Dubois. There are other people involved too, but we don't know exactly who they are. That's what we still have to find out. We suspect the real key is in the Caribbean. Maybe Miami, but more likely Saint Theresa or somewhere pretty close."

"While I sit terrified in my flat, waiting to be burgled again. Thanks!"

"Oh, I think that phase is over. I'd relax, if I were you."

"Why?"

"We thought that someone might have you in mind as a way to get to the laundered money, but that now seems unlikely." Allardyce smiled. "I'll tell the local police to keep an eye on your place for a while, but I doubt if you'll be bothered again."

"But why do you wait until Tony's gone to tell me all this?" I persisted. "We've decided to get married, you know. We're absolutely together in everything!"

"I see. Well, in that case, congratulations are in order."

"Aren't they just!" I knew my attitude was ridiculous, but this cool policeman was driving me crazy. It was like mulling over the details of your life in the company of a very personable robot with an excellent taste in coffee.

"Sorry, but I never usually comment on other people's relationships," Allardyce said. He paused. I fancied he managed a slight grimace. "I have enough trouble with my own."

"What's the matter?" I pouted. "Don't the parameters compute?"

"In my case? No, not really."

There was a silence. He actually looked bleak. I wanted to hug him. This was not the correct response for a soon-to-be-married woman, but then my life was changing fast. Anna . . . Jilly . . . Mulcahy and the computer disk . . . Zena and Johnny . . . Tony proposing . . . Australia . . . and now Allardyce loading me with this new burden.

"I've got to go, actually," Allardyce said then. "Keep hold of my direct number, won't you? If I'm wrong, and someone does try to approach you, or something disturbing occurs, do ring."

He offered his hand. Not knowing what else to do, I shook it. Then he walked out of the café. One of the Greeks looked at me and winked. I scowled back. He nudged his friend, obviously considering that this indicated encouragement. I picked up my bag and left.

I was halfway home before I realised that I'd left my trashy paperback in the Greek café. I didn't turn the cab around, however. I simply got the driver to drop me at the Waterstone's on the corner of Bayswater Road, and bought the damned thing again.

One of the advantages of being well off is that with money, everything can be replaced. Everything, that is, except life itself.

★ ★ ★

Shortly after moving in, I had cast-iron grills installed on all the basement and street-level windows of my flat. I was grateful for their protection, however illusory, that evening. It got dark early, and with the darkness fear returned.

Tony called at six, to say he was on his way out to dinner with Di and other cast members from *Intensive Care*. There wasn't much I could say. I could have mentioned that Allardyce had followed me to the station in order to insist there was nothing to worry about. Tony would have been thrilled about that, I don't think! So I just said, "Fine, have a lovely evening."

An hour later the phone rang. It was a man whose voice I didn't recognise at first.

"It's Peter," he said. "Peter Mattheson."

It still didn't register, which shows how disturbed I had become.

"*Jilly Mattheson's brother*," the caller explained, half-amused and half genuinely upset. "I know it's only a few weeks, but I hope you haven't forgotten us already."

"Oh God," I said. "I'm so sorry. Of course not. It's just that I've been up to my eyes in . . . you know, what with Anna . . ."

Peter had this very crisp voice — upper-crust, of course, but with a no-nonsense, scientific edge. He was something in derivatives.

"Look," he cut in gently, "I'm in the area, visiting someone, and I wondered if you'd fancy a snack. Nothing fancy — pub, wine bar, that sort of place. I want to talk about Jilly. And Anna."

I thought about it for a second, then agreed. So much for my promise to Tony that I wouldn't undertake any more freelance solo investigations. But this was just supper, wasn't it?

Peter suggested the pub in Edwardes Square, which was a fifteen-minute walk away. I said I would see him there in half an hour.

* * *

The pub was crowded with evening drinkers. I must have peered around for a minute or two before I saw Peter Mattheson sitting quietly at a table in the corner. He didn't look up until I was standing right by him, then he just made a little gesture for me to sit. Peter was wearing an old sweater and jeans; whatever he had been doing on his 'visit', it certainly hadn't been business of the city-gent kind.

There was a half-empty bottle of Beaujolais and two glasses on the table. Peter poured me some, then thoughtfully topped up his own.

"My wife's left me," he said. "My sister

is dead. Funny things are happening."

I had been raising my glass to my lips but at this I froze. His thin, boyish features were absolutely serious. He must have been a bit drunk, but nothing in his voice or expression gave it away or meant that I took him any less seriously.

"Your wife?" I echoed, starting with her first.

"A month ago. She's been having an affair with her boss."

"Do your parents know?"

He shook his head. "I'll have to tell them soon, I suppose. Because she ain't coming back. What a fuckup." He looked at me steadily. "For all of us."

Peter, usually such a calm, rational young man, was a mess. I touched his hand and he shuddered, as if he had suffered a mild electric shock, then shook his head.

"I didn't call you up just to bitch about Pru. I wanted to talk to you about Jilly and Anna."

My heart skipped a beat. "What about them?"

"There was something wrong with their relationship. Something unhealthy." Peter looked around briefly, as if to check whether anyone was listening. "The police came round to see me on Monday. They claimed that Jilly had been up to something. They wanted to know if I knew anything."

I nodded again, preferring not to comment at this stage. But Peter smiled humourlessly; he'd got the message.

"They've been to see you too, haven't they?" he said. "They wouldn't confirm that Anna was involved, but I bet she was."

"Peter," I began hesitantly, "I think Jilly was laundering money, and I believe Anna was killed because she stumbled on the truth. I'm not saying Jilly was behind it directly. Not at all."

"You think she killed herself because she felt guilty?"

"It's possible."

"My sister did not commit suicide!"

"Peter — "

"Shall I tell you why?"

I gave up any thought of arguing. "OK."

"Because . . . " A glug of red wine in my glass and in his. The bottle was empty now. "Because . . . she left the car unlocked on the Downs."

"Peter, I don't know how to say this, but if Jilly was going to kill herself, she'd hardly be caring about locking her car."

He looked at me with a kind of grim triumph. "Who said anything about *her* car? It wasn't her car, it was mine," he concluded, his voice a low, painful rasp. "BMW Seven Series. Her little Italian thing with the lawnmower engine was playing up again, so I said she could borrow my motor for the weekend. So you see, Jilly being Jilly, she would never have left my valuable car vulnerable to thieves, no matter what she was planning to do. That would have been totally against her nature, believe me, Saskia."

At that Peter's lip started to tremble and he burst into tears. A few rugby-club types drinking nearby exchanged patronising grins. One of them caught my eye and winked, as if to say, "If this is too much for you, darling, I'll take you off Crybaby's hands right now."

"What are you saying?" I whispered. "That someone else pushed Jilly off that bridge?"

"Yes," Peter stuttered between sobs. "Listen, I realise Jilly liked girls, not men, and I know she would do whatever your sister told her. Plus there was that black girl, Zena, the one who came to the funeral but didn't stay to talk . . ."

"You knew Zena?"

"Of course. She and Jilly were an item, weren't they? One of the first things I did when Jilly died was to ring Zena. It seemed only natural."

"And you invited her to the funeral?"

Peter nodded. "At first she said of course she would come. Then she rang back and said she couldn't possibly. Then in the end she turned up unannounced on the day."

"Why do you think she changed her mind?"

"I don't know." Peter blew his nose noisily. "Zena seemed like a pretty nice girl on the whole. Smashing-looking. A bit moody, as she herself admitted. Told me Jilly kept her on an even keel." He let out a sad little laugh. "Jilly was honest and conscientious, her whole life," he said with sudden fervour. "Ever since we were tiny. She never cheated, not even the harmless way kids cheat at games. *Never*."

"People change, Peter. There are pressures — you know how it is."

"Not Jilly. She was my sister. I knew her better than I know myself."

Peter got to his feet and lurched over to the bar. I saw him putting another bottle of Beaujolais on his tab, a lost child with a top-of-the-range BMW and a Gold American Express Card.

There was no escape from the quandary. If not Jilly, as Peter maintained, then could it have been Anna? Of course not, I told myself. But if it was neither of them, then who else was there?

At that moment, I believed that Tony was right about Australia being the answer. I wanted to be far away from these sad spirits and restless ghosts. I wanted to be reborn. To enter the world again, healed and whole, without the phantom pain of a dead twin calling to me from some lost world of childhood innocence.

14

I ROLLED back home about eleven, approaching my front door cautiously, grateful for the photo-sensitive cell that turned my porch-light on automatically. I let myself in, kicked off my shoes and padded through into the living room. The light was blinking on the answering machine.

Grabbing myself a whisky-and-water from the drinks table — I had sipped sparingly at my single glass as Peter got through the second bottle of red wine, and now I needed something to buoy me up — I hit the replay button and collapsed on the sofa.

The first message was from Daisy Tyler, wondering if I was available for a shoot in France just before Christmas. Sweet of her to think of me. Still trying to get me to 'snap out of it', bless her. Daisy thought of work as the ultimate therapy. Very American.

The second message was from Tony.

I could hear people laughing in the background — or maybe just one — and the television was on. You can tell from my description that I was still harbouring irrational fears about his new chumminess with Di Winstone. Irrational because she and Cal were a golden couple, and Tony and I were engaged. On the other hand, even at my most optimistic, I always bore in mind the chillingly cheery actors' term for on-set affairs: 'LDC' — 'Location Doesn't Count'.

Tony said he was just checking in. A bit of gossip about his day, meeting the director and the other cast members, that kind of thing. Then a big signing-off kiss. By that point I had convinced myself everything was fine.

The third message? Well . . . it was Maggie.

"Darling Sass," she said, as if we were having lunch together, "I'm fed up with the weather already, so I've decided to go off to Lanzarote with some friends for six or seven weeks. They've got this marvellous little house, dirt cheap. Lovely weather guaranteed. They're leaving the day after tomorrow, cheap flight at some unearthly hour, which they've also booked me on. So, I thought I'd shoot up to London on the morning train tomorrow and stay overnight. Any chance of a late lunch, or preferably dinner? Be lovely to see you, anyway. Do let me know . . . Oh, and if you should feel like coming down to Trerose while I'm away, please do. Good to have the place heated and the damp kept at bay. You know how it is!"

Then came the beep. No more messages.

I took a sip of whisky, lay back in the forgiving lap of the sofa and let the spirit burn down through me. Then I picked up the phone and dialled the Trerose number.

Maggie was still wide awake and made no comment on the lateness of the hour. Her matter-of-factness was one reason why I had always been fond of her.

"Darling, hello. Are you free tomorrow?" she asked.

I hesitated; a wild idea was forming. "Actually, I shan't be here for the next couple of nights," I said. "Tony's in Bristol until the end of next week, filming a guest appearance on *Intensive Care*.

Yes, he's got a job! So dinner's not on. But I'd like very much to spend some time at Trerose."

"Oh good. I'll be sorry not to see you, but never mind. Everything all right?"

"We're getting by. Are you well?"

"Oh . . . " A minx-ish purr came into her voice. "Having a pretty good time, considering. Lanzarote should be even better!"

"Not another Wing-co!" I said, trying to match her zest. A dashing retired RAF ace had had a thing for her a few years back. She had darned near gone up the aisle with him before she found out that he had been married four times previously and appeared to have had an affair with every woman in west Cornwall under the age of eighty. Every time Maggie showed signs of becoming attached to another man, there had been a chorus of "Wing-co!" from me and Anna.

Maggie laughed coquettishly. "He's an artist. And we're just good friends. I've learned my lesson."

Anything less likely was hard to

imagine, but I said nothing further on the subject.

"I'll probably come down in the next few days," I said. "Then maybe Tony would like to spend Christmas at Trerose. Get away from the hectic festive scene up here."

"Do you want to? Darling, you only live once."

There was a short silence. "Of course," I said. We had both thought of Anna, and we both knew the point didn't need to be expressed. "I'm tired of London, though, Maggie." I paused. "Tony's keen on going to live in Australia. Clean air, fresh start. And I've agreed to marry him."

I don't know why I phrased that last sentence the way I did, making marriage to the man I loved sound like a sort of health measure. Perhaps because I knew Maggie would have her doubts and I wanted to disarm her.

She did hesitate for a moment. Then: "Well, Sass. Congratulations. Was this your idea or his?"

"Maggie! He proposed to me!"

"Darling, one never knows these days.

Marvellous. He means it then."

"I should hope so."

"When's it going to happen?"

"I don't know. We discussed it the other morning. Then he was called off to do this TV job."

"I'll give you the address of the house on Lanzarote," Maggie said. "No phone, I'm afraid. Let me know, and I'll make sure I'm in town for the happy event."

There was another pause.

"I'm floating on air, actually," I said, as if I was sixteen years old and justifying some unsuitable boyfriend. "It feels very good."

"Darling, I'm thrilled for you. The best thing is that he's in work. It evens up the financial aspects, that kind of thing. All the sorrier to be missing having dinner with you. So do let me know, won't you . . ."

We agreed I would pick up the key for Trerose from Mrs Williams in the village, who had cleaned the place ever since I could remember. We giggled a bit about marriage generally and Tony in particular, which made me feel a bit better.

But after I put the phone down I felt churned up, fragile. I suddenly didn't want the whisky any more. I went straight upstairs to bed.

★ ★ ★

The voice came back again. I lay awake listening to it.

Sassie. Sassie . . .

Then it went, in the automatic way it did. This had become routine. Frightening, but not overwhelming. When the silence returned I got up, put on my robe, and wandered down to the ground floor. I didn't know what else to do. I wanted to call Tony, but I felt ridiculous. If Anna had still been alive, I would certainly have rung *her*. But then if she had still been alive, I would not have been going crazy, I thought feverishly as I retrieved the half-drained glass of whisky from the table beside the sofa and topped it up from the bottle.

Fortified by Scotch, I did something I never do. I turned on the television at two-thirty in the morning. It was a choice between a weeks-old American pop-charts show or a Brazilian vampire film. Each lasted about five minutes. Or rather, that was my attention-span.

In a sudden burst of paranoia, I decided to roam around a little, check the rooms. For the first time in the couple of days since the window had been fixed, I went up to my study and switched on the light.

Everything looked in order. Until I glanced in the direction of my computer.

The disk was back. Anna's disk. The one stolen in the burglary just a few nights ago.

For a moment I just stared at the little square of black plastic and metal. Then, my heart beating like an artillery barrage, I went over to the computer and clicked it on. My hand trembled as I inserted the disk into the slot and told the computer to load it. Then I flashed its contents onto the screen.

I read the first sentence and froze in shock. Instead of Anna's nervous, affectionate beginning, here was something else. Something vile.

Well, bitch, you really have been talking to the wrong people, it said.

Talking too much. So here's a warning to you and that pretty-boy of yours, that we are watching. We want to, we find you.

And then we do what we need to do. Never forget: you can run, but you can't hide.

I looked around for signs of forced entry. None. Impossible — unless they had a key! Maybe they had found one last time, made a copy. Oh my God!

I *had* to talk to Tony. I needed the sound of his voice. If I could speak to him, he would be with me — and when he was with me, bad things stopped happening . . .

In blind terror, I ran downstairs and scrabbled around beside the phone until I found the scrap of paper with Tony's number in Bristol on it. I dialled, then let it ring, and ring, and ring. He wasn't there. And it was almost three in the morning.

The conclusion I drew was the obvious one. All my suspicions of Tony's relationship with the glamorous Di Winstone flooded back and overwhelmed me. Location Doesn't Count. I was on my own, just when I really needed him. Maybe only for tonight. But maybe for ever.

Finally I stopped hoping and put down the phone. I sat still for some time, then realised I had to do something.

Summoning up some last reserve of strength, I fled to my bedroom and got dressed. Fifteen minutes later, I threw a suitcase and my camera-bag into the Suzuki, got in and started the engine.

The words of the poisoned message placed with such exquisite cruelty on my disk were seething in my head. *Never forget: you can run, but you can't hide.*

Try me on that one, I thought with desperate determination. Just try me.

I headed out through the empty, dark streets of West London towards the M4. I would be in Cornwall for breakfast. Alone at Trerose, where no one would find me.

Where I would be safe as houses. So the saying goes.

15

I WAS about half an hour out of London before it occurred to me that I might be just a fraction over the alcohol limit. I wasn't terribly worried about being stopped, but didn't want to risk falling asleep at the wheel so I made myself pull in at the new service area near Reading.

After buying myself a filter-coffee and a ham sandwich, I sat down in a corner of the snack-bar. Catching sight of my reflection in the window, trapped in the unflattering overhead light, I hastily turned away and studied the human ecology of the place.

The cafeteria wasn't crowded, but it was somehow extra-alive, in the way places are that have stayed awake when the rest of the world has chosen to sleep. There was a rock band on their way back from a gig, some truck-drivers taking a break, and a surreal party of old-age pensioners who obviously had some schedule of their own.

It wasn't that the world held no more danger for me now. But these were the usual, run-of-the-mill dangers that face any woman alone at night, on the road. I was used to it, even got a faint buzz from it. My safe place wasn't being invaded.

I thought a lot about Tony as I drank my coffee. For an instant, sure of his sexual treachery, I harboured the wild idea that he might also have been involved in stealing Anna's original disk and then leaving the poisoned one in its place. After all, there was no sign of forced entry this time. Except *why* on earth would he do such a thing? None of it made any sense. I dismissed the whole possibility. Just showed how far my paranoia had a grip on me. No, the key-copying theory was far more plausible. Unfortunately, my other suspicion — Tony's double-cross with Di Winstone — still made hideous sense He wouldn't be the first man to press ahead with marriage to his steady woman while maintaining the right to have others on the side, before and after the wedding.

I set off again at four-thirty. Then,

after Newbury I saw a pair of headlights hovering behind me. I slowed down. I speeded up. They were fixed in my rearview mirror, as if they had been stuck there.

I've had the odd road-crazy before. I'm blonde, considered nice-looking, and I drive around a lot on my own. And you get them. Hanging in behind you, overtaking and making gestures. But not at night like that, without ever having been close enough to see who you are, locked in at a distance like some slow, heat-seeking missile.

Of course I was spooked. But I wasn't trapped at home any more, wondering who had got in here, or worrying about voices in the night. I was in my speedy little Jeep, free to go wherever I liked. I had my mobile in its cradle, ready to summon help, and there was the strictly illegal can of Mace I had picked up in New York the year before, snuggled in the glove compartment. I put myself on autopilot. I waited, watched, kept driving.

The following vehicle came slowly closer and closer, until it was no more than twenty feet behind. I studied my rearview mirror again. A mist of sweat was spreading across my forehead. My hands were clammy, though it was a cold night and I never put the heater on when making a long drive, for fear of drowsiness. But my brain was clear, and my eyes sharp. The tailgate was on dipped lights. I started to make out details.

It was a Suzuki just like my own, I realised. And the driver had a shock of blonde hair.

I was being followed, in other words, by a mirror.

And then the car-phone rang. I put my foot down, and pulled away. It kept ringing. I glanced up again. The Suzuki — if I had been right and the whole thing hadn't been a trick of my mind — was making no attempt to keep up, and there was suddenly at least a hundred feet between us.

I picked up the phone, my left hand trembling. The plastic of the receiver felt cold as the grave.

"Hello?" I said in a choked whisper,

"*Sassie,*" came the familiar voice. "*Sassie, Sassie . . .* "

I snapped it off and tossed the phone away from me as if it were a vicious snake. It clattered against the gear-stick and spun off into the legroom-cave below the dashboard. Then I don't remember anything except timeless, overwhelming terror until a sign loomed up — it could have been five seconds or five minutes later — announcing that there was just one mile to the next service area. I glanced behind. The headlights were still there and starting to gain once more. I must have been doing ninety when I reached the turnoff. God knows how I managed to pull over and slow down sufficiently not to kill myself or anyone else as I hit the blessedly lit, garish and peopled forecourt of the service area. I jammed on the brakes and squealed to a halt just before I reached the ranks of parked cars next to the restaurant complex. With the engine still running, I sat slumped over the wheel, waiting for my heart to get back in my chest and my hands to stop trembling.

Then I heard a vehicle drawing up behind me. A door opening and shutting. Unhurried footsteps. A tap on my window. Someone trying my door, which I had locked from old London habit. Leaving the engine running, I turned slowly, easing open the glove compartment as I did so. My hand felt for the can of Mace, found it. I relaxed a fraction. I could have the spray operative in a second. Then I finally looked up.

Into the face of a uniformed policeman. Quite young, a little overweight. Trying hard to look stern. He tapped again and I heard him say in a West Country accent: "Excuse me, madam. Are you all right?"

I straightened, hastily withdrawing my hand from the glove compartment. No way did I want to be found in charge of an illegal weapon tonight. I turned off the engine, then reached down, picked up the phone from the floor of the car and replaced it in its cradle. A little bit of batty housekeeping in the night. Finally, taking a very deep breath, I wound down the window. The cold pre-dawn air hit me like a blow. I gasped.

"I'm sorry," I mumbled then. "Someone was tailgating me. I panicked."

I ventured a quick glance behind. The

car he had got out of was not a patrol vehicle but an unmarked white Ford saloon. Another cop was sitting in the driving seat with the light on, reading.

The policeman looked at his car and smiled wryly. "We don't always like to make ourselves too obvious." He was fiddling with something in his jacket pocket. I realised it was a notebook.

"I know I was speeding," I confessed. "Sorry. I just put my foot down. You know how it is."

He glanced around. "Yes. Listen, why don't you get a cup of coffee? Sounds as if you need to take a break. How far are you going?"

"Oh, just to Bath," I lied instinctively. I didn't want him giving me a long lecture about how I was in no fit state to drive to Cornwall. "I'm a photographer. Wanted to take some pictures."

He did look at me a bit searchingly then. When policemen come up against someone like me, a capable, presentable woman with a fairly posh accent, it either gets their backs up or they go all deferential. Luckily my policeman's reactions put him in the latter category.

"Well, take a break. I understand why you overdid the speed there, so no harm done. I see you've got a phone in the car, so just ring the emergency number if you get any more hassle, OK?"

I nodded. He half-turned away, then seemed to think of something else.

"You say you had someone tailgating you, madam. Where was this?"

"I'm not sure," I said. "It was some time back, but she got close . . . " I remembered the shock of blonde hair and shivered. "That was a mile or two back. That's when I freaked."

Of course, I didn't mention the phone, and Anna's voice. The policeman was nodding, smiling faintly.

"A woman driving, eh? What kind of vehicle was this?"

"A Suzuki Jeep just like mine, actually."

"Right," he said. "Well, I suppose we were behind you for about three miles. You were driving along OK, but then you suddenly took off like a bat out of hell." He frowned. "And I never saw a Suzuki Jeep. Now you be careful, madam. Take it really easy. Promise?"

He hesitated, perhaps wondering if he

should take me in for my own good — a possibility that was already occurring to me. But then he tipped his hat and walked back to his car.

I watched the unmarked police vehicle circle the car park slowly, checking out the scene there, then pull away, heading for the petrol station behind the restaurant. After it disappeared from sight, I locked the door again and sat stock still at the wheel for several minutes.

Of course, I told myself, he thinks I'm crazy. At that moment I thought I was crazy. My hands were trembling, and I was gripping the steering-wheel as if it were my one anchor in life. I relaxed my hands slowly, like a sick person doing an exercise, eased them away and slid them behind my head. Then I lay back and closed my eyes.

Bad things have happened, I told myself yet again. If you must accept that you are mad — temporarily mad — you know there is a reason. In fact, there are a dozen reasons. Deaths. Break-ins. Threats. Confusions and intrigues. And now Tony's betrayal. The final straw.

Oh God, Tony, why weren't you there when I called, and what does it mean? Are you in love with Di Winstone, or is it just about sex? And even if this was only a one-night stand, could I possibly marry you and then live with the knowledge that you've done this once and you could do it again . . .

I opened my eyes again. The terrors in my head were too much to handle. I flirted with the temptations of the brightly lit restaurant, the lure of the company, the illusive security of the normal.

But a conviction was growing. All I wanted now was to be at Trerose. If I was about to go finally, definitively crazy, I might as well do it there. Among the scenes of my childhood. With people who were familiar to me, and whom I knew to be benign. If I really had to heal myself, alone, without Tony, where else but Trerose could that be possible?

Suddenly I felt very strong. I let out a weirdly triumphant little laugh. Without a second thought, I started the Suzuki's engine once more.

If you're out there, my phantom twin,

I thought, I'll race you. And if you're only inside my head, then I'll be racing my bloody self won't I, and that's fine too, because it's probably what I've been doing all my life.

★ ★ ★

Of course I didn't drive straight down to Cornwall without stopping.

I knew Maggie would be getting a train from Truro at about ten, which meant she probably wouldn't order a taxi for earlier than nine. I didn't want to risk showing up just as she was leaving.

So the purple late-November dawn found me at a greasy-spoon halfway across Dartmoor, worrying at a bacon roll and trying to stomach enough of the weak black liquid that called itself coffee to keep me awake until I could safely tackle the remaining drive into Cornwall and then on to Trerose.

I knew this café. It, or something similar, had been on this site for at least twenty-five years. In those pre-motorway days, driving down from Buckinghamshire to Cornwall in Daddy's stately Rover was a seven, eight-hour business. Often he would tip us into the back of the car at ten p.m., wrap us up in blankets, and chug off into the night. On he would drive, careful and slow, and he never took the Tamar Bridge route, or the toil through Launceston. He loved to turn off at Moretonhampstead and detour across Dartmoor in the early morning. He would stop at this place, by an old bridge and a stream and a string of sturdy cottages, sit for a few minutes, then lean over the back of his seat and give each of us a shake, murmuring: "Girls, girls, breakfast-time."

Of course we were hardly ever asleep, but we would never let him know. It was a joke between Anna and me. Already long-since woken by the early morning chill, we would feel the car stop, cut its engine. We would hear a big sigh from Father in the front seat. Then a squeak as he turned on the leather seat and half-clambered up so he could reach us.

"Girls, girls, breakfast!" Anna and I would whisper our chorus. Then we would open our eyes and smile at Daddy as he smiled down at us, eager to show him that we had just emerged from the land of dreams at his all-powerful behest.

I often wondered why Daddy stopped so near to our destination just an hour-and-a-half to go, even in those days. He was like a tortoise, the way he drove, slow and remorseless. I knew him even in his sixties, just before he died, to drive 600 miles in a day, from Cornwall to the Scottish Highlands, without stopping except for petrol, and never show the slightest sign of tiredness.

The penny only dropped after Grandma Freeling's death. From then on he never bothered to stop. Previously, it became clear, he had broken the journey because he needed to 'spruce us up' before presenting us to his mother. The routine never varied. A cup of tea for him and Robinson's Barley Water for us, and a snack. Then 'some fresh air to put some colour back in your cheeks' — this usually consisted, weather permitting, of hopping around the stones that littered the bank of the stream crossed by the ancient bridge. Then a rub with a flannel, a comb of the hair, and on with cardigans that he kept ready for the purpose. Only then could we continue, down the zig-zag road to Gunnislake Bridge and the romantic, narrow entry to Cornwall that felt like a scene from *The Prisoner of Zenda*. At ten we would be coming up the drive to Trerose, ready for another breakfast provided by Grandma Freeling, hungry or not . . .

All this came back to me that morning with a corruscating vividness. I even hopped around the stones, though now they were adjoined by an ugly Visitors' Centre, and a sign expressly forbade any latterday little girls from following our long-ago example. As I jumped I pursed my lips. I shrank to three feet tall, and I was automatically wary of getting my sandals wet. I leapt around like a mad thing. It was a kind of lonely, bleak ecstasy, a willed nostalgia, like drawing on some treasure you have always had but know you must not spend because, once lost, it can never be restored.

The funny thing was that I felt marvellous. Free, because I didn't care if I died at that moment. Everyone I loved and hated — and aren't they often the same — had gone, including, I was sure, Tony. Nothing mattered. Except the stones, hopping from this one to that one and trying not to get my feet wet . . .

★ ★ ★

In Cornwall the trees were finally bare. I always kept up with the weather down here, and I had read in the paper of a big sou'westerly a week or so back, which had evidently torn the last of the leaves from their fragile anchorages. But as I drove down the spine of the county and into its heel, I saw that everything was still green, as always in south Cornwall, and there were lilies and nasturtiums in roadside gardens, even a few sturdy rose-bushes still blooming behind sheltering walls.

It was an overcast but calm day, and the sea had settled into a grey uniformity untroubled by wind. I stopped on the hill just before it dipped down into Gillan and looked out over the Helford Estuary. I wound down the window. One breath of the soft, mild air and I knew I was home. I inhaled it, sprawled like a cat in my seat, and I think I was really smiling for the first time in days, even weeks.

A glance at myself in the Suzuki's rearview mirror wiped the smile off my face. I looked worn, wild-haired, altogether deranged. I opened my bag, dug out my make-up kit and hairbrush, and performed a quick repair job before starting the final drive down to the village.

Five minutes later I knocked on the door of Mrs Williams' council house. Her son, Gary, answered. A pudgy boy in his mid-thirties' just as he had been a pudgy boy twenty years before when we played on the beach together, he lived, like many local men, off the dole and a bit of socially acceptable, cash-only moonlighting. Gary greeted me with a vague affability that was also unchanged from childhood, invited me into the hall, and called through to his mother.

The familiar petite figure of Mrs Williams appeared from the living room. To the terrified, exhausted woman who had driven down from London that night, her welcoming smile was worth a year of therapy, a bucket of pills. She immediately ushered me into the kitchen and put the kettle on.

Of course, all the time I could tell that her clear blue eyes were examining me, checking for damage or distress hidden behind my quick cosmetic disguise, my attempted air of naturalness. Not that Mrs Williams wanted to know my reasons for being here, or why I had arrived without warning just hours after Maggie's departure. She simply pressed a cup of hot sweet tea into my hand. A quiet, austere woman, she was far from the stereotype of the apple-checked gossip, which was why my grandmother had employed her all those years ago, when Mrs Williams was still a young mother. Not that Grandma Freeling had any secrets, I think. She just liked her privacy.

"Mrs Freeling left about two hours ago," she said when she had me established in an armchair by the fire. "Harry from the garage took her to the station. Doesn't want to pass another winter here, your stepmother. Too much rain. None where she's going." She paused. "I'm sorry about Anna," she added softly, and touched my arm. "You'll miss her."

I sipped the tea. It tasted good. And it felt easy being with Mrs Williams, hearing what she said about Anna, because I knew her own husband, John, had disappeared on a fishing trip twenty years ago, leaving her alone with Gary to bring up. She knew what the sea could do, what loss meant, and also how the bereaved just had to carry on living.

"I do miss her," I said. "It's the suddenness. But then you know — "

"Yes," Mrs Williams said. "I know. My John, God rest his soul. And they haven't found Anna either?"

I shook my head. "We're still hoping. I suppose we'll keep hoping until they do."

There was a long silence, filled with sadness, but not uncomfortable or awkward.

"And how's young Tony?" Mrs Williams asked. "Been a great support, I daresay."

"Oh yes," I said quickly.

"I talked to Mrs Freeling first thing. She told me he's working on that hospital programme, so we shall see him on the screen soon."

"Soon," I agreed. "A few weeks' time."

Mrs Williams' alert gaze missed very little. I could tell she knew something was wrong, but she made no comment. Instead she sighed, and got to her feet. I could see now that she moved with a slight limp, and she noticed that I noticed. "Osteo-arthritis," she explained with a wry smile. "Got me name down for a hip replacement. Once they finally get that bit of plastic in me, I'll be the bionic woman."

As Mrs Williams spoke, she reached a chest of drawers and started rummaging through the top one. Finally she produced an envelope and turned to face me again.

"I've got something for you," she smiled, opening the envelope and taking out a sheaf of small photographs. "Had some copies made at the photo place in Helston. Doesn't cost much these days, you know. I was going to give you these when you came down at Christmas, but since you're here, you may as well have them now."

I took the photographs from her, and

fanned them out on the little table. There were a dozen of them, with that slightly washed-out look that cheap colour-prints had in the late 1960s and early 1970s. There was one of my father, fiftyish, smoking his pipe and holding a pair of garden shears, smiling unconvincingly for the camera. Then one of all of us — me and Anna at about five or six, our mother and father, Grandma Freeling, and the car in a supporting role. The house. My mother reading . . .

"John took all these with his Instamatic," she said. "That would be in 1971."

"The year Mummy died." Mr Williams himself still had three or four years to live.

I carried on sorting through them until I arrived at one that showed either Anna or me as a six-year-old with Mother. This snap was slightly out of focus, with a tilt, where the others were competently if unimaginatively shot.

"Ah, I was going to ask you about that photo," said Mrs Williams. "Which one of you would that have been?"

Something long-suppressed and long-avoided was coming back to me.

Something terrible. Something totally and inexplicably at odds with the smiling faces and innocent scene in that sunlit garden from the mid-1970s.

"You all right, dear?" Mrs Williams asked.

I looked up sharply. "This picture feels spooky. The others are OK."

She looked at me shrewdly but with immense compassion. "That picture was taken the day your dear mother passed on, Saskia, my dear," she said softly. "'Twas just a few minutes later she felt tired and went to lie down, and while she was asleep her heart gave way. That's why the picture feels like that for you."

Silence covered us like a net. The clock's tick marked out the path of time. Those few seconds took me back twenty-five years. The net lifted. Memories writhed like deep-sea fish dragged up into the light.

"No, that's not all. You see, it was me who took it!" I blurted out. "Suddenly I remember!"

It was true. Details of that afternoon had begun flashing back to me: the photo-session in the garden, John Williams wielding his little camera, wanting one more picture of us to finish his roll of film, and me pleading with him to let me hold it and see how it worked . . .

"I remember I took that photograph of Mummy and Anna!"

So, in fact, I had actually first used a camera years before I had always thought. Of course, all recollection must have been obliterated by what happened later that same day: my mother's death. I looked down. My mother's eyes were shaded slightly by an overhanging laburnum branch, but even in so poorly focused an image I could see the slightly sour expression on Anna's face, the look that said: "Why does Sassie get her way and not me?" My mother's hand rested on her shoulder, protective and comforting, but not enough to assuage that jealousy. Except, it occurred to me now, that it was probably Anna who had been the last to feel my mother's living embrace, captured here in this tilted image.

I put the photograph back on the pile, and quickly picked up another. The car again — John Williams' pin-up. He had always admired Daddy's Rover.

Fishermen who lived in council houses didn't have cars in those days, especially not three-litre luxury saloons.

Ten minutes later, with the envelope of photographs on the seat beside me and the key to Trerose in the pocket of my jacket, I manoeuvred up the steep drive towards the home of my childhood. Here were all my childhood's joys and its one vast, incomprehensible tragedy. I was still trembling from the recent revelation, still fighting an impulse to burn the poisoned image of that fatal afternoon and unmake my whole life as a photographer, a capturer of memories.

As if such actions would bring my mother back to life. Or my sister. *As if.*

16

I THINK I already mentioned that Trerose is a wood-framed house, built during the 1920s in the American style. No cob walls or quaint, tiny windows or gloomy, poky rooms: everything about the place is designed to trap the warmth and light of the sun. The only parts of the house which don't fit this pattern are the two rooms under the eaves built, Grandma Freeling always thought, as servants' quarters. These became Anna's room and mine when we were children and remained so for almost thirty years, until we went off on that fateful holiday to Saint Theresa.

Opening up the house, I prowled for a few minutes around the plain but pin-neat ground-floor rooms, and found a note on the mantelpiece from Maggie, wishing Tony and me a happy Christmas stay. If only she could have seen me, invading this house just hours after she had left! I even checked the kitchen, altogether like a nervous animal ensuring no predators have sneaked in while she was away. I could still smell a whiff of Maggie's Chanel in the atmosphere. Perhaps she was travelling up with her mysterious artist-friend; perhaps he had even stayed the night here with her.

I took my bag up to my old room under the eaves. The scent worn by my stepmother lingered on the landing even more strongly than downstairs. The reminder was both comforting and disturbing; somehow it made more painful the thought of Anna and my dead mother, and the photographs Mrs Williams had given me.

The room received me like an old friend. Across the low-ceilinged landing lay the closed door of Anna's room. It was exactly the same size and shape as mine, a mirror-image except for its window, which had been pushed to one side and reduced by the substantial chimney on that side of the house. To me the division of the rooms felt like a fixed thing, a fact, something which had always been so. Although, in fact, Anna and I had fought over them. More flash-recollections came to me. Anna's angry eyes. Accusations. *Why does Sassie always get the best? I want it! I want it!* I knew then that this stay at Trerose was about summoning up old memories. No matter how difficult or even dangerous, if there was a key, this must be it.

I didn't go into Anna's territory that morning; couldn't face it. Instead I pushed quickly into my own room and tossed my bag into the far corner by the threadbare Lloyd-Loom chair, just as if I were thirteen again and returning from school for the holidays.

Then, again as in my childhood days, I flopped down on top of my bed and stared at the bumpy Artexed ceiling, looking for secret patterns and shapes, searching for sense.

★ ★ ★

I remember nothing more until I heard the phone ringing down in the living room. Propping myself on one elbow, I listened dopily, and even as I listened the ringing stopped. I lay down again.

Through my east-facing window, I could see that the sun had moved round to the other side of the house; it was afternoon. I felt quite chilly; that is what drove me out of bed and along the landing to adjust the central-heating thermostat. A glance out of the window there confirmed that the day was well-advanced, perhaps almost over. I heard the oil-fired boiler kick up and shambled back to my room.

From inside my bag came a chirrup, like the cry of a small, trapped animal. I unzipped the flap and pulled out my mobile phone.

"Yes?" I mumbled. "Saskia Freeling."

There was a sharp intake of breath at the other end.

"Thank Christ I found you." The voice was Tony's, harsh and yet concerned, like a worried parent.

"Hi," I said coolly.

"Where the hell are you, Sass? I called Maggie's place . . ."

"I know. That's where I am," I said.

"You're at Trerose? What are you doing there? What made you take off like this? I've been worried sick."

"Is that right?" My voice was sarcastic, defensive.

"Yes, that's right." Tony paused. "What are you pissed off about?"

"I called you again last night. I needed you, but you weren't at the flat." I paused. "I . . . I suppose you were with Di."

"You're absolutely right," Tony confirmed. I froze, unable to believe his easy, almost jocular dismissal of my feelings. Then he said: "I was with her because Di had to take me to hospital."

"*What?*"

"I was chopping a lemon to put in her gin and tonic, and I damn-near sliced the end off it. My finger, I mean. She had to drive me into Casualty. You can imagine the remarks from the staff when they recognised the famous Dr Hilary from the telly. Asked why she couldn't sort it out herself . . . Anyway, I didn't get back to the flat until well after four."

There was quite a long silence.

"Oh God, I'm so sorry, darling," I said then. My voice was trembling, whether from relief or embarrassment I had little idea — and cared less. "I misjudged you. Oh God."

"You thought I'd gone to Di's place? You thought — "

"Tony, I can explain. I had a terrible fright last night, really terrible. Anna's disk was returned — by someone. Somehow. And now, instead of the letter she wrote, it's got a . . . horrible message on it."

"When did you find this thing?"

"After I'd finished talking to you. That's why I called back, and freaked out when you weren't there. I thought — " My voice began to wobble.

"I'd gone back to Di's for coffee and a spot of nooky," Tony finished for me. "Actually, Di's a mess at the moment, estranged from Cal and needing to be on her own."

"Can you forgive me?"

"Yeah. Easily." Tony laughed. "You need a holiday, sweetheart. So you bolted down to Cornwall. Don't blame you."

"I'm feeling a bit mad, darling. I warn you."

"Come on, you headed for where you

feel safe. What's out of order about that?"

"When I was driving down here, someone called me on the car-phone." I forced myself to say the words. "It was like the voice in the night at home. Anna's voice, you remember."

This time Tony went very quiet. Then he said: "That's not funny, not funny at all. Listen, once I've finished shooting today, I won't get called again until Tuesday, so I'll be down tomorrow morning to fetch you. You're coming back here with me — right?"

"Oh, Tony. There's so much — " I was nearly weeping with love, and relief.

"No arguing. I'm not going to let you out of my sight again. But right now I have to get my ass back on the set or I'll get fired. Just sit tight, take it easy and rest."

"I will."

"I love you."

Before I could answer, he hung up.

I put down the phone. My poor, anxious body was singing with joy.

From now on, nothing would shake

my trust in Tony, nothing, I told myself. Until death us did part.

★ ★ ★

I just had time to drive down to the village stores, where I bought some bread, milk, some instant pasta sauce to go with the spaghetti in Maggie's cupboard, and a bottle of Australian wine.

When I got back it was dark. The wind had started to pick up from the south-west, whipping the tops of the trees like an unpopular uncle ruffling the hair of a gaggle of long-suffering children. I could feel rain in the air. It wasn't the sort of night to be alone in my current state, but then I had no choice. Better at Trerose than at the London flat, where I knew I had been observed, and where I knew my privacy had been violated.

Meticulously, I locked all the doors and windows. I took one last look over the soft, serpentine contours of the Helford Estuary, still visible in the last glow of the setting sun, then it was time to draw the curtains on the big picture window and settle down for the night.

I watched a little television; first the local news, then over to Channel Four for the world's misfortunes. That did me until eight, and helped drown out the gale that by now was hurling branches at the seaward windows of Trerose. It took me back to the bed in Howell's office-bungalow at the Emerald Key Resort, the night after Anna disappeared. Except that this was familiar, dear Cornwall, where I had always felt safe, and not the dangerous Caribbean.

Leaving the TV on, I walked through into the kitchen to prepare some supper. I was suddenly ravenous, and possessed of a spiky nervous energy, the kind you often get after an unaccustomed afternoon nap. To the comforting sound of an over-the-top Northern soap blaring through from the living room, I chopped up an onion, started sauteeing it in a skillet, and put a pan of water on for the pasta. Then I poured a generous glass of wine and told myself that I was, if not happy, at least coping.

There is a sloping area of garden outside the kitchen window. It provides about thirty or forty metres of neat lawn and flowerbeds leading to the top boundary, a hedge behind which meanders a right-of-way used by ramblers and dog-walkers as a short-cut between the village and the coastal footpath. Behind this, woodland rises to the crest of the hill.

I was gazing out into the darkness, where the silhouette of the copse up there was just visible in the night sky, and was taking another sip of wine, wondering if it was time to mix the sauce with the freshly sautéed onions.

Then the shot came.

It sounded like a fuse blowing. But blown fuses don't make round, star-edged holes appear in glass windows. And they don't repeat themselves a couple of seconds later . . .

I did an assignment in Sarajevo years ago, when the trouble first really got under way and the civilised people of that city were still learning how to cope with indiscriminate Serb sniper-fire. I learned along with them. Which was why, when the second faint *crack* came, and the second bullet smashed through the kitchen window, I was already dropping automatically towards the kitchen floor, oblivious to potential bruises or to the fate of my stepmother's crystal wine-glass.

I hit the quarry-tiled floor hard, then rolled over. There was a moment of unreality, a sense that this couldn't be happening, not here, then my brain started to work like a computer, calculating first that the shot must have come from the footpath at the top of the garden, and next that whatever else I did, I had to switch the light off, or the moment I showed myself — say, in trying to escape through to the living room — the sniper up there would have his shot made immeasurably easier.

I lay there for about ten seconds, breathing hard, gathering my nerve. Then I squirmed on my belly towards the skirting board below the light-switch. I reached it in one piece, waited for a reaction. None, and no sound outside. I eased myself up onto my haunches. Taking a deep breath, I threw myself upwards towards the brass-plated lightswitch and flicked, almost punched it off, before ducking down again. Instantly the kitchen was plunged into darkness, with only a pale emanation coming through the half-open door of the living room, where there was no overhead light, only lamps.

The TV was still blaring away. Another show had succeeded the Northern soap. I heard American male voices arguing. Lots of conflict. Then, bizarrely, given what had just happened to me, a volley of shots was fired on the screen. Fake, sound-effect shots, by which I mean hard-sounding, clear 'bangs', not like the almost comical, pop-gun-sounding shots that kill people in real life. Not at all like the sounds made by the bullets that had just smashed through the kitchen window of my childhood home.

I crouched there for a moment more, then decided that it really was time to move. Maybe he was already in the garden and coming closer if a 'he' is what the would-be assassin was — so I had to act before he managed to take fresh aim, or decided to get into the house to finish me off.

Keeping low, I took another deep breath and dashed through to the living room. Nothing happened. I was tempted by the phone on the table, but it was right by the window. I would be a brightly lit target if I paused there to make a call. And my mobile was upstairs.

In that moment I switched from logic to instinct. Instinct told me that delay could be fatal. The only thing I could do was trust to luck and make a run for it.

They were having yet another scripted argument on the television as I slipped out of the living room, aiming not for the front door, but for a way out that only I and those familiar with the house would know: the slightly rickety lean-to conservatory on the west-facing side of the house.

The route to the conservatory was through the old utility room, with Maggie's washing-machine and drier in one corner, and in the other the big, battered Belfast sink where I remember young Mrs Williams doing our laundry when Anna and I were little girls. I padded cautiously into the darkness, not daring to switch on the light. My trainers squeaked — in my nervous state almost seemed to scream — on the linoleum as I edged towards the glass-panelled conservatory door, praying that Maggie had left the key on the ledge above it, as we had done ever since I could remember.

My hand went to the spot with the swiftness of long practice, but my fingers found themselves scrabbling only at bare wood, scouring dust.

A moment passed as I cursed silently and listened to the howl of the wind. Then I heard someone banging at the front door. I froze. There was a pause. For a moment I thought it was the wind. Then the banging resumed, loud and persistent. It must have gone on for a full thirty seconds. By now the unnatural calm that had descended after the shooting had evaporated, and my whole body was shaking with terror. I was a trapped, helpless animal. Then the banging stopped, and the fear got even worse. I had a brief, wild notion of fleeing upstairs, hiding in the loft and taking the ladder up behind me, but if whoever was outside decided to do a thorough search, they would find me — and then there really would be no escape.

I ran out of time to think of any other bright ideas, because as I stood there, wondering what to do, the beam of a powerful torch became visible through the panes of the conservatory door. The torch pointed right into the conservatory, and probed towards the door behind which I was standing. I flattened myself against the wall, anxiously imploring God to make me thinner, more invisible. The beam flitted briefly through the utility room, licking at the implements and machines, the shelves of housewares and detergents, revealing the worn lino at my feet.

And also the door-key that had fallen from its ledge to the floor.

The torchlight lingered for an endless second, then disappeared. Shortly afterwards, it went from the conservatory too, as the searcher continued on his windswept way.

Without another thought, I ducked down to a squat and ran my hands gently over the lino in the dark, feeling for the key. I found it. Blindly, I felt for the keyhole in the conservatory door and noiselessly inserted the key.

I calculated I had a few minutes before the man with the torch took another turn around the house — presuming that he did. I was given new confidence when I heard the banging at the front door start up again. *Right*. Out the side while he's busy at the front, then through the vegetable garden to the drive.

The outer door of the conservatory was locked, but the windows were openable from the inside. I struggled with one, which was sticky, but eventually got it open. The wind came in with a blast that threatened to bring down the stack of pots on my father's old workbench, but I was heedless as I pushed the window open and launched myself first onto the sill, then out into the darkness.

I landed in some weeds, a bit heavily. I looked up. The big ash-trees on the far side of the vegetable garden swayed wildly against the night-sky.

I moved forward quickly across the soggy winter ground, keeping my eyes on the trees. I felt impervious to the wind-chill, all panic banished as suddenly as it had come. I was an animal on the run now, not a trapped one, and that made all the difference. I stumbled over a cold-frame, slid to one side, then righted myself and stumbled on.

But then the torch-beam cut through the darkness and caught me. Someone shouted. I kept going, but a large shadow was on the move there too, heading me off. *There were two of them. I hadn't thought of that.*

I changed direction, but it was futile. The bulky shadow approached unerringly, anticipating my every move as I tried to weave and dodge in the stormy dark. A moment later a large and unmistakably male figure crashed into me, and strong arms pinioned me, held me tight. The man was panting; he reeked sourly of sweat and exertion. He was saying something, but in the storm and my terror I couldn't or wouldn't listen. I just concentrated on kicking and struggling.

The dazzling beam of the torch seared my eyes, blinding me. A terrible moment of helplessness and terror followed. Then the man with the torch shouted something, and suddenly the arms around me relaxed. The torch turned away from my face and, as my eyes recovered from

the dazzle, I started to be able to make out the plump, concerned-looking features of the man holding it.
It was Gary. Mrs Williams' son.

★ ★ ★

Soon we were back inside. Gary was keen to get on the phone to the nearest police station, in Cambourne, twenty miles away. I said I'd prefer to deal with the law later on. Meanwhile, I pumped him about what had brought the two of them to Trerose just when I needed them.

"Mum had been getting sort of worried about you," Gary explained. "Thought you looked worn out, not your usual self, so she asked me and Harry to drop over on our way to the pub, make sure you were all right." He turned to his companion, Harry Bolitho, the big man who had grabbed and held me out there in the vegetable garden. "Bloody lucky, right?"

Harry, a man of few words, nodded. "Right."

"Because," Gary continued, warming

to the drama, "as we came up here, this flash motor comes bombing down the lane from the direction of Trerose and all but runs us off the road. The bloke's driving like something out of *Die Hard*, in't he?"

"Right," Harry agreed.

"That got us worried, which is why we searched around when you didn't answer the door."

"I don't think I've ever been so frightened in all my life," I said. "Or so grateful." I could see that some kind of explanation could no longer be postponed, and that it would have, unfortunately, to be a lie. "Someone's been stalking me," I said quickly. "There's a special number I have to call, OK? It's sort of . . . personal."

Gary nodded gravely. My explanation was plausible and noble. He knew how to behave.

"You can stay in our spare bedroom tonight, Saskia," he said as he led Harry out to the car so that I could make my call in privacy. "It's what Mum would want."

"That sounds like heaven," I said

gratefully. "I'll see you outside in a few minutes."

The anti-climax of my actual phone call was almost laughable. Allardyce's direct line gave me an answering machine. It featured Gwen Carver, his assistant asking the caller to leave the usual message, in response to which DI Allardyce would get back to them as soon as possible.

"Inspector Allardyce," I said shakily, "this is Saskia Freeling. I'm in Cornwall and I think someone just tried to shoot me. I'm going to stay with some friends now. Please call me there when you decide to make yourself available."

I gave Mrs Williams' number and slammed down the phone. Then I had a little weep, just enough to lighten the burden that was pressing against my heart. And finally I collected my things and went out to the drive, where two honest, decent men who knew nothing of what had really happened in my life were waiting to escort me to safety.

17

SLEEPING in the security of the Williams' house, knowing that the one constant adult figure left from my childhood was in the next room, did truly feel like heaven after the terrors of the previous days. In a way, this was what I had really been looking for when I jumped in my car the previous night and set off on my mad drive to Cornwall.

When I awoke, with Mrs Williams' clean sheets against my skin, there was no wind rattling the window, only the noonday sun flooding in. All was peaceful except for a gentle knocking at the door.

"Yes?" I called out lazily.

Mrs Williams opened the door and popped her head in. "You've got a visitor, my dear."

I smiled. Tony must have left before dawn. We had pinned a note to the front door at Trerose, explaining that I was at Mrs Williams' place.

"Show him in," I murmured.

I was still wearing a broad smile when Mrs Williams moved aside and admitted a familiar figure in a windcheater and jeans. Familiar, but not the one I had expected.

"Morning, Saskia," said Detective Inspector Allardyce. He looked at his watch. "Actually, it's five past midday, so good afternoon."

I was wearing a long T-shirt with a high neck, about as revealing as an overcoat, but that didn't stop me instinctively pulling up the bedcovers like a frightened virgin.

"I thought you were Tony," I said. "You're quick, Inspector."

"All part of the service," Allardyce said with an easy smile. "So you summoned Mr Patterson. Is he aware of what happened last night?"

I shook my head. "He was coming anyway." I paused. "The people you said would leave me alone have not. In fact, it looks as if they just tried to shoot me. Can you explain all this — please?"

"I don't know what to say, except that the game we're dealing with here is obviously not the one we thought."

At that moment Mrs Williams walked in with a tray. On it were two flowered mugs filled with tea, a milk-jug and a sugar bowl. She put the tray down on my little bedside table, and glanced enquiringly at Allardyce.

"Just milk, thanks," he said pleasantly.

She handed him his mug, then turned to me. "Milk for you too, my dear?"

"Not for me, Mrs Williams. I need waking up."

She tenderly passed me a black tea, then left the room as discreetly as she had entered it.

"I've known Mrs Williams since I was a little girl," I said. "We used to play here, with her son. This house is almost as familiar to me as my own." I paused. "So. Which game are you talking about, and how has it changed?"

"Describe yesterday's events, and I'll try to work it out, Miss Freeling," Allardyce said. "OK?"

I obeyed, leaving out only the personal bits to do with me and Tony. I went through my conversation with Peter Mattheson, my return to the flat and my discovery that Anna's disk had been returned to me, cruelly amended. My terror, and my hurried flight down the motorway. The incident with the 'phantom' Suzuki. And finally the shots through the kitchen window at Trerose.

"Quite a twenty-four hours," Allardyce conceded. "Well, I owe you an apology. I was obviously wrong in thinking these people had finished with you. In their unpleasant way, they're back in contact." He picked up the pot and offered me a refill. I said no. He poured a little more into his mug. "The question is, why?"

"I can't work out what they want from me," I said. "And if they do want something, why try to kill me?"

Allardyce shrugged. "Sometimes thieves fall out. We could have two groups operating against each other, one of whom wants you dead, the other to use you. Either that, or this is a sustained campaign to frighten you, soften you up."

"Yes," I said desperately. "But *why*?"

Allardyce looked at me for a long moment, as if wondering whether to confide in me. "I think we have to remember one thing," he said slowly.

"This was not something I wished to burden you with at an earlier stage, when I was still unsure how important you were in this affair ... but the fact is that you are Anna's legal heir. This may be why the people for whom her company laundered this money are interested in you."

"You seriously think she was involved? My sister Anna?"

"I'm not sure if she was consciously part of the conspiracy, but she may have signed documents without really considering their import at the behest of Miss Mattheson, her partner — whom she trusted implicitly. Do you follow me?"

I nodded slowly.

"Mr Patterson's working in Bristol, I hear?"

"Filming a cameo for *Intensive Care*."

"Good show."

"He's a good actor," I retorted. "He's going to come down and get me later. We'll be going back up to Bristol. I don't plan to be more than touching-distance from Tony for the next few weeks, possibly months. Whenever I'm alone, something very scary happens."

"So it seems." Allardyce paused. "It would be quite understandable if you wanted out of this situation," he said. "Unfortunately, it's unlikely that these people would let you drop out just like that. I mean, if you tried to go away they would find you eventually. So, if you feel up to it, we'd like you to keep going."

"Who are these people who seem to be targeting me — this *they* you keep talking about?" I asked.

"They're a gang with political contacts in the West Indies."

"Is Johnny Dubois involved?"

"He's in there somewhere."

"And Zena? She seemed like a decent human being."

"We're all at the mercy of our families, aren't we, Miss Freeling?" Allardyce said softly. He shrugged his shoulders, cocked his head slightly and looked at me with a kind of stern affection, like a teacher persuading a star pupil that the extra homework is worthwhile. "Well, what's the decision? Are you willing to stay in play?"

"Tony said right at the beginning that

you were just using me as bait. I'm beginning to think he was right."

"Maybe that's how it looks," Allardyce said with an apologetic shrug, "but if so, we would have watched you far more closely. From now on we definitely shall. That's a promise."

I nodded slowly. "You make it sound as if I don't have much option. But that's not it. I've always wanted to know what happened to Anna. I still do. After the events of the past few days I can't really rest until I know the truth." I smiled. "So here I am now, a piece of bait. Waiting for the fish to bite."

Allardyce downed the rest of his tea and got to his feet. "Ah well, back to the Smoke," he said with a sigh.

"That's it?"

He stared back at me with bland surprise. "Yes. I have to get our intelligence sources working, try to make sense of what's happened. I'll be in touch in a day or two. What's your address in Bristol?"

I didn't have that, but I did have the phone number. He took it, then left.

When Allardyce had gone, I got up

and padded over to the window. From here I could see Allardyce's car, parked just across from the house. I watched as he took his leave, painstakingly polite as ever, from Mrs Williams, then walked across to the car. It was then that I noticed movement in the passenger seat. As Allardyce got in on the driver's side, someone leaned over to greet him. Someone with long, fair hair. I recognised his assistant, Gwen Carver. And I could see her hand snake over, stroke his and squeeze it.

I had wondered about their extra-curricular relationship. Well, now I knew.

★ ★ ★

Half an hour later, I was up and dressed. Mrs Williams had shopping to do in Helston, but she stayed around, making little excuses for delay. Gary and Harry had gone off to deliver a load of wood for old Mr Bolitho, who called himself an agricultural contractor, which meant that basically he would do or sell anything for cash. Mrs Williams had clearly decided to stay with me until her son came back or Tony finally arrived, whichever happened sooner.

I was starting to get anxious, though since Tony knew nothing about the previous night's dramatic events, there was no reason why he should rush down here. I was irritated that Inspector Allardyce had managed to get his dapper, infuriatingly cool self down from London while Tony was still stuck playing pretend doctors with Di Winstone and company in a TV studio.

In fact, it was Gary who arrived back first from the morning's delivery trail, via the pub, with Harry in his wake. They both looked secretive.

"You can go into Helston now, Mum," Gary said. "We'll stay here with Saskia till Wotsisname . . ."

"Tony," I put in helpfully.

"Right. Till Tony turns up."

Mrs Williams looked at her son with some suspicion, but picked up her bag.

"Will you be all right with the boys, dear?" she asked.

I nodded. "Never had any trouble with them."

She laughed, but shook her head and gave Gary a disapproving look on her way out.

"OK, what is it?" I said, when we heard Mrs Williams' old Ford Fiesta coughing into life out in the road. "You look like you just lost a pound and found a fiver."

Gary exchanged knowing glances with Harry. "Went and had a quick beer," he said.

"I can tell that. So can your mother."

"Thirsty work, loading wood. Anyway, we got talking to Jim Kelly from up at Roskadden Farm. He was out last night on his tractor, taking hay to his livestock, when he saw that flash red car parked up by the crossroads."

"When was this?" I asked sharply.

"He thinks eight o'clock, because he was just about to go home for his dinner."

That was half an hour before I had gone out into the kitchen and started to prepare my own evening meal.

"Yeah," Gary continued, enjoying himself. "And he really took notice, did Jim. Not just because it was a pricey motor, but because the bloke sitting in it was coloured."

"Surprising he could see him in the dark then, right?" Harry chuckled.

Gary gave him a shove. This was the double-act they had been rehearsing all the way back from the pub, I could tell.

"Nah. He had the interior light on, this black chap, looked like he was reading something."

"Or studying a map," I suggested. A chill crept down my spine, though the room was warm. "Looking for Trerose."

Just at that moment, there was the sound of an engine outside as a car drew to a halt. Harry went over to the window.

"Taxi," he reported. "Must be your fiance, Saskia. Wotsisname . . . "

"Tony."

I ran into the hall and wrenched open the front door. Tony was already on his way up the front path, past the last of Mrs Williams' nasturtiums, carrying an overnight bag and looking troubled.

Just short of me, he set the bag down. "Christ," he grumbled. "Do you know how hard it is to get here by train? And why are you at Mrs Williams' instead of Trerose? Luckily, I saw the note fixed to the door and managed to call the taxi back just as he was turning round in the drive . . . "

"I can explain," I interrupted. "Calm down."

Tony sighed. "You got me worried again. You've done a lot of that lately."

I could sense Gary and Harry listening and watching.

"Let's put your bag inside," I said, "then go for a walk, OK?"

Tony nodded reluctantly. "OK."

I fetched my jacket and we set off through the little council estate. A German Shepherd dog barked frantically from a garden. Tony was very silent. I took his hand but he didn't encourage further intimacy.

"All right," I said then. "Here's why I slept at Mrs Williams' house. Last night I had the fright of my life. Someone took a pot-shot at me — two, in fact — through the kitchen window at Trerose."

Tony stopped, spun on his heel. "*What?*"

"And according to a local that Gary

and his friend met in the pub just now, a black guy in a smart car was sitting at the crossroads half an hour before, obviously looking for something, or someone. How do you like that?"

"You're bloody joking."

I shook my head.

"The Saint Theresa connection," Tony said.

I was suddenly paralysed, struck dumb. The fear had come back — the feeling of what it was like to be sprawled on the kitchen floor, surrounded by broken glass, with bullet-holes in the window and someone out there in the darkness trying to kill me. But I admit that I also felt a strange triumph, a kind of twisted elation. Because the man with the gun last night, Allardyce, the unknown beneficiaries from Anna's death — they all wanted me for their purposes, and only me, Saskia Freeling, whether dead or alive. That sense hit me as I faced Tony in the lane near Mrs Williams' little house, with the thin late-November sun hanging in the sky above us, and the energy in it was more frightening than the fear itself.

It must have showed. I think my face had frozen in a strong mask of mixed horror and exultation.

"Are you all right?" Tony said.

"I've just realised that sibling rivalry sends you mad," I whispered. "I wonder if Anna was mad, too. Whether I caught the craziness from her, or whether it was always there in both of us, the rivalry under the closeness . . ."

"I don't understand." Tony took my hand firmly now. "Let's just concentrate on practicalities, shall we? The psychodrama can wait."

"One more thing — Allardyce. He thinks these people are interested in me because I'm Anna's next of kin."

"Screw Allardyce," Tony said with feeling. "He's using us. And especially he's using you."

"Well, I trust him."

"You're biased," Tony said with a laugh. "You always did fancy him."

I was in no mood for jokes about either illicit lust or DI Allardyce. "Don't trivialise this, it's serious," I hissed.

"I didn't say it wasn't. And you *do* fancy him."

I took a deep breath, collected myself. "So what do we do now?"

"Simple. We grab some lunch at the pub, then we drive back up to London and get some more clothes and stuff. Can you bear to stay at the flat overnight?"

"I don't know."

"Darling, I'll be there."

"OK," I murmured. "One night."

"Fine. We leave first thing for Bristol. I've got the flat for a week. I'll be on set here and there over the next couple of days, but you can either come in with me or just amuse yourself around the neighbourhood. And with a bit of luck, nobody will know where we bloody well are."

"Except Allardyce. I gave him the number — I thought I should."

Tony shrugged wordlessly. We started to walk down towards the pub, which was at the bottom of the hill below the council houses. I put my arm around Tony.

"I'm sorry," I said quietly.

"About what especially?"

"About accusing you of doing the dirty with Di Winstone."

"Don't worry. She's having it off with the director, to tell you the truth."

"The bitch," I said. "I never trust someone who says they want to be alone."

Shortly afterwards, we arrived at the Millwrights Arms. Tony ducked down into the little pub's thatched porch and eased up the latch on the door.

"Speaking of vitch," he murmured in his smokiest Greta Garbo voice, "gimme vissky. And a liddle ginger ale on the side."

18

IN fact, Tony just ordered a mineral water, plus a giant sandwich. He was even more jumpy than I was, and eager to get me away from there.

"You're in no fit state to do anything heroic," he argued. "Hearing voices, being shot at, having an identity crisis. I mean, you have to be pretty together to put up with all this shit, and together is what you, my darling, are not."

I nodded. He was very persuasive. "But it's hard to give up the idea of finding out what happened to Anna," I said. "To think I'll . . . never know."

"OK, OK. Maybe later. But for now give yourself a break. First you need to be settled, you need to be secure. Then we'll think about the quest for truth."

"What if these people Allardyce mentioned do get in touch with me?"

Tony went very quiet. He seemed to

have no answer to that. Then, after a while, he said gently: "Did you like Anna?"

"What an odd question."

"Well, did you?"

"I loved her," I said. "A feeling that goes beyond liking or not liking. I felt ... still feel ... incredibly close to her. I mean, sometimes it's as if now she's physically gone, somehow she's taking root in me. That she's moved in ... because there's only one physical body left for us to share now, not two."

"You're different since she disappeared, you know," Tony said.

I nodded. "I haven't picked up a camera, have no desire to. I don't even know if I could. I feel as if I've forgotten everything about the craft that I ever learned."

Tony got to his feet. "Come on," he sighed. "Enough theorising for one day. Let's collect your stuff and hit the road. If we get a move on, we can be in London before bedtime."

★ ★ ★

While I packed, Tony talked with Gary about arranging for a glazier to come and fix the kitchen window at Trerose, as if the damage had been done by skylarking kids. Practicality is a calming thing.

All the same, it was a difficult farewell from a bewildered Mrs Williams. I couldn't possibly come up with a satisfactory explanation for what had happened, not without telling her everything. All I could say was that Tony and I had decided to go away, and that I was sure this was just a one-off incident. With luck we would be back for Christmas.

"Married," I added, smiling a bit manically. "We're going to get married as soon as we can."

Mrs Williams glanced at Tony, who was being regaled by Gary with an embellished account of how he and Harry had 'saved' me the previous night.

"I hope you'll be happy," she said quietly. She looked back at me. "You're very troubled, my dear. Something funny with Anna, isn't it?"

I nodded slowly.

Mrs Williams looked at Tony again,

long and hard, as if trying to penetrate some invisible shield around him. We had always joked about how she was a 'Cornish witch', and more than once I had suspected she might be a touch psychic; the day before her husband John was reported drowned, she had dreamed it all, I remember her telling us after it happened.

"You'll find out about Anna," she said softly. "And he'll have something to do with it."

"Tony?"

She nodded. And then she went placidly out into the kitchen to make some more tea. A last, strong pot for the road.

★ ★ ★

We had just pulled out of the council estate when Tony, who was driving, said suddenly, "Have you still got the key to Trerose?"

"Yes."

"Let's go up there. I want to see where all that mayhem happened. Just for a few minutes, OK?"

I hesitated, then nodded.

Tony skilfully manoeuvred his way up the narrow driveway, with the creek to our left, just as I had a little more than twenty-four hours previously.

From here we could see up behind the house. There was the stand of trees on the brow of the hill, below it the footpath from where the shots had been fired. Everything looked so peaceful. I know people always say that about places where killings or atrocities have taken place in the past, but it's true. The only thing that wasn't still was my heart.

Tony took my hand in solidarity as we walked to the door. I handed him the key, and he opened up. He was on full alert.

The curtains were still drawn in the living room, and the house was gloomy. Despite the fact that this was a fleeting visit, I opened them, to let in some light. Tony pressed on into the kitchen, where I joined him.

He was already checking the bullet-holes.

"I'm surprised the guy missed — I mean, if we're talking about a professional hit-man or whatever," Tony said. "It's fifty yards, tops, from that lane. You're standing here in a brightly lit kitchen. He's got eternity to set up his first shot."

"I did react pretty quickly," I retorted with some pride.

Tony grunted sceptically.

"Well," I said, "it has occurred to more than one person I've spoken to that the marksman didn't intend to kill me, just to give me a fright."

"Oh, that's the lovely Inspector Allardyce's opinion, is it?"

I laughed. "If you mention him once more, I'll . . . I'll . . . "

"You'll hit me with your handbag," Tony finished with a harsh laugh. "But what I don't understand is, why would they put the frighteners on you while you're down here? If they want to contact you, you'd think Cornwall would be a good place to do it."

"Maybe they wanted me in London."

"Which you had left in a panic because you thought your flat had been broken into. By these same villains, presumably."

"*Thought* it had been broken into? The

stuff was missing and there's absolutely no other explanation. None at all."

"OK," Tony said, and clapped his hands together. "Then it's clear that what these bastards are really trying to do is to frighten you into not helping Inspector Allardyce with his enquiries. I can mention him again, can't I?"

"In the correct context, yes."

"Thanks." Tony thought for a while. "My first instinct, naturally enough, is to tell you to pull off the case and fly away with me. Then again, maybe this is contemptible and I'm just playing into their hands."

"Darling, what could be more natural than wanting to protect me?"

Tony shrugged. "Sass, I still think that on balance you shouldn't involve yourself with this business. You've got too much self-healing to do."

On impulse, I told him about the photograph of my mother and Anna that Mrs Williams had given me the previous day — the one I had taken, aged six, with her husband's Instamatic on the day my mother died.

"Jesus. Spooky."

"I often wondered why Anna hated me so much when I got my first camera," I blurted out. "Because she . . . I don't know, because in her little-girl way she thought the photograph I took that day *killed* Mummy. You know, like — "

"Well, that was then, darling. Twenty-five years ago. This is now. Don't torment yourself with it. *You* know it's not true. And so did the grown-up Anna, surely."

But I wasn't going to let this ghost go until I had exorcised it. "The thing is, I'd completely forgotten I ever took the picture," I persisted. "Suppressed the memory, perhaps. No wonder, with all these things coming back to me, that I'm suddenly not so keen on photography. But God knows what kind of business I'll have in Australia if I don't do that!"

I stopped suddenly, aware that I was babbling like . . . like a six year old. Tony was staring out of the window, up at the sniper's vantage-point.

"We'll think of something," he said absently. "Right now, though, I want to go up to the top of the garden."

We opened the kitchen door and

trudged up the slope. I swung round as we walked and glanced down towards the kitchen garden and the little lean-to conservatory where I had emerged the previous night after being surprised by Gary. In the still, bright daylight, there was no hint of that drama either. Tony was already at the top.

"See?" he said, turning to check the angle on the kitchen window. "He must have stood about here. Actually, it's less than fifty yards. Thirty-five, forty. Even I could have hit you from here. First shot."

"All those long afternoons on the firing-range with the army chaps when you were doing *The Regiment*," I said. "And I thought you were just wasting your time . . . "

But Tony wasn't really listening. He had shifted sideways a few feet and was peering intently at the ground.

"Look," he said.

I followed where he was pointing. I saw a cigarette-end. Another. Three in all. As I watched, Tony reached through the fence-wire and poked around them.

"People do walk their dogs here, and

they smoke while doing so," I pointed out.

"Yeah, but this is a grouping. Three cigarette-ends close together. And recent. As if someone chainsmoked while waiting here at this spot. They've not really collapsed or discoloured. And one of them's only half-smoked."

Tony managed to retrieve it and held it up to our view. In fact, the discarded cigarette was even less than half-smoked. Tony examined it minutely, squinting.

"I can see the brand-name," he announced. "Lark — American cigarettes. I don't think you can get them in this country."

"I thought you wanted out of this," I said. "Now you seem pretty eager to get back to playing the detective."

"Can't help myself. Listen, darling, it was your sanity I was worried about." Tony indicated the evidence of the sniper's presence. "What you thought happened, happened all right. That's what I wanted to establish. Now let's head for a little rest and recuperation."

"London, you mean?"

"Just for one night. Anyway, my love,

how restful has dear old Cornwall been?"

"Point taken."

We walked back to Trerose hand-in-hand.

★ ★ ★

I was beginning to feel like the Flying Dutchwoman — someone haunted by what the Chinese call a 'Hungry Ghost' — as we drove back up over Bodmin Moor to the Devon border. Ever since that day in Saint Theresa when Anna had vanished into the sea, there had been no chance to relax, no sense of a safe place to settle. And I was getting tired, in a profound way that had little to do with weariness of the body and everything to do with a diminishment of spiritual energy. I was aware of the crumbling of my confidence, even my sense of identity. Boundaries were blurring at their edges. I seemed to have become porous.

Tony told me these things were just down to stress. All the same, it was hard to avoid all consideration of madness, the 'm-word' as I started to think of it. Somehow this, or other related words, kept cropping up in conversation between me and Tony, then being avoided for a while, like embarrassing smells or ominous symptoms we didn't dare acknowledge.

At Taunton we stopped for coffee and a sandwich, then quickly pressed on. Despite my tiredness, I insisted on taking the wheel for a bit. That day Tony had done a four-hour train journey, then three hours straight driving up from Trerose. He dozed too, but woke just before Swindon.

"Time I took over again, love," he said.

"Male stereotyping," I said, though it was now twilight, always the most treacherous time of day to be driving, and the motorway was starting to swim gently in front of my eyes.

"Bollocks. You're all-in," Tony insisted. "Pull off at the next service area."

I had to concede. We stopped in the car park in front of the restaurant. As I cut the engine, I felt a shock of recognition.

"This is where I had to stop — after the weird phone call I told you about.

And the Jeep following me . . . and the policeman who said he hadn't seen anything. Remember? Of course, it wasn't on this side, it was over on the westbound carriageway . . . "

I had disclosed all that in the pub at lunchtime. Tony had been remarkably matter-of-fact about the whole story, whether because he really believed me or just decided to treat it as part of the general insanity, I couldn't tell.

"I remember," he said. "Let's not worry about that. Come on, swap over."

I climbed out and jumped down to the ground, then paced around a bit to stretch my legs.

"More coffee?" Tony said, joining me.

"No. I'm happy to press on."

He patted me on the shoulder and headed back towards the Jeep, but I didn't make an immediate move. There was a police patrol car parked just a couple of spaces away with two officers inside. On impulse I walked over and bent down.

The nearside policeman looked up slightly nervously. I smiled. He smiled.

"Evening," I said.

He was still smiling. Haggard I may have been, but I could still impress a hick cop.

"Evening, madam. Anything wrong?"

"Not really," I said. "It's just that the other night I had a problem. One of your colleagues helped me out. It was in the small hours. I was alone ... you know. Anyway, I didn't get his name, but I wanted to send him a thank-you note. Could you tell me where you're based? I'm sure that if I send it there he'll realise who it's from."

The two policemen exchanged knowing smiles, and I could read their thoughts. A girl with a thing for cops. *Right.*

"What did he look like?" the driver asked. "Good-looking, like me and my friend here?"

I laughed. "Not bad. Quite young. Could lose a bit of weight. Oh, and he was in one of your unmarked cars. A white one, a Ford Sierra, I think."

More glances were exchanged, a little less jolly this time.

"Regional crime squad?" the offside man suggested.

"Plainclothes, was he, this bloke?" the other one asked.

I shook my head. "Uniformed."

"Madam," said the nearside man, "we don't use white unmarked Sierras for routine motorway work. They are too similar to your ordinary patrol car."

"It was definitely white. And a Sierra."

He turned to his friend, who shrugged.

"Another bloody impersonator. We'd better report it."

They asked if I could remember the registration number, and where and when it had happened. They took notes.

"You're sure?" I pressed him. "It couldn't have been a policeman?"

"No way."

"Well, that's a bit creepy," I said with a well-feigned laugh. "Lucky there was no harm done."

When I got back to the Jeep, Tony had a face like thunder.

"What the hell was all that about?" he demanded.

"Just having a word with the local constabulary," I said. "I won't tell you what it was about. It will only feed your fantasies."

"If only," he said, trying to make light of it, though I could tell he was still very annoyed. "Seriously, what were you doing?"

"Trying to find out about the cop I met the other night."

"And?"

"Drew a blank."

I don't know to this day why I didn't tell Tony the truth. Maybe I was just tired of impossibilities and loose ends, and starting to worry that he really would decide I was crazy.

Tony shrugged, got in and started the engine. We headed off on the last leg of our journey to London.

For the next hundred miles the patrolman's words echoed in my brain. *We don't use white unmarked Sierras.*

Which meant that either the policeman in the unmarked car in the early hours of the night before last was a figment of my imagination, or he hadn't been a policeman at all.

I tried to decide which was the more frightening explanation. Every time I ran the contest in my mind, I came up with a dead heat.

19

"I COULD murder a nice full-blooded red!" Tony exclaimed, the moment we set foot back in the London flat.

"There's a very good Chilean in the rack," I said. "Whether it's butch enough for the likes of you, I don't know, but it'll have to do. You open it while I pop upstairs and check my messages."

While Tony went to the drawer for the corkscrew, I switched the stairs light on and headed up towards my study.

I put my study light on a little nervously, for I thought I could smell the remains of my own fear in the room. Or something indefinable that created unease.

There were three messages. One was from Maggie, just before she boarded her plane, saying she was worried about me; I had seemed 'stressed' the other night on the phone. Jesus, if only she knew. Then the voice of a creative director I knew, offering me a series of print ads for swimming costumes. It felt like a visitation from another planet. And finally came the voice, halting and slurred, of Zena Dubois.

"Hello, Saskia Freeling," Zena said. She sounded drunk or stoned, but not in any happy way. "Hello from hell in the sun, Saskia. This is the friend of Jilly . . . dear Jilly . . . and of Anna — not so dear, but . . . Well, I'm home. I want to talk to you, tell you something that will help you, will save you." She swallowed hard. "I — "

Then came the sound of someone entering the room with her. A male voice. Zena muffling the phone, probably with her hand, though I thought I could make out her words, switching to strong Saint Theresan patois: "I'm not a fucking prisoner man, this is my family's house. You know I want to talk on phone, I fucking do it." But then there was a scuffle and the phone was slammed down thousands of miles away, a beep for the end of the message and the rustling silence of the unused tape.

I located the beginning of the message

and played it back again. Then I stood, rooted to the spot, and took some deep breaths. I looked around the room.

The computer was still on. Of course — I had left it running the other night when I had fled the flat in panic. There was the diskette in its slot, the display still running on the screen. I stepped forward and forced myself to reread the abusive message. In a moment I would go downstairs and bring Tony up here to see it, to prove that this terror, too, hadn't been an imagined one.

Except that these weren't the short, brutal paragraphs I had found two nights ago.

My heart in my mouth, I sat at my computer and started reading.

Darling Sassie,
I hate to be melodramatic, but the fact is that if you ever read this, it will be because I am dead.

There it was, back in the machine's memory. The final message that Anna had left with Mulcahy.

When I got back to the living room,

Tony was sprawled on the sofa, nursing a half-finished glass of red wine.

"Hi, love," he said. "I was starting to think about forming a search party. Fancy sending out for a curry?"

I just stood there, shivering, until it dawned on Tony that something was wrong. He put down his glass and swung round to face me.

"What is it?"

"Something . . . something very strange," I said hesitantly.

"A message? Bad news?" Tony got to his feet, came over and took me by the shoulders. "Tell me, darling. Come on."

I shook my head, feeling as if my brain was about to explode. I also had a pain between my shoulders, as if someone had stabbed me.

"Take your time. What is it, Sass?"

"I . . . " I swallowed hard. "First there was a message from Zena Dubois, calling from Saint Theresa. I think she was drunk. She wanted to talk but someone interrupted her and they slammed down the phone . . . "

Tony's grip on my shoulders tightened until it hurt. I winced and he let go. For all his brave talk, he must be almost as frightened as me, I thought.

"You said first, darling," Tony coaxed, like a doctor or a priest. "What else? Don't worry. You know you can tell me anything.,

"The computer disk. Anna's computer disk," I finally blurted out. "It's up there. And the copy I made onto the hard disk is there too. But I know . . . " I hesitated. "I *knew* that it had been wiped the other night. I checked and double-checked! Both the floppy and the file in the computer had gone. I *know* it! Then there was the other disk. The nasty one that made me so afraid — " Tears sprang into my eyes.

Tony steered me to the sofa and sat me down. I watched as he poured me a glass of red wine and pressed it into my unresisting hand.

"Here's what we do," he murmured. "We send out for a curry, and we get a good night's sleep. In the morning we deposit that disk into the safe-deposit where you keep the jewellery you inherited from your grandmother, then you won't need to worry. It'll help if you don't have to worry, won't it?"

"I think I'm going mad, Tony," I said hoarsely. "I keep imagining things. Until now I didn't really believe I was losing my mind, but — "

"Hey, you didn't imagine those bullets, Sass. I saw the holes in the window, OK?" He put his hand under my chin, turned me round to face him. "And remember the old saying. Just because you're paranoid, it doesn't mean they're not out to get you."

"Us," I said, my voice shaky. "You mean they're out to get us. The horrible message that was left here mentioned you too."

"You and me. The Beast and the Blonde. Together."

I fell into his arms, nestled into his neck. "I'm frightened," I murmured. "What if the voice comes back tonight?"

"It won't," Tony told me, stroking my hair gently.

"Are you sure?" I said in a timid little voice, craving reassurance.

"I'm sure. Trust me. Tonight you will sleep like a baby, Sass. Like a little baby."

* * *

And when I did awake the next morning, it was from a slumber just like the one Tony had promised: undisturbed, dreamless, refreshing. Thank God, no voice in the night. No Anna to haunt me. For now.

Tony was already up. I padded downstairs in my old terry-cloth robe, feeling for the first time in days at home and safe — even though I knew we were supposed to be travelling down to Bristol that day.

I heard Tony on the phone in the living room and went through to investigate.

"Right," he was saying. "Eight sharp. Perfect. Yeah . . . I've ordered it." He half-glanced at me, waved. "OK, Di. Cheers . . . see you later."

Tony put down the phone. "How're you doing?"

I kissed him on the forehead. "Better. Not perfect, but much, much better. What was that you were talking about?"

"Arranging something with Di."

We went through to the kitchen. I poured coffee for both of us.

"When I get a good night's sleep and nothing crazy happens, I start to feel better," I confessed. "I go back to wanting to aid the police in their enquiries."

"One promise," said Tony, spooning sugar into his coffee. "I want one promise from you, which is that you'll wait until after we get married. Until then, Dr Patterson prescribes complete rest."

"And he is never wrong."

"Never." Tony looked at his watch. "The scripts for Tuesday are at the flat in Bristol. I should be looking them over. OK if we leave pretty soon? Or are you so comfortably re-established here that you've changed your mind and want to stay?"

I shook my head. "It's true, I am feeling at home again, but I don't want to be alone, so I'll come with you." I paused. "I hate being dependent, darling, but it seems to be a fact that when you're with me, everything is OK. It's when I'm alone I get into trouble. I've learned that lesson."

"Blimey. Watch it, or I'll phone the *Guardian*'s Women's Page and reveal that you're showing trad feminine tendencies."

I smiled. "I'm starting to enjoy traditional role-playing. Especially you working and me hanging around. Actually, I think I might go back to bed for a bit before I start packing for the road."

"Feel free."

"And I'm afraid I don't want to be alone there, either. Do you think you could help me out?"

"Oh, I think so."

We made languid love in our bed. It was very pleasurable but with a touch of ritual, of performance. Nothing wrong with that. Except at one point, just before Tony reached his peak, I turned my head to the left and caught sight of our lovemaking in the wardrobe mirror. Usually this was a bit of a turn-on, glimpsing my own nakedness, my lover's body from a different angle. But in the mirror I saw Tony staring at my reflection in a strange, intense way, as if he was looking at someone else, *being* with someone else.

"Look at me!" I said, pulling him back down to me, the real, physical me. For just a fraction of a second he looked angry, but then the moment passed, and he smiled, and moved down to kiss me on the lips, and to move intently inside me, towards climax. I forgot that moment in the passion of the next. He was absolutely mine again.

Absolutely.

20

I DIDN'T take my camera down to Bristol. It was a conscious thing, an admission of the change that had occurred in me since returning from Saint Theresa. I felt as if I never wanted to pick up that familiar bag, with its neat array of lenses and filters, its film-pouches, ever again. Or not until I had managed to banish the monster of guilt and self-loathing that the tragedies of the past few weeks seemed to have awakened within me.

All the same, it had been a good morning. We were almost cheerful as we nosed through the early-afternoon traffic on Hammersmith roundabout, and performed the miracles of precision ducking and weaving that are required to get onto the M4 approach. Tony had put his new Blur CD on the Jeep's in-car stereo, and there was a crisp winter sky overhead, duck-egg blue with fluffy clouds straight from a Turner painting.

He had work for the moment. I had my sanity back — maybe also just for the moment — but it felt good.

After an uneventful journey we arrived at the Bristol flat, which was in a Victorian house just off White Ladies' Road. Tony said a lot of BBC people lived round here — the studios were within walking distance — so it was a nice, lively area. Not quite as nice as Clifton, a mile or two up the hill, but pleasant enough.

Clifton. I shuddered briefly at the memory. The Suspension Bridge. The hundred-metre drop to the gorge's deadly floor. Jilly's death. Such a short time ago, but seemingly an eternity. I put the thought out of my head, with difficulty but no less firmly for that. This was my new beginning. *Our* new beginning. Tony and me.

The flat wasn't exactly fabulous, but it was OK. It was rented by one of the regular stars of *Intensive Care*, Ted Quinlan, who like most of the cast, owned a house in the London area. Ted was taking a break from the show, subletting the flat to guesting actors like

Tony to cover the rent in his absence. Apart from a few prints and a decent TV set, everything was as basic as you might expect. Thank God the building itself was light and airy.

I unpacked in the bedroom while Tony hit the phone to check up on what had been happening in his absence. I could tell he was talking to Di Winstone. Lots of chuckles and mechanical flirting. Then he wandered through.

"Di wants to take us out for dinner at the health club her brother owns," he said.

"Oh my God," I answered, popping some underwear into the battered chest of drawers. "Do we have to?"

"Do you good. We can take a swim in the pool first. It's a very upmarket place."

"I didn't know Di's brother was a health nut."

"He's not. He's a businessman. Do you have any idea how much money there is in these places?"

"You say that with respect."

"I've come to care about dosh since not having any of my own."

I giggled slightly nervously.

"I've been to the health club almost every night," Tony continued. "Done out like a Roman villa. Yuppy heaven."

"Omigod. They still have yuppies down here, do they?"

"My dear, you will see more Porsches than you could shake a stick at. And they still discuss property prices at dinner parties!"

"Good grief. But I didn't bring my cossie," I objected.

"Don't worry. Di keeps half a dozen at the club, so you can nick one and apologise later. She's a bit shorter than you," he patted my rump in passing, "but about the same build, so there's no escape. Surrender, my love."

"I do."

"Unconditionally?"

"Nobody does that these days, darling," I said with a giggle. "Didn't you know?"

★ ★ ★

The health club owned by Di's brother was every bit as classy as Tony had promised. Even I was impressed. The pool, especially, was terrific: of Olympic-proportions, in a space the size of an aircraft hangar, with mosaic tiles, high windows, and lots of painted and stencilled wood. Plunging in alongside Tony was like a liberation. I tore off a length before I surfaced and cried out in sheer animal exhilaration.

Tony came level with me a moment later.

"After what happened to Anna, I thought I'd be frightened of water," I said. "But it feels wonderful. I could stay in here for ever."

Assorted youngish accountant and doctor types were padding damply around the edge of the pool and chatting. One or two were even in the water.

Tony took off again, doing his usual enthusiastic but not particularly well-coordinated breast stroke. I followed and was level with him by the time we touched the far end. I did a racing turn and arrived back where we had started several seconds before him.

Up Tony popped again, like a seal checking out a boat, his thick dark hair matted to the top of his head.

"I'm marrying Superwoman," he spluttered. "Why am I doing this?"

"Who knows?"

"You're probably after her money, Tony darling," a feline voice wafted down from the poolside. "The BBC pays peanuts."

I looked up and there stood Di Winstone, a vision in a Speedo-type number cut high in the thigh — so high that it scarcely had any sides at all. She wasn't quite as tall as me, but she was slender and her legs seemed to take up two-thirds of her body. She tossed her wet dark tresses and laughed gaily, with the kind of confidence that few except a woman adored by fifteen million viewers twice a week can muster.

"I didn't see that one when I was rummaging through your kit," I said, eyeing her costume. "Do you keep it somewhere safe?"

She nodded. "Darling, some things are too precious to make available to the general public. I keep this in my brother's office under lock and key."

"Coming in for a splash?" Tony asked.

Di shook her head. "Been there. Done

that. Saskia, darling — lovely you could come. You look as though you need a break." It could have been a bitchy remark, but wasn't. "We all know what you've been through. Tony's told us everything. So relax — have a good time. I'll see you at dinner. We're going to try to make this evening suitably special," she added mysteriously.

"I didn't tell them quite everything," Tony said quietly. "Just about Anna and Jilly. Everyone's really sympathetic, Sass. Really."

We had dinner in a little bistro with high-backed chairs, each table enclosed by designer-rattan screens to ensure privacy. And as Di had hinted, she wasn't the only guest. We also had the director, Barry Spenser, a Jeremy Irons lookalike, with whom La Winstone was having a scene, according to Tony, and Morag Macrae, who played Bea, the Scottish theatre sister. She had brought her boyfriend, a shaggy-haired, completely non-actorish person called Ian who smoked all the time.

It was a bit of an odd experience for me. I mean, being Tony's appendage for a change. I was suddenly very sensitive to that. Especially as I had taken on no work since coming back from Saint Theresa and was seriously considering giving up photography. Here was a foretaste of what it would be like to be Mrs Anthony Patterson. I could see that it might be wonderfully relaxing in one way; in another it might be frightening — having to trust someone else so very much, and having to make a real effort to fit into their world.

On the outside, I probably appeared to be perfectly calm, but inside I was fighting a sense of rising panic. I didn't want to be with all these people. I didn't want them scrutinising me, *pitying* me.

But while I may not be an actor, I'm certainly a trouper. I didn't say much that evening. I smiled wanly, listened, ate and drank sparingly, though both the food and the wine weren't bad. For all the little ripples of fear that kept passing through me, I felt like the still point, the eye of things, while all around me the happy boozers and adulterers and poseurs partied up a storm. And slowly the panic went away.

Then, just as we had finished ordering dessert, Di banged on the table with a spoon.

"Now, lads and lassies, we all have to get our beauty sleep." Moans and titters. "Early start tomorrow." Di smiled meaningfully. "Except for Tony and Saskia here. They'll be too busy getting married."

There was a silence. Then Di burst out laughing, and for a moment I thought it had all been a joke. Until Tony squeezed my hand.

"Naughty, I know," he said, "but Di's not kidding. I've booked us into the register office in Broadmead tomorrow morning."

"How?" I stuttered. "I thought you were making enquiries about doing it in London."

"Special licence. We've neither of us been married before. I nicked your birth certificate as proof you're over twenty-five. That's it. They changed the rules recently. Special licence means you can get married at two days' notice so long as you've got the documentation and the extra readies and the registrar's got a spare slot. Which it happens that she has."

The others had been listening eagerly. A cheer went up. Someone shouted out: "The year's best-kept secret, or what!"

"The registrar told me gentlemen often do this, to surprise the ladies," Tony continued, mimicking the official's prissy voice. "The ladies can get a little cross. No time to put on nice make-up or clothes." Tony turned to me. "All right?" he murmured.

I nodded.

"What does that nod mean, Sass? You're cross, happy — what?"

"I would have liked Maggie to come. And some of my friends . . ."

"We'll put on a really humungous party for them later! The party to end all parties!"

At that point, the waiter brought in a magnum of champagne, courtesy of the other cast members. There was another round of applause. The cork was skilfully popped; foaming Bollinger poured into flute glasses. I was still stunned. I kept a hold of Tony's hand; in fact, I tightened my grip. I was about to become a dependent woman, legally linked to the charming, spiky, sexy and surprising man beside me.

Di raised her champagne glass.

"To the happy couple," she said. "May they have many happy years together." She grinned foxily. "I'm sure Tony's technique has improved since we had that fling all those years ago!"

Whoops of delight. I managed a smile as they toasted us, although I felt as if I had been pushed onto a roller-coaster. It was unnerving, exciting — full of the promise of happiness. But definitely out of my control — and that was a sensation I wasn't used to, one that I hadn't experienced since Anna and I were children together.

21

AND so, Lord save us, just after lunchtime the next day we were married. In a perfectly pleasant room in the main shopping centre. Which was convenient, because that morning I was able to have my hair cut and styled and then to slip into a choice little shop and acquire an off-the-peg Nicole Farhi suit for the occasion. Witnesses were Morag Macrae's silent boyfriend, and Ursula, an elegant lady in her seventies who was playing a stroke victim and didn't have a scene until the afternoon.

Then we went to the pub with them and had a nice little drink. I enjoyed the low-key quality of it all, and the romance of the actorly, gipsyish milieu.

Despite my misgivings of the previous night, it was true that I had no close family to invite. No blood relations, anyway. Just Maggie, who was in the Canaries and probably already suspected this might happen. The same went for

Tony, of course, though in a more roundabout kind of a way. As we shook hands with the witnesses and they went their separate ways, I felt genuinely happy, but that happiness was shot through with an inevitable sense of loss, of what might have been.

Afterwards, when the witnesses had gone, we took a walk along Welsh Back.

"How does it feel?" Tony asked.

"Still strange," I had to admit. "I've never been married before," I kissed Tony on the cheek, "but I think I like it." We walked on a little further. "I just wish my parents were alive to see this. And Anna. God knows what she would have thought, but I know she would have wanted to come."

Tony looked at his watch. "Christ," he said. "Time to be getting back."

"Anna and I were very, very close," I continued, as if talking to myself, "but sometimes that closeness could get in the way. Sometimes I felt she resented everything I had, every nice thing that happened to me, every nice person I met." I reached out and touched Tony's arm. "Perhaps she wouldn't have minded in your case."

"Yeah. Maybe."

It was all Tony said. Then he announced that he had to get back to the flat and read his scene through. He couldn't afford to fuck this up. A job was a job was a job, and since he had not been born independently wealthy, he had better get it right.

Of course, I said, feeling puzzled and slightly crushed. I understood completely. It wasn't the time for psychoanalysis. We would have plenty of other opportunities to talk these things through.

By the time we arrived back in White Ladies' Road, Tony was all charm and concern. Did I want to come out to the set? I could pick up a book, drink tea from the catering truck. Everyone would look after me. I was an honorary member of the team after last night.

I shook my head. "I'd rather stay here, thanks."

"Darling," Tony said, taking me in his arms, "you know what tends to happen these days when you hang around on your own."

"I'll be fine. And I think I should ring Inspector Allardyce, don't you? Tell him that Zena Dubois made that strange phone call. And that the disk's been returned."

"Up to you. Just don't go chasing around too frantically, and if you feel anxiety coming on, or the world seems like it's generally slipping out of control, just come right over." Tony fished around in his coat pocket and took out a card featuring a phone number and the legend *Your friendly reliable car-hire service*. "This is the minicab firm *Intensive Care* use. Any of their drivers will know exactly where to bring you. Promise?"

"Promise."

"Sorry I'm touchy." Tony forced a smile. "Stress."

"I think we should simplify our life, stop worrying so much. We'll always have my money to fall back on, as long as we're careful."

"You used to be the one who talked big. You were the one for the lifestyle."

"I know," I said. Let him taunt me. "Now I just want to be happy. I don't think I really care about money. Or glamour. Or my career. Not any more. I think that's what losing Anna has done."

"You'll get over it," he said. "I recommend a strict policy of rest over the next few weeks. Please believe it, because I'm never wrong."

"Never?"

"Have faith in your husband." Tony looked at his watch. "Listen, Mrs Patterson, tonight we'll go somewhere really nice. Just us."

"The simple life." My tone was gently ironic rather than sarcastic.

"I understand why you feel like retreating from a lifetime of comfort and indulgence," Tony said. "You were born to it. Personally I'm your working-class boy eager to make good, practising to be a millionaire with a beautiful blonde wife."

I laughed. "The Beast and the Blonde."

"Yeah . . . that notorious couple."

A peck on the cheek and Tony was out the door. Perhaps he was right — I *was* just rundown. Ambition would return when I had recovered.

Strange. As I've said, I was the

outgoing, pushy, ambitious twin, while in contrast Anna seemed self-effacing. On the other hand, she *had* chosen to work with money. Perhaps she liked her power to be wielded quietly, out of the public gaze. Anyway, it seemed to me as I made myself coffee and prepared to phone Inspector Allardyce, that since Anna's disappearance I seemed to have taken on many of her characteristics. In fact, I felt in danger of being overwhelmed by them.

I dialled the Inspector's number. Gwen Carver answered, but put Allardyce on immediately when I identified myself. First I told him about the mysterious reappearing disk.

"Get your locks changed," he said.

"Yes, of course. But why did they put it back?"

"Maybe to spook you again. Maybe ... I don't know, I can't work it out. Give me time. It doesn't make a lot of sense. Do you have the disk?"

"Yes, but I put it in the bank for safety."

"We'll make a copy as soon as you get back to London."

So then I told him about Zena's call.

"Let's get this straight, Saskia," Allardyce said. "She didn't actually make any big revelations?"

"No, but she sounded as if she would like to. And she was frightened, I could tell that."

"Did you keep that tape too?"

"Oh God, no. I had so much else on my mind . . ."

There was a short silence. "Any chance it's still there?"

I bit my lip, once more feeling like a fool. "I automatically flipped the tape back to the beginning, as you do. If anyone's called since yesterday, it will have recorded over it."

"Can you check that? Are you in your study now?"

"Actually, I'm in Bristol."

"Oh." His disappointment was clear even over the phone.

"I came straight down with Tony last night," I explained. "That's why I didn't ring you then. And by the way," I continued, "Tony and I got married this morning. And now that I'm a married woman, I'd like to know when

I go off-duty from helping the police with their enquiries."

"Whenever you like," Allardyce said quickly. "It was always voluntary. Except you still want to find out what happened to your sister, don't you?"

"Of course," I said grudgingly.

"And there's still the question of what to do if these people approach you."

"You really think they will?"

A pause, and then: "I still have to say I don't know. Saskia, it's possible the story's not over yet. It's also possible that the story isn't quite what we originally thought it was . . ."

"That's it!" I snapped. "This is all I ever hear from you. I'm finished, bushed, wiped out. Tony is right — I need to get myself straight before I do anything. You said I could pull out whenever I liked. Well, I like!"

"Just ring if anything happens," Allardyce said calmly.

"Good luck with the investigation," I said brusquely. "And goodbye!"

I slammed the phone down. Trembling all over with unexpected emotion, I went and sat on the utilitarian sofa. After a while I realised I was waiting for Allardyce to ring back. Furious with myself, I got up and walked around for a bit, made some more coffee and sat down again by the phone. Still Allardyce didn't call. He must have given up. Or this time God really was telling me I had done the right thing.

When I had finished my coffee, on impulse, I dialled my own number in London. I waited while the phone rang the pre-programmed eight times and Tony's comforting recorded voice came on the line, just as it had when I called from Saint Theresa the previous month. Then I pressed the recall bleeper against the phone and kept it there until the machine in my flat went into rewind mode. I listened to the chatter as it ran back to the beginning. A click as it touched the beginning of the tape. A beep to indicate the first message starting to replay.

Then silence. As I listened, there was only a faint whistle and a rustling. I swear to God the sound on the tape 120 miles away immediately made me think of leaves stirring in a tropical breeze, heard through an open window. I could see it in my mind's eye, almost smell the soft salt wind. I stood there with the phone in my hand and listened and listened.

"Hello?" I said foolishly as the tape kept inexorably playing.

It kept on and on for a total of four and a half minutes. Until Zena's message was safely wiped. Then the beep went again.

A cheerful voice came on. A friend from an agency, wondering if Tony and I would like to come on a jolly skiing trip to Italy with her and some other advertising types. We had been to Austria with them the previous year. Tony had spent the whole time arguing with a particularly Thatcherite account manager about politics, but the skiing itself had been fun.

"Hope you're well, Saskia, and recovering from the tragedy with your sister. How's that wonderful boyfriend of yours? He's a tower of strength, I'm sure. I'll understand if it's too soon for you to go gallivanting again with the crowd, but do think about it. Might even do you both some good to get away! Give me a call, anyway. *Ciao!*"

That was the only message left on the tape, made after Zena's had been carefully wiped.

Ciao, I repeated to myself. *Ciao. Zena Dubois.*

★ ★ ★

By the time Tony came home from filming, my resolution seemed to have hardened. I had definitely done the right thing, seeing Inspector Allardyce off, I told myself. I gave Tony a complete description of the phone conversation.

"Good for you," he said.

I gave him a big kiss. "Darling, I don't know what I'd do without you. I'm so glad we're married. I'm thrilled that you arranged it all, with the register office and everything." I giggled. "I'm rather enjoying being dominated for a change."

Tony poured himself a whisky "Excellent," he smiled, "because I've also taken the liberty of talking a bit more to a guy at the Australian High Commission, about emigrating in the

Business Skills category. We can start the process, Sass. He told me they'd be happy for us to get a tourist visa — valid for up to six months — and tootle over there and take a look. They'll set up meetings with business groups, banks and so on. Just think! This time next week, we could be there." He paused. "You look blank. I know you were hesitating before."

"Darling, I'm listening really but now — "

"For now, all we'll be doing is taking a holiday. We don't have to go through with the emigration, but I think it would be psychologically good to know we can do it if we want to. I mean, if we really do decide to get out of England and start afresh, away from all these sleazy people."

I didn't know what to say, so — as you do — I mumbled something about yes, he was right, and we could always pull out if we changed our minds.

So much had happened so fast. Too fast. I wanted to tell the world to stop and leave me — us — alone, but maybe we would have to be halfway round the world before that could happen.

Tony and I starting again in some tropical Eden. Adam and Eve. What a fantasy. But was it any odder than what had already happened in the past few months? Wasn't a drastic solution the answer to a drastic problem?

After dinner we filled out the tourist visa forms. I signed my application and Tony his.

"Mr and Mrs Patterson go travelling," he said.

"Mr and Mrs Patterson make themselves scarce, more like it," I joked.

We laughed a lot about that.

22

THE next forty-eight hours — days two and three of my brief married life with Tony — were deceptively peaceful. It was as if for all these weeks a storm had been battering at my windows, shaking my house, and suddenly it stopped and I could rest, collect myself, and really start to become strong again.

One thing still bothered me, though, even then. Was this because I had won, or was someone just *letting* me think I had?

Whatever. Tony trotted into the location to do his bit on *Intensive Care*. I sat around the flat, did a little shopping, read newspapers and magazines. It was in one that I chanced on an article about twins. Research into identical twins, I learned, was all the rage, firstly because they were being heavily focused on in gene research, and second because by studying the behaviour of twins who had been separated, scientists were able to make progress in the so-called 'nature-versus-nurture' debate. You know the kind of thing: twins are separated at birth, go to completely different adoptive families, and thirty years later turn out to have the same taste in food and clothes, go on holiday to the same part of the country, and to have married similar people, even with the same *name*, for God's sake.

Well, I had never bothered much about the theory of things while Anna was still around — I mean, we were both too busy being identical twins to worry about what it all actually meant. But one thing in this article did give me pause for thought, and I hit Tony with it when he plodded in at night from a long day's filming.

I popped a couple of chilled gourmet dinners from Waitrose in the microwave, poured the exhausted actor a glass of wine, and said casually: "Twins fight in their mother's womb for space and nutrition, did you know that?"

He took the drink, frowned. "I've never really thought about it, but I suppose it's quite logical."

"And did you know that often a twin

will die in the early stages of pregnancy," I continued, "leaving the other to go to term and emerge into the world, but suffering all his or her life from a sense of loss and incompleteness, except nobody knows why because the doctors never realised the other twin existed . . ."

"I suppose that's reasonable too, though a bit more surprising. Well, you and Anna had your rivalries, that's for sure. No matter how close you were."

"Yes," I said, "but the funny thing is, although she must be . . . dead, instead of feeling this aching vacuum in my life I almost feel as if Anna's personality has become part of me. You know, like someone whose house — I mean, her physical body — has been repossessed, and she decides she'll move back in with her family. Maybe that's why I had those hallucinations of her voice and stuff."

Tony raised an eyebrow, knocked back the rest of his wine and held his glass out for more. "Definitely a two-glass problem." He smiled crookedly. "Even a two-bottle one."

It occurred to me that Tony was drinking a lot lately. Not so surprising, I thought. We all have our ways of dealing with stress. But I decided that I would watch my newly minted husband. Didn't want to lose him to the bottle. I had seen it happen to people before.

"Well, what do you think?" I queried. "Am I still crazy or is something actually going on?" I handed Tony his second glass.

"Well," he said, "it's an interesting idea. You mean some kind of a telepathic thing?"

I nodded. "In a roundabout way. I really do feel I'm becoming more like Anna. I'm changing."

"Did you say anything to Inspector Allardyce about this? If you did, it's no wonder he's gone all quiet."

"Oh, I think he's just given up, don't you?"

"Could be."

I took away Tony's glass and placed it out of reach on the table. Then I put my arms around him and nestled into his shoulder.

"It's a comfort, in a way," I said. "Even though it's a bit eerie. Do you mind?"

"Why should I?"

"Two women for the price of one," I murmured.

I looked up. Tony's face expressed a kind of nervy concern.

"I'm glad you're able to make jokes about Anna," he said hesitantly. "So soon afterwards, I mean."

"I'm sure I'll have ups and downs from time to time," I sighed, "but what I'm saying is, all I want now is to live with you and have a normal life. Everything — including maybe those bits of Anna that are me and vice versa — will get a chance to integrate."

"Blimey, Sass." Tony gently disentangled himself and reached for his wine. "You've been thinking, and I'm not sure whether that's a wonderful idea or a terrible one. Maybe a bit of both."

The microwave made its little 'ping'. Dinner. We started to talk about his day. Everything was fine again.

★ ★ ★

The next morning, after seeing Tony off for what was to be his last day's filming,

I was on my way towards a deli I had located just down the road from the flat when a blue Ford saloon slowed down and started to keep pace with me. I kept walking, not looking to the left or right, at the same time ready to move fast if need be. I've lived in cities a lot. I know how to do it.

Then, when a bus-stop provided a gap in the row of parked cars that edged the street, the car suddenly turned in and stopped. Its passenger-side door opened and a man got out and started to walk towards me. I quickened my pace.

"Saskia!" he called out.

I recognised the voice and halted in my tracks. It was Inspector Allardyce.

"Kerb-crawling," I said. "Has it come to this, Inspector?"

Allardyce stood with his hands in the pockets of his jacket, rocking on his heels. "Call me Harry, will you, Saskia? I feel we know each other well enough by now, don't we?"

"No. And for God's sake, do you have to keep popping up like the Demon King in a pantomime? You've got my telephone number — couldn't you just ring?"

"Get in the car. Please. I need to take you somewhere."

"We spoke about this. I'm finished with being your patsy."

"Come on, Saskia. I just want to take you somewhere."

I looked at him. The expression on his even features was the nearest I had seen him come to beseeching. I glanced beyond and saw a young, shy-looking driver trying to look cool while he waited for his boss to sort out the angry blonde on the pavement.

"Where's Gwen?" I asked with more than a faint trace of sarcasm.

"Busy."

I sighed. "Nice, is it, this somewhere you mentioned?"

"Some people think so. Please — no funny stuff, I promise."

My curiosity got the better of me, as I'm sure he knew it would. "OK," I said.

I sat in the back like Princess Diana out on a shopping trip with her police escort. I had expected Allardyce to join me, but he got in the front with the driver and evaded conversation with me by telling the boy where to go and what to do and to a great extent how to drive the car. I was calm enough until we reached a roundabout at the top of a long hill and I recognised where we were.

"This is the approach-road to the bridge over the Avon gorge," I hissed through gritted teeth. "You can't do this to me. I've been avoiding coming here ever since I got to Bristol, and I'm not changing my mind for you." I tried to sound commanding, but I knew it came out as simple panic. I raised my voice: "Either turn round and go back, or stop and let me out. *Now!*"

Allardyce turned and looked at me intently. He jerked a thumb to our left.

"Jilly Mattheson got out of her brother's car here on the Downs," he said harshly. "Ten minutes later she was dead. I don't believe it was of her own volition. And I'll tell you something else, Saskia — *you* don't believe it either, so why don't we talk this one through together?"

"I'm finished with it!"

"No, you're not!" he snapped back at

me. "We both need to deal with this one, so we can get on with our lives."

There was a heavy silence; I didn't say anything more. The driver kept his eyes on the road and drove on. Once at the bridge, we pulled in behind a couple of other cars at the toll-booth.

"We're getting out," Allardyce said to me. To the driver: "Go and take a look at the other side, will you, Simon? I'm sure there's somewhere over there they'll sell you a cup of tea. See you back here in half an hour."

The fight seemed to have gone out of me. Or did it have something to do with the man's deadpan intensity? I followed him, unresisting, out of the car. Moments later, there we were, him with a hand on my arm, guiding me gently towards the pedestrian path that runs alongside the road bridge. Towards the barrier where you can look over and see the gorge.

A damp wind was chilling the parapet as we leaned on it, a thin mist obscuring the more distant parts of the view. I shivered.

"Cold?" Allardyce asked.

I shrugged. "It's OK."

"Tony working hard, is he? What do they call you, a TV soap widow?"

"I don't mind. I'm getting a chance to relax. In any case, it's his last day on set today."

"Right. There you go, I needn't have driven all the way down here. I could have talked to you when you got back. You are going back to London, aren't you, Saskia?" Allardyce paused. "What's wrong?"

"I should warn you, I'm not crazy about heights." I turned to him. "But that's the idea, isn't it? You're trying to scare me into doing what you want."

Allardyce said nothing for a bit. He was looking down towards the Gorge Hotel, which nestled in the rock halfway down the cliff. Its terrace was closed for the winter, all the tables and chairs stacked away in storage. From here it looked windswept, bleak and dangerous.

"I chose here," he said eventually, "because this is where Jilly Mattheson died. They're killers, these people. You have to understand that."

"Tell me about it. Remember last week in Cornwall — the bullets through the kitchen window?"

"If they'd wanted to kill you, they would have," Allardyce said calmly.

I tensed. This man was driving me crazy. And I couldn't keep looking down 300 feet to that muddy river, feeling my eyes popping and my brain tipping, and above all I didn't want to remember the horrific way Jilly had died. With a shudder I pictured the brief struggle, the strong, pitiless hands that must have sent her on that last, whirling journey through the dark.

"Yes," I said. "But why just pretend to? To frighten me? I don't understand!"

Allardyce shrugged wordlessly.

The cold hit me again, made me tremble as if afraid, which perhaps I was. I think I was unconsciously wondering if Allardyce was going to bundle me up and push me over, as someone had done to Jilly perhaps even someone she trusted as I was supposed to trust Allardyce.

"If you're not going to come up with any new suggestions, Inspector, could we at least take a little walk, so I can warm up?" I said.

Allardyce nodded. I hated him when

he came over all silent. It was usually a bad sign. So I just set off towards the far side of the gorge, looking ahead and not to my left. He followed, then after about fifty yards took me by the arm again. I noted to my satisfaction that he was blushing. Or perhaps it was just that cold wind.

"I understand your feelings, believe me," he said. "There's nothing worse than only seeing a limited amount of the picture. Think how we feel."

"Nothing you've said makes me change my mind from what I said on the phone. I'm giving up."

"Doesn't it bother you that these people might have killed Anna and Jilly, and in some way be damaging Zena Dubois?"

"Of course it bothers me!" I exclaimed. "But I don't know whether it makes me want to risk my life, my marriage and my sanity. You're the police — *you* catch them!" I stamped my feet, which were starting to go numb.

"Listen," Allardyce said with what seemed like a jab of real emotion, "I want to catch them so bad it hurts, OK?

I understand what you're saying. We all have our limits. But I just want a promise from you, Saskia. If someone contacts you — about anything at all to do with Anna or Jilly or any of this stuff — call me, will you? That's all." He paused. "I cannot emphasise too strongly, that you are your sister's heir. I'm sure that's why they're after you."

"Whether or not I inherit from Anna is irrelevant! Her body hasn't been found!" My voice was halfway between a sob and a shout.

A passing motorist looked over his shoulder. I threw up my hands to indicate *everything's fine*. He frowned and drove on.

Allardyce's hand was still resting on my arm. "But if they do find Anna?" he asked slowly.

"Then . . . " I pulled away, put my hands over my face, like a child hoping that because she can't see danger, it can't see her. My voice had subsided to a low, reluctant mumble. "That would make things different."

We listened to the wind whistling. "I'm sorry I had to be so brutally frank,"

Allardyce said, "but if my suspicions are correct, that may be the next thing to happen."

I sniffed back tears, nodded. "I'm freezing."

"Will you ring me if I'm right — please?"

"All right."

"Thank you, Saskia. Thank you very much. I'll let you go now."

Allardyce pulled out a mobile phone, punched in a number. "OK, pick us up," he said. He put the phone back in his jacket pocket in a brisk, final movement. "Simon will be over in a couple of minutes. We'll take you home."

"I was going to the delicatessen when you intercepted me. To get something for supper."

"Very domestic." Allardyce had his confidence back now. He was cocksure again in that seductive yet maddening way he had.

"Well, that's right, because I'm planning to go domestic from now on," I retorted. "I've got a good man, and I'm sticking to him."

Allardyce didn't answer. He glanced

up the road. I followed his gaze. The blue Ford was approaching at a sedate limousine pace. I was suddenly reminded of a scene from *The Godfather*.

"Well, well. Here's Simon," he said. "He must have parked just up the road."

He made a little gesture towards the car. Simon was sitting with the engine running.

"Actually, I think I'll find my own way back to the flat," I said on impulse. "I might have a little stroll around the shops in Clifton."

"Suit yourself, Saskia. Take care."

I watched Allardyce get back into the car and disappear in the direction of the Downs, presumably en route to the motorway and London. I shivered and set off at a brisk pace.

I didn't go to the shops, actually. I found my way down to the Gorge Hotel, bought myself a double brandy, and sat alone in the lounge, struggling to recover.

I stayed there for, oh I don't know, an hour or so, looking through the locked doors out onto the grey, empty terrace overlooking the gorge. Imagining the sheer fall beyond the terrace wall. Rehearsing Jilly Mattheson's last moments. Dying a hundred times. Trying, as if by grim magic, to catch the truth that might still be floating out there, in the air, that tiny echo of memory that outlives a scream.

I asked a hotel staff member if it would be possible to open the terrace doors so that I could go out and see the view properly. He looked edgy, said he had to find the manager and it might take some time.

When I realised he thought I was a potential suicide, I smiled and said it didn't matter. And it didn't, not really, in light of what was waiting for me when I got back to the flat in White Ladies' Road.

★ ★ ★

I had picked up plenty of food from the deli, put the ingredients for supper in the fridge and then made myself a little salad for lunch with real fetta cheese and olives. I was wondering whether to go and have a doze and dream of Australian beaches, so that I would be nice and refreshed when Tony got home.

First, I decided, I would find my bleeper and call up my answering-machine again. But it wasn't in my bag. Terrified that the thing was about to start disappearing and reappearing like the computer disk, I searched frantically around the living room and eventually found it under a copy of the *Radio Times*. I almost wept with relief. At least I didn't have to agonise about being crazy.

There were two new messages on the machine at the flat.

The first I don't remember, but the second I will never forget.

It was a gentle West Indian voice, a woman from the Saint Theresa High Commission in London.

The voice was sorry it had no good news for me. It said that the body of a blonde Caucasian woman had been found washed up on a beach near Emerald Point.

Would I, the voice asked, call back as soon as possible? Their government would like me to fly out to Saint Theresa and confirm whether the remains were indeed those of my sister, Miss Anna Freeling, missing believed lost in the area some weeks previously.

My world tipped on its axis, and suddenly all promises to Tony, all bets on the future, really were off.

23

I WAITED until Tony got home from filming. He held me while I poured out my tension and my despair in a torrent of tears. I think my mind had already accepted that I wouldn't see Anna alive again, but my body needed one final, cleansing release. Then I wiped my eyes, drank some coffee, and got on the phone.

Tony was wonderful. No more talk of avoiding involvement with the police. No more discouragement. I had to go to Saint Theresa. And he would come with me.

When I rang him, Inspector Allardyce was beautifully sympathetic. He didn't rush me, but when it came to the point he didn't hesitate to ask the hard question.

"So, are you going?" he asked gently.

"How could I not?"

"Yes." Pause. "I'll be on Saint Theresa too, though you won't see me unless the situation calls for it." Another pause. "I'll give you a local number to ring. If — when — something happens, just call that contact."

"You ... you promise you'll be there?"

"Yes. And Saskia, once you're on Saint Theresa don't confide in anyone else, whatever you do. There are people in the government and in the police that you can't trust."

He gave me the number. And that was it.

Tony and I drove back to London the next morning, and took the first available flight.

Early evening saw my new husband and I holding hands as our 737 took off into a clear winter sunset. On our way to a final accounting in a place of sun and death.

★ ★ ★

As our BWIA turbo-prop made its approach from the sea, the twin peaks of the island's famous volcano lay straight ahead, their contours shadowy in the evening light. We knew the airfield was close at hand, but until we suddenly glimpsed its postage-stamp clearing of green, we had the uneasy sense of dropping inexorably onto a thick, perilous carpet of forest.

Night comes quickly in the Caribbean. The shadows had lengthened, and the scenery was smudging into pastel as we taxied in towards the little terminal building.

The first shock came when we joined the queue for passport control with the rest of the passengers, mostly tourists from the US and Canada. I had been shuffling forward obediently for a few seconds, passport in hand, when I froze.

"It's him," I hissed, gripping Tony's arm.

"Who?"

I pointed to the other side of the barrier, where a Saint Theresan in a neat khaki officer's uniform and cap was standing beside the passport control official, his keen gaze sweeping the ranks of arrivals. He was a little taller than I remembered, and he seemed to have grown a beard, but I knew it was him.

"Johnny Dubois," I mumbled desperately. "Zena's brother. The one who slapped me."

Before Tony could say anything, the officer pushed through the barrier with a nod to the passport official and strode straight towards us.

"Oh, my God," I gasped.

"Miss Freeling?" he said. "I am Chief Inspector Dubois."

"Johnny?"

A puzzled but still polite smile. "My name is Valence, though I have a cousin by that name."

I recovered quickly. Of course — family resemblance. Allardyce had told me that the Dubois clan was large and influential in politics and the administration here. Why wouldn't one of them be a senior policeman? But they were also a close family; he had warned me about that too, in his cautious way . . .

"Thank you so much for meeting us," I said. "Actually, I'm Mrs Patterson now." I indicated Tony. "This is my husband, Tony."

Valence Dubois shook hands with Tony. "Pleased to meet you, Mr

Patterson." He made a courtly gesture of invitation. "And now, if you would like to come through with me . . . Formalities will not be necessary. You have already been cleared for entry."

"It's very kind of you," I repeated clumsily. In fact, it was rather unnerving, as I'm sure my manner showed all too clearly.

"Oh, the least we can do, Miss — I mean, Mrs Patterson." Valence Dubois was solemn and superficially gentle. I wanted to believe he was on our side. "A tragic situation, the death of your sister. For these few days you are our guest."

I exchanged glances with Tony. The last thing I wanted was to be saddled with a mincer, someone who could monitor our movements on behalf of the shady political and governmental figures we had been warned about. But we could hardly refuse this man's help without risking offending a powerful section of the island's elite. So I smiled in a dignified way and told him yet again how grateful we were. We were waved through the barrier by some of the most polite customs officials I have ever encountered — a hundred times more respectful than I remembered them being when Anna and I arrived for our holiday. On the other side, two policemen came forward to carry our bags.

A few minutes later, we were hunched in the back of a top-of-the-range Landcruiser, with our greeter and his driver up front, and heading out along the airport approach road, passing traffic at a lick that told us these were people who didn't need to obey speed restrictions.

"If you'd like to just clean up at your hotel and take it easy for a while," Valence Dubois said in his serious way, "we'll give you a call to arrange the actual identification." He paused, frowning. "The mortuary has closed for the day now, so it will be tomorrow morning."

"We'd like to get it over with, actually," Tony said through gritted teeth. "I'm sure it won't take a second."

For a moment the policeman's eyes flashed, giving the lie to that gentle exterior, but then he nodded thoughtfully. "I should warn you and your good lady, when someone's been in the sea for this long, they don't look pretty. Also, they are not necessarily that easily recognisable. That's another good reason for leaving the identification until the morning. Unless, of course, you insist."

"It's OK," I said quickly. "Tomorrow is absolutely fine."

There was no easy way to do this. On the one hand, as Tony had said, we wanted to get it over with, but on the other . . . Who in their right mind would be in a hurry to find themselves in a room with their sister's half-destroyed corpse?

"Suit yourself," Tony mumbled.

With great politeness we were dropped at our hotel in the centre of Port-Choiseul. Our police helper even came in to make sure we got a good room. Which we did — a ground-floor suite away from the street noise and overlooking a pretty tropical garden with a fountain. Then he departed with a smart half-salute and a wish that we pass a comfortable night.

Ignoring the air-conditioning, I flung open our French windows and breathed in the warm, bougainvillaea-scented air. I turned to Tony.

"Maybe we're here for nothing. Did that ever occur to you?"

He was sitting on the bed, his chin resting in his hands, looking at me with a kind of baleful disapproval. "Take it easy, love," he said.

"Why? You don't seem so relaxed yourself."

"Too right. I'm dazed and confused, as they say," Tony admitted. "Lord Lucan could walk through that door and I'd not turn a hair. Martin Bormann could appear with a tray of Martinis and I'd just take one and say thanks."

I laughed, a little too long and more than a little too loud.

"I did say to take it easy," Tony cautioned. He got up, padded over and took both my hands in his. "Are you sure you don't want the hotel doctor to prescribe you something to help you cope?"

"What? Valium? Prozac? No. I'm into experiencing what I'm experiencing. Whatever it is. However bad."

"You really mean that?"

I nodded.

"Well," Tony said, "I wish I could

share your stoic attitude. Personally, I need a drink. I think I'll just change into something more Caribbean and trot down to the bar. OK?"

"Aren't you exhausted?"

"No."

"Do you need to drink?"

"Maybe."

Tony turned with the air of a very, very tired man who is nearing the end of a journey. He swung his suitcase up onto the bed with a kind of grim determination and started to unzip it.

"I might join you later," I said, deciding not to force the issue about the drinking. "Maybe I'll have a bath. That'll make me feel better."

"Sure, love. You do what helps you through. I'll do what helps me."

★ ★ ★

After my bath I stretched out on top of the bed in the humid night, tried to relax, and thought about going down for a drink and dinner.

The next thing I remember is snapping awake, to hear the door opening and someone stumbling around in the darkness.

"Tony?" I whispered.

"Yeah." He sat down and kicked off his loafers. I could tell he was pretty drunk. "What happened to you?"

"I fell asleep," I yawned. "What time is it?"

"About half-eleven. Jesus, you left the doors to the garden open. Anyone could have wandered in, love."

"Have you eaten?"

"A ham-and-cheese sandwich," he said with the bizarre precision of the inebriated. "Toasted. With a slice of pineapple. And, I must confess, quite a lot of whisky." He paused. It was so quiet I could hear him unbutton his shirt, then unzip his slacks. "Want to get something from room service, Sass?" he asked then.

"No. No appetite, thanks."

Tony laughed as if at some secret joke. Then he rolled over and began to stroke my naked back, half-soothing, half-exploring. I shuddered with unexpected delight. There was something almost touchingly desperate about the way he did it, like a blind man judging a strange and precious thing, storing a memory of it. He moved closer, drew me to him. Normally I find any man, even one I love, a turn-off when he's had a lot to drink, but tonight there was something in Tony or in him and me — that made me want him all the more. My hand slid down to his flat, hard belly, lingered for a few moments, then ventured further down. There he was even harder. Proud and insistent.

"I said I was dazed and confused. But never about this," he murmured. "Never about this, my lovely blonde creature. Not even for a moment."

And he touched me too, and pleasured me with his mouth, and we made love in every way we knew, and one or two more, until we were both slippery with tropical sweat and heady with exhaustion.

I think Tony already knew this was the last time we would make love. Was that why it was so fine, so intense, so strangely beautiful? I have relived that night a thousand times since, and now I think that maybe I knew it too, somewhere in the depths of my twin-haunted heart.

24

THE Hotel Aux Quatre Vents in Port-Choiseul was a faintly decaying nineteenth-century building, all tropical hardwoods and faded green shutters. A charming and well-run establishment, but neither of us was in the mood to appreciate its virtues.

I sat in the breakfast room the next morning in my best white linen dress out of respect for where I was going, toying impatiently with my papaya slices and waiting. Tony kept checking his watch.

All the guests but us had finished eating and disappeared on their holiday jaunts when a young man walked through the door and asked for Mr and Mrs Patterson. I braced myself, got to my feet. Tony took my arm.

"I'm Mrs Patterson," I said. There was a quaver in my voice that I could not disguise.

The young man nodded. "How do you do. My name is Henry Lasalle. I will drive you to the coroner's office."

"Thanks," said Tony. "Well, you're the first local I've met this trip whose name doesn't begin with a 'D' and end with an 's', so there's something."

The young man didn't miss a beat. "Oh, Lasalle is my father's name. My mother is a Dubois. Please just follow me."

★ ★ ★

It was a half-mile drive to the coroner's office, in a bronze Buick that was straight out of *The Streets of San Francisco*. Except that these were the streets of Port-Choiseul, colourful thoroughfares thronged with, it seemed, more tourists than locals, and more dogs than either. Henry Lasalle explained that it was very high season. The native people of Port-Choiseul were either working in the shops and hotels, or staying indoors out of the heat. Finally he pulled into a cement-surfaced car park next to a two-storey 1960s official building that wouldn't have looked out of place in the English Home Counties.

Polite as ever, Henry came round and opened the car door for us. We paused in front of the building. A battered plaque informed us that it had been opened by a minor British royal in 1967.

Inside, it was all institutional smells — tobacco, disinfectant, and a faint aroma that I thought belonged to stale food until I remembered the building's purpose. I took a deep breath as Henry knocked on a door marked *Coroner's Office. Please Wait.*

Well, he knocked but he didn't wait. And we followed him in. At a desk sat a very pretty young woman with plaited hair in the fashionable African style, clicking away at an old IBM Golfball typewriter. Beyond her was another door marked CORONER.

Henry shot the secretary a dazzling smile. "Mr and Mrs Patterson. Case of Miss Anna Freeling. The coroner is expecting them."

She nodded. "He's already in the pathology room, Mr Lasalle. You want to go and check with him? The gentleman and the lady can stay here for now."

Henry came back a couple of minutes

later, then ushered us through some swing doors into a big, sterile room illuminated only by strip-lights. An autopsy table stood at one end. By this waited a bespectacled middle-aged man in a lightweight suit and tie, who I took to be the coroner, talking quietly to a mortuary attendant in a white coat. I advanced slowly into the room. Tony hung back. This was, after all, sisterly business, but he would be there if I needed him. Seeing us, the suited man broke off his conversation and came towards me, hand outstretched. I shook it.

"Miss Freeling," he said heavily. "This is a most distressing duty for any family member to perform. We'll try to make it as easy as possible."

"Mrs Patterson," I repeated for what felt like the hundredth time. "I got married just last week."

He raised an eyebrow. "Are you ready?" he asked softly. He hesitated. "I should add that the body may be difficult to recognise immediately. So do take your time. We want to be certain."

I nodded, then moved forward as if in

a dream. *Get it over*, I thought. *Tony's right. Get it over* . . .

The man walked across to some steel drawers set in the wall. He pulled one out. I saw a matted-blonde head, a body under a sheet.

"Please," he said.

I gave a long, shuddering sigh, then looked. At first I could just feel the cold of the refrigerated unit where the cadavers were kept. Then a faintly sour smell hit my nostrils, a shock after-scent, almost tipping me back. I started to take short, quick breaths, to minimise the contact with death.

The face of the woman in the body-drawer was like melted wax. Greeny-blue and almost featureless. Her hair was genuinely blonde, there could be no doubt of that. The shoulders looked just a tiny bit beefier than Anna's or mine, unless somehow the muscle had become bloated in the process of drowning and drifting. This was by no means the first corpse I had seen — I'd been to flashpoints in Africa, done the war-correspondent's tour of Sarajevo, shot a photo-essay about terminal illness for one of the serious weekend supplements — but this was a victim of the sea, an unfamiliar phenomenon. I just didn't know what happened to a body during weeks in the sea, what changes it would undergo.

I stared at the body until the coroner's voice imposed on my horrified meditation.

"Well?" he coaxed.

"She's . . . about the right height, and her hair's like Anna's . . . "

Most of me had already accepted that this was my sister. The coroner nodded solemnly. I saw him exchange a knowing glance with the man in the white coat.

Then something in me resisted their certainty. I gulped in some air. "Could . . . could I see her arms, please?" I asked, my words emerging in a dry rattle.

A momentary cloud of irritation passed over the coroner's dignified features. Then he nodded. He gestured to the man in the white coat, who carefully lifted the corpse's arms out and laid them on top of the sheet.

Behind me, I heard Tony cough. The coroner folded his arms.

I surprised myself by my own coolness. I leaned in close, inspected the arms. Both were faintly but definitely scarred in several places. And one forearm bore a tattoo.

"This is not my sister Anna," I said, and now my voice was strong.

The coroner was looking past me at Tony, as if to say, *Can't you get your wife to do the right thing, man?* I stepped back in a very definite way. I felt relief flooding my body. I was floating, serene.

"It's not my sister," I repeated. "Those are not her arms. And she doesn't have a tattoo, not anywhere on her body."

"Madam, are you sure?" the coroner snapped, quite aggressively. "That this is not her, and that she did not have a tattoo?"

"To your first question: absolutely. To your second: my sister was an *accountant!*" I hissed. Then I turned to the orderly. "Please close that drawer. I can't bear to look any more."

He rolled it slowly shut on its casters and the corpse slid out of sight with a dull, metallic and very final clang.

Then Tony was with me, holding my hand. "Let's go and get a cup of coffee, love," he said in a subdued voice.

I nodded. The coroner was still looking at me. My absurd, polite English instincts were to apologise. To apologise for their mistake, if mistake it was. But I just shrugged and walked towards the exit, trying to keep my dignity while my brain raced with a hundred versions of the same problem: *what the hell do I do now?*

★ ★ ★

We declined Henry's driving services and headed for a bar near the main square. I ordered an espresso, Tony a beer.

"You really are certain?" Tony said.

"You sound like that po-faced coroner. Yes, of course I bloody well am!"

"You don't think Anna had that tattoo done but didn't tell you?"

"I spent nine days with her before she disappeared," I said irritably. "I would have seen it, don't you think? I saw her getting up, getting out of the shower . . . "

I gulped down some of my boiling hot coffee. The floaty euphoria had subsided; now I was feeling puzzled and oddly let down, as if I had been cheated of a resolution, however painful.

"OK," Tony said. "Back to square one."

"And you know what else?" I said. "I could see little scars and bumps all over that dead girl's skin. You know what they told me? *Junkie*, that's what! I've seen tracks like those on the arms of working girls in New York and Miami."

Tony looked shocked.

"I'm starting to think," I persisted, "that we're dealing with genuinely evil people. People who might find some blonde junkie, maybe a prostitute, here or in Miami or somewhere, and who might just dump her in the water and hope she got found, and I'd somehow be confused enough or stupid enough or still shell-shocked enough to identify her as my sister." I eyed Tony fiercely. "How does that sound to you? Crazy?"

He made a helpless gesture. "Not exactly. Of course, she may have been a tourist, and this may be just an unfortunate mistake."

"I wouldn't put it past them to kill," I said again. "I would believe anything of these people — Johnny Dubois, whoever. Anything."

★ ★ ★

The man at reception greeted us with a sympathetic smile. He was well aware of my reason for being on the island, and our destination this morning.

"Mr and Mrs Patterson," he began, "you go sit through in the lounge and we bring you a drink — on the house — "

"It wasn't my sister in that morgue," I interrupted him. "No way." Before he could respond, I went on: "I'm absolutely certain of that, and I don't want anyone to query me ever again, do you understand?"

I ducked through into the lounge, sat down heavily in a cane chair, put my head in my hands and just blanked out. When I opened my eyes, moments or minutes later — I saw the same receptionist standing over me. He was holding out an envelope.

"Letter for you, Mrs Patterson," he said. "Some street-kid brought it in."

I nodded wearily and motioned for him to put it down on the low table next to my chair.

"Sure you wouldn't like a drink, madam? Your husband has already gone through to the bar."

"Not for now, thanks," I said. "And I'm sorry I snapped at you. It's been a tough morning. Not as bad as if it had been Anna in that mortuary, but bad enough."

The receptionist made a little bow and left me on my own.

I picked up the envelope, languidly ripped it open. Maybe it was the coroner asking me yet again if I knew my own sister, I thought bitterly. Then I saw that it was a page torn out of an exercise book. I made out the jerky handwriting, and my pulse quickened. My body interpreted the signals before my mind got round to reading the message:

Saskia, I've only got a moment to write this. I found out it's going to be just me and the servants here today, so we have a chance to see each other. Not here or in town, though. Too dangerous. I can bring the boat to the beach at Eugénie Bay and we can talk. I know what's going on, and why Jilly and Anna died, and it's awful. Please meet me there at one o'clock. Go to Gene Peters' place in the port and he'll get someone to bring you.

It's our only chance. If I can't get the boat, I may come by Jeep, but anyway just wait on the beach and I'll be there.

The note was signed Zena.

"Jesus, sweetheart, are you all right?" asked Tony when he got back with a large rum cocktail.

Wordlessly, I handed him the note. He read it slowly, then read it again.

"Whose side is she on?" he asked.

"I don't know," I said. "But I think we have to follow up on this, don't you? Allardyce said something would happen and it has. At last. I mean, for once he got it right."

Tony nodded. "Or we could just walk

out of here and take the plane back to London."

"Then we'd never know, would we? I couldn't face Allardyce again if I muffed this chance."

"Your decision," Tony said. "We've got an hour and a half to get to where Zena will be. If you want to go." He looked at me questioningly. "Well?"

I felt a wild rush of energy, a yearning for certainty. "How can we not?" I said. "Go and ask the hotel people where to find this boat-hire place she mentions."

"Not necessary. It's the same outfit who rented me the boat when we went exploring after Anna first disappeared."

"Right." I rummaged in my bag, fished out my personal organiser and looked up the number Allardyce had told me to ring in case of emergency. "I'd better get changed into something more suitable than this frock, but first I'll call the number Allardyce gave me."

"I'll do it," Tony said crisply. "You go and get changed. I'll tell them where we're going and when and why — OK?"

I hesitated, then handed him the organiser. "Thanks. Meet me in our room," I said. "Maybe this is the end, darling. Not that body in the mortuary, but the truth from the mouth of the single solitary *honest* Dubois."

I kissed him quickly on the cheek and left. Tony, drink still in hand, hurried off in the direction of the payphone in the hotel lobby.

The moment I opened the door of our room, I knew something was wrong. A breeze was running through it, yet we had closed the French windows before we went out.

I stood on the threshold for a moment, peering round the half-open door. There was nobody there. But yes, everything was open to the garden. I searched the room. All our possessions had gone, from the alarm clock on the bedside table to the sunblock cream in the bathroom, to the suitcases and clothes in the closet. Everything except . . .

I felt around on the top shelf of the closet and retrieved my beloved pair of Gap khaki shorts and plain white top. Thank God Tony had insisted I pack them — in fact, he had tossed them into the suitcase just before I closed it.

So at least I had a change of clothes.

I went over and closed and locked the French windows, but the room door was still open. When I heard a footfall in the hall outside, I whipped round in alarm, but it was only Tony, still carrying that damned cocktail.

"Hi," he said, looking around the room. "What's happening?"

"We've been robbed," I said. "Everything's gone except my cheapest top and shorts. Our local thieves only go for the best stuff."

"Shit," Tony said. His expression darkened. "We'd better report this to the police."

"Forget it," I sighed wearily. "After what Allardyce told us about them? Maybe we'll mention it to the management on the way out. OK with the boat-hire people?"

"Yup. They were really helpful. No sweat."

"And Allardyce?"

"I got Gwen. She said they'd be there to keep an eye on us. They sounded pretty well organised."

Quickly, I pulled off my dress and slid

into the shorts, tugged the top over my head. I had to wear the sandals that went with the dress, but what the hell. Tony had no choice but to go to meet Zena in his good slacks and shirt, and his best docksiders. Too bad, too.

The receptionist promised to call the cops about the robbery in the room. He was genuinely horrified. This had never happened in the hotel before, he swore. They always tell you that, said Tony. But as we rushed out, the man called after us: "Take care!"

He seemed to mean it. I thought I could tell.

25

IT was all very straightforward, that first part. Down to the port, among the yachts and the fishing craft, a quick conversation with a fat man who looked as if he would be surprised by nothing, and there we were, stepping onto a little motor-boat and greeting the taciturn Roland, the same man who had steered us all those weeks before to the remote beach where we had found Anna's flipper.

It was a calmer day than I had seen before on Saint Theresa, where there was usually a breeze. As the boat chugged away from the quay, with a handful of figures watching us, still as sentries, I said to Tony in a low voice, "Saint Theresans make me nervous."

He shrugged. "I have a feeling they think we're crazy," he whispered. "Either that, or they know we're connected with the Dubois in some way and they don't know which way to jump."

I nodded slowly. Roland gazed ahead, his sinewy hand steady on the tiller, face as unreadable as an Easter Island statue.

"How far to Eugénie Bay?" Tony asked him, putting on his innocent tourist voice.

"Twenty minutes," Roland said.

And those were the last words we had from him. Tony and I didn't talk much either. We were shy about discussing possibilities in front of a local, and so we just sat. I took Tony's hand. He seemed to flinch slightly with the shock, showing how nervous he was. Then he gave me a tight smile which was meant, I think, to encourage. And that was how we stayed as the boat cut through the water, carefully keeping its distance several hundred yards from the shoreline.

Soon we were out of sight of the harbour and moving round a forested headland. It was amazing how quickly the bustle of Port-Choiseul, its people and its yachts and busy little local craft, gave way to a feeling of remoteness, of pure, unexplored territory. There was a little hamlet in sight for a short while, and then just trees and foliage and the occasional silver strip of beach. Another little headland came up, and we rounded it. I looked at my watch. Just over fifteen minutes had passed since we left port.

As if on cue, Roland flicked the tiller and we started to curl back in towards shore. We were heading for a small clearing that came down to the water, a patch of beach, a few posts that must once have supported a jetty, and a wooden shack. A little closer and I could make out the sign, peeling letters against faded wood, saying: PLANTER'S RESTAURANT & BAR. The building revealed itself as seriously dilapidated. The even more badly decayed remnants of a wooden-hulled boat sat a little further down the beach, to the right of the wooden posts that marched feebly into the sea. There was not a soul in sight, as far as I could see.

"Planter's Bar?" I said enquiringly to Roland.

He didn't grant me a direct look but kept his eyes on the beach we were steering towards; when he did speak, it seemed to be to Tony.

"Banana plantation near here," he said.

"There you are," I told Tony. "She said she might come by road. I was wondering how. Must be tracks criss-crossing the plantation."

He nodded. "Yeah. I don't see anyone waiting, though."

"Neither do I. But then she's hardly likely to be jumping up and down on the beach, waving a red flag," I said not unreasonably.

A little snort of amusement or exasperation came from Tony; it was hard to tell which. I squeezed his hand. He returned the gesture briefly, but then pulled away and gripped the side of the boat with both hands as we started our final approach, bobbing in through the gently-lapping surf.

As we reached the nearest of the stumps that had once been jetty-posts, Roland ran the launch up alongside it and gestured for Tony to tie up there. My husband obediently picked up the painter on the floor of the vessel and looped it round the rotting post. I looked at it dubiously — how could we guarantee that the mooring would hold? — but didn't argue.

Roland cut the engine, reached over and tied Tony's temporary landlubber's loop into an efficient knot. Then he sat back and folded his arms.

"Is not deep. Three foot mebbe," he stated.

There was a silence.

"Well, he brought us here," Tony said then. "That seems to be where he feels his responsibilities end. Shall we go ashore?"

I took a deep breath, nodded.

"I'll go first, Sass."

Tony rolled up his slacks to the knee, then slid over the side and lowered himself gingerly until he found a footing. The water came almost to his waist.

"It's OK," he encouraged me. "The sand's pretty firm. It'll be an easy wade from here."

He held out his arms for me and I joined him in the water. Hand in hand, we headed towards the beach a few yards away. The slope got steeper and the going softer and more difficult, so we were fully preoccupied until we finally squelched our way onto dry land.

There I paused and checked my watch again. "We're five minutes late. And I didn't see another boat out there."

"She did say she might come by Jeep," Tony reminded me.

"I wish *we* had," I said. "I find Roland a bit creepy, to tell you the truth." I half-turned. The boatman was looking out to sea, as if he didn't want to catch our eye, in case anything was demanded of him. "Maybe he's just not one of nature's communicators."

We walked the last few yards to the ruined restaurant. Close up, it was clear that the place hadn't served up a lobster tail or a rum sour for years. The building sat on wooden piles that raised it two or three feet above the sand. Tony clambered up some wooden steps to the doorless entrance, peered inside, then descended once more.

"Nope," he announced. "I thought she might be hiding in there, but it seems not."

"So we wait."

"Sounds like it's difficult for Zena to

get away. We have to give her the benefit of the doubt."

I nodded uneasily and swiped at a buzzing insect that had taken a fancy to blonde, pale me. Already my skin was starting to dry in the warm wind. Tony looked almost comically uncomfortable in his waterlogged, rolled-up slacks, like a day-tripper who had misjudged the incoming waves. Under any other circumstances, I might have laughed.

We sat down on the little raised platform. Time passed. Four, five minutes.

"How long do we actually give her?" I asked.

"I don't know, Sass. How long is a piece of string?"

"Show me it and I'll tell you. I don't see anyone else either, by the way."

"Allardyce, you mean?" Tony said.

"That's exactly who I mean."

Before Tony could reply, we heard a sound from inland. At first I thought it was the call of a bird or an animal. Then it came again, and I realised it was manmade. A car-horn.

Tony looked at me anxiously. "Do you hear what I hear?"

"Yes."

"Maybe I should investigate." He nodded vigorously. "Yes, I'll go and take a look. Maybe she's driven here and she's lost."

"What? She grew up here! She must know these parts as well as I know the countryside around Trerose."

"All right, all right," Tony said. "Then maybe she doesn't want to come down to the beach where the likes of Roland will see her talking to us."

"Let's go and see," I suggested.

"No. No." Tony was visibly screwing up his courage. "I'll sneak up to the road and take a look. It's obviously not that far. If it's not her, I'll just sneak back here again and we'll decide what to do next."

"I want to come with you." I reached out and seized his hand.

"Darling . . . please . . . that's just being silly. What if it's not her on the road? What if Zena comes round that point in a boat while we're away? She'll see Roland on his own and may not recognise him. Maybe she'll be frightened off. Then we'll have wasted the opportunity."

"But I don't want to stay here on my own."

"Roland's within hollering distance."

"I know. That's what worries me."

"For God's sake, Sass," Tony pleaded. "Don't be irrational. I'll just be a couple of minutes."

There was a brief standoff. The distant beep sounded again. I studied Tony's anxious face, his fearful, darting eyes that belied his determination to be brave. He had helped and protected me ever since Anna's death, had been right about so many things, even the voices I had heard, the voices that had almost driven me crazy. He had saved my sanity, I thought, and possibly my life. The least I could do was trust him.

"OK, but be careful," I said, swallowing hard. "God, I'm a feeble creature, aren't I?"

"No, not at all." Tony pulled himself free of my grasp. "I'll go quickly, so I don't have a chance to think, OK?"

I watched, bemused, as he turned awkwardly and, without further hesitation, hurried up the beach. When he reached the little clearing, Tony glanced back very quickly, not especially at me. Then he quickened his pace to a run. Within moments the foliage had swallowed him. I shivered at that moment, despite the heat of the early-afternoon sun. Mrs Williams would have said, *Someone just walked over your grave.*

I sat down on the platform once more and gazed determinedly out to sea, as if by keeping my eyes fixed in that direction I wouldn't be able to worry.

There was only the lazy lapping of the waves on a tranquil day. The noisy little flying insect returned to pester me. I waved it away. The sun was pleasant on my skin. I forced myself to close my eyes, to pretend calm, mimic a pose of peaceful waiting. If you had materialised on that beach, knowing nothing, you would have seen me as a laid-back beachcomber resting from her unimpressive efforts, without a care in the world. In fact, the effort of resisting the urge to get up and go to the edge of the forest to look for Tony was so extreme that my shoulderblades had clenched rigid and the hairs on the nape of my neck stood up like bristles.

The insect had come back for another attack . . .

Or had it? The buzz wasn't like the insect, more like a motor. I opened my eyes, shaded them with my hand against the light and looked out to sea. Nothing was moving.

Until suddenly, out of the corner of my eye, I glimpsed activity. Roland was quietly but quickly untying the rope from the mooring post. In fact, the rope was already snaking back into the boat. In a moment it was all gathered in and Roland was moving to other duties.

I stood up, and at that moment the launch's gently purring engine roared into life.

"Roland!" I shouted. "What are you doing!"

But he didn't react. He just sat, shoulders hunched, and steered calmly away, looking neither to the right nor the left. His whole being was concentrated on taking that machine away from the shore.

"*Roland!*" I started to run down the

beach. I reached the edge of the water, but by now there was only the stern of the boat, its foaming trail, and the back of Roland's head. The sixty, seventy yards between me and the launch rapidly became eighty, ninety, a hundred . . .

I sobbed in helpless terror. I tried to shout again, but the boatman's name died on my lips, because now I could see something else, coming towards me even faster than the launch was leaving. A real speedboat this time, the kind I had seen used in races on Lake Windermere — or by cigarette-smugglers in the Adriatic. In it were two men, one black and one white. The black one, who was the passenger, pointed towards me.

Allardyce, I thought feverishly. *Is this Allardyce at last?*

Then I recognised the black man. It was Johnny Dubois.

And I thought I understood everything. The memory flashed back of that other sun-drenched beach weeks ago, when I was woken from my nap by a fast speedboat out at sea. To find Anna gone.

They could have swooped in on her

before she was able to escape, just as they were about to do with me. Oh God, poor Anna.

For a moment, terror cast its paralysing spell. Then, by a titanic effort of will, I managed to restore movement to my limbs. I turned unsteadily, then stumbled blindly back up the beach.

"Tony!" I screamed. "*Tony!*"

But I knew even then that to call out my husband's name was worse than futile. It was a mistake.

★ ★ ★

I had no idea what was in the forest, how far it was to the road, or what lay ahead when I got there. But every instinct shrieked at me to get away from Johnny Dubois at all costs.

I followed a rough path, once presumably capable of bringing tourists down from the road but now seriously overgrown. Creepers threatened to trip me, spiky little plants pricked my calves, but I half-ran, half-jumped up that path. The long legs that had put both me and Anna in the school relay team all those years ago carried me quickly and surely, despite the obstacles. My heart was pounding ready to burst, but some kind of animal survival instinct had taken over; during those few minutes as I crashed through the forest, my body worked more perfectly than ever before or since. The fear, I recall, had gone completely, even though I knew that soon Johnny Dubois and his companion would have made landfall and be after me.

This strange exhilaration lasted until I rounded a corner in the path and found that I was approaching a fork. I stopped abruptly, my chest heaving, desperately wondering which way to go. I fancied I could hear the sound of my pursuers behind me.

I closed my eyes. *Tony*, I whispered, despite my earlier misgivings. I prayed to him, I swear I did. *Tony, don't let me down now. Give me a sign* . . .

And from somewhere a sign did come, in the form of a distant voice, raised briefly in protest or celebration, it was impossible to say. And it came, I was sure, from the left-hand fork. I locked onto that sound, and started running again.

I had chosen correctly. As I pounded through the forest, the sounds became louder, more distinct. Male voices. And a female one. Tony had found Zena, I thought excitedly. Maybe everything was all right. It sounded as if she had people with her who would see off Johnny and his friend. I gritted my teeth, and began to run even harder, summoning up every last ounce of my strength. I could see a clearing ahead now. And a vehicle of some kind.

My spirits leapt. As I brushed past a final, chest-high fern and emerged into the open like a winner breasting a tape, I heard myself shouting in a high, disembodied voice, half-war cry and half-warning: "Tony! TONY!"

And there he was, standing by the open front door of the vehicle, which was identifiable now as a red Range-Rover, along with a black man and a woman. The woman was laughing. She wore shorts just like mine. *And an identical T-shirt to mine* . . .

Not Zena.

Not black, but white.
Blonde, long-legged, tanned.
Anna.

I'll never forget the range of expressions on those faces as the three of them turned to see who had erupted so suddenly into their private world. Tony, a frozen smile. The black man, angry puzzlement. And Anna, at first still laughing, but then her mouth forming an awkward 'O' of surprise.

For a moment I stopped, wheezing with effort, hands on hips, staring at the mirror-image of myself that stood just fifteen feet away over by the Range-Rover. She was identically dressed, her hair just the same as mine, with my husband by her side. I was spooked. Wild as it may sound, for that instant I doubted that I existed any more. It felt possible that somehow I had entered another body, that it was actually me over there with Tony and the unknown man.

"Anna," I stuttered between breaths. "You're alive. Thank God." I held out my arms towards my sister.

Even then I knew it was a foolish thing

to say, and an even more foolish thing to do. But old feelings don't die easily. And old instincts need hard lessons before they change. A hard lesson was what I was about to receive.

For Anna made no move towards me. Her mouth had formed itself into a kind of smile, but her body-language — tight, defensive — told me everything I needed to know. This was not a miraculous, happy reunion. Something was horribly wrong.

"Tony! Johnny Dubois is after us!" I panted. "Anna — where's Zena? What's going on?"

Tony shook his head. "This shouldn't have happened," he said dully. "Not like this. Not like this."

Anna glanced at him with a frown of pure contempt. "Johnny screwed up. She's here, so just face up to it!" I felt a rush of anger and stepped forward. Anna reacted quickly. She reached into the Range-Rover and pulled out a small, snub-nosed automatic pistol.

"Get back," she said coldly. "Keep your distance, Saskia!"

I froze, temporarily stunned into silence.

Now I knew as much as I needed to know. She had never been kidnapped — she had gone willingly with Johnny Dubois in his speedboat that afternoon weeks before. It had all been part of a long-laid plan. Everything I had done since had been manipulated. By Anna . . . and . . .

"Tony?" I whispered. "You were part of this, weren't you? Everything. Here. London. Cornwall . . ."

Tony looked around wildly then shrank back against the Range-Rover like a child trying to disappear by sheer force of wishing. He had started to sweat. It was all coming together for me as I looked at him now. His mood-swings as the pressure grew, the lies piled up. The escalation of his drinking, rising up to meet this moment of unbearable truth. Unbearable for both of us.

"I wanted her, Sass," he said meekly. "Those were the terms. To help her keep the money. Our money. Our freedom. You know, when you really want someone . . ."

"Bastard," I cut in, voice hard as steel. An odd calm was settling over me; the calm that's needed when you want to give yourself a chance, even a slight one, of survival in an impossible situation. "I loved you, trusted you. And all the time it was a set-up. How could you do it?" I shook my head. "But then, of course, you're an *actor*! You can make anything seem real, can't you?"

The full, agonizing horror lay not just in their treachery. The deepest pain was knowing how they had planned to have me killed at the beach, by Johnny and his friend, out of sight and mind. Tony in particular would have been able to walk from one identical woman to the other, without having to go through the messy business of watching one being killed. He would almost — I know he was a great self-deceiver — have been able to persuade himself that nothing had happened, nothing had really changed. Same clothes, same body . . . which is why he had looked so absolutely horrified when I appeared on the edge of the clearing, robbing him of his coward's comfort.

"Leave him alone, Saskia," Anna said. "I wanted him from the first time I set eyes on him, and I got him. We worked out a way to be rich and free. Together."

"Why didn't you just take him?" I hissed. "Why do this to me?"

Anna shrugged. "You don't get it, do you?"

She stepped forward until she was just a few feet from me. The gun was still pointing at my midriff.

Keep her talking, I thought. Just delay the moment when that gun goes off. "No," I said, edging a little closer, totally focused on Anna, feeling the intensity of her cold blue eyes, fighting once more that sense of shrinking identity, the loss of self that, if I gave into it, would kill me. "Explain."

"It's not enough to get Tony," Anna said. "I also have to become someone else — you. So that I — " Anna glanced with casual affection at my husband and corrected herself with a humourless little smile. "I mean *we* — can spend all the money I worked so hard and cleverly to make. Because if I were still me, I might be arrested. And they might confiscate it."

"I understand. So now I die. And you and Tony drive back to Port-Choiseul as if nothing has happened . . ." I edged forward a little more. "The police — Inspector Allardyce — thought it was because I stood to inherit your money, but that's not it. The idea is, you *become* me. You even organised the robbery at the hotel, so you'd *know* what I would be wearing and could match it, right?" I took another step towards her. "Why, Anna? Was it just the money?"

"No." Anna glanced past me. I knew she was expecting Johnny Dubois soon. She didn't realise that I was waiting for Inspector Allardyce. "That's just a symbol, Saskia. All my life you worked so hard to suffocate me. You thought your life was so glamorous. I was the little, downtrodden mouse. But I just quietly went my way, developed skills of my own. Skills that have made me a millionaire. And I got new friends."

"Including Jilly, the innocent friend you killed?"

"I didn't want to. I was very fond of her. But we were afraid that when she realised what had happened, how

I'd put her signature on the stuff, she might tell them about Tony and me, and everything would unravel. You see, she saw him leave the flat a couple of times in the early morning." Anna sighed. "It was safer . . . kinder, in a way, because imagine how upset she would have been if she'd known the truth."

"I never wanted to make you feel bad, Anna. I loved you." The words tumbled out, and I realised that I meant them. *Really* meant them. Whatever was about to happen, I wanted her to know. "I can't help the life I grew up to live. I was good with a camera, that's all — "

"Ah, the *camera*!" Anna interrupted me. It was bizarre, as if we were chatting in a room alone, not in a lonely tropical forest with my sister holding a gun on me and my husband waiting for her to kill me. "Where's your camera now?" she taunted. "Could your camera stop me doing what I want to do? If you took a picture of me now, would it make any difference? I'd just show it around. Photo of Saskia Patterson."

"Like the photograph we found in your flat. Tony and you, pretending to be me.

You were tempting fate there, weren't you?" I looked into her bright, hard eyes. "Just tell me. When was it, Anna?"

"About six months after Tony moved in with you. You were away on another of your stupid trips. He took me to a party where I was 'you' the whole evening. That's when we *really* got into it." Anna's voice dropped to a throaty whisper. "And into each other. The delicious danger. The secrets. The things only we could do together."

I knew now that there was no dissuading Anna; she had long since gone beyond the caring emotions where I was concerned. She wanted me dead. Badly. But the longer she kept talking, the better the chance that Allardyce would arrive before that happened. For God's sake, where *was* he?

"We're *sisters*," I said. "Doesn't that mean anything to you?"

"Oh yes." Anna's green eyes flashed with cool amusement. "I've thought about that a lot. One egg's tight. You learn to be ruthless, to bide your time. You learn to hate." Her eyes bored into mine. They were almost hypnotic. "But that's enough talking, Saskia. I've had enough of being dead. I'm eager to start living again."

"So you're going to kill me?"

Anna shook her head. "Oh no. I'm waiting for Johnny. Johnny does that stuff. Quick and easy. He's good at it. And he's on his way . . ."

"So's Inspector Allardyce," I said.

Anna smiled thinly. I froze. Of course. I had left it to Tony to phone Allardyce. Oh God . . .

I knew then that if I didn't move immediately, I was finished. Oblivious to the gun in Anna's hand, or the other people in the clearing, I sprang forward at her. From deep within me I drew on the same store of anger and frustration against my twin that Anna had been using, nurturing, but until now I had never known existed.

When I launched myself at Anna, I caught her completely by surprise. I think she just never conceived that I'd have the courage, or the self-belief, to do what I then did. With that initial onrush, I knocked her off-balance. Then, before she could bring the gun round again and aim, I grabbed the wrist of her weapon-bearing hand and squeezed it ferociously. Anna grimaced but held onto the gun. I kept the pressure up until I heard her yelp with pain, but still Anna clung on, as if waiting for me to weaken — or for someone else to intervene.

I don't know how long this grunting, wordless trial of strength went on before the next sequence of events. Probably just a few seconds. I sensed a crushing blow to the back of my neck as Anna brought round her left hand and started pummelling wildly at me. Stung into new action, I increased the pressure on her wrist until all circulation must have been cut off, until her fingers splayed and finally the weapon went spinning away...

When she dropped the gun, I grabbed Anna round the waist and tried to pull her over, hoping wildly that I could roll over together with her, disentangle myself and then run away before Tony and the other man had a chance to react. She resisted, and in that moment of impasse, as we grappled, a gun went off very close nearby.

Anna and I both turned in a sort of bizarre mimicry, still locked together, and glimpsed the same thing: Johnny Dubois, newly arrived in the clearing and holding an automatic weapon that he had just fired once in the air to get our attention. And now that weapon was pointed straight at us.

For a moment all was silent except for our agonised panting.

"Anna — move," Johnny said then. "Get away from her."

Something told me what to say. "I can't, Johnny." I was amazed to hear the words coming out of my own mouth. "The bitch has got me."

I saw the look of outrage that passed over Anna's face.

"That's not me talking. That's Saskia!" she hissed. And she pushed me off-balance. I swayed, she twisted, and then we were apart.

"She's lying!" I gasped, knowing it was my only chance.

We stood there, feet apart, neither daring to move lest it be construed as an attempt to escape, proof of being the dispensable twin. Johnny shook his head uncertainly. How could he tell the difference? We were identical women, identically dressed. Only one of us could be Saskia, and Saskia under the circumstances was not the twin to be . . .

"Hey," he growled. "Hey, hey. What d'you say, Tony? Which one is Anna?"

For the first time since I had attacked my twin, I noticed Tony again. He had moved halfway across the clearing and was closer to Johnny than to us. My husband still wore that look of abject horror, and he was shaking his head.

"I . . . God, I don't know."

"Tony! Help me!" Anna screamed.

"I'll kill you, you liar!" I shouted, staring at her with fury. "Tony, come and get me. Quick!"

Nobody spoke. Tony just stood there, dumbstruck with indecision. Suddenly the clearing was filled with the growling throb of an engine overhead. A *whoosh* of rotor-blades ruffled the tree-tops above us, and in just a few seconds a shadow was cast on the sunlit grass of the clearing. We all looked up like amazed children. A helicopter hovered overhead, maybe a hundred feet up; a man in a khaki uniform was leaning out of the cabin, a loud-hailer raised to his lips.

"Shit," Anna spat. She seemed genuinely astonished. "What *is* this?"

"Run, Saskia!" the man with the loud-hailer called down. "*Run!*"

And the helicopter began to slowly descend towards the clearing.

I suppose I was transfixed with amazement. Or perhaps I didn't trust my own ears. But the fact is — and this is what you have to believe — it was *Anna* who moved first, Anna who, without a moment's hesitation, bolted for the edge of the forest. *Anna who was now pretending to be me* . . .

There was a thud. I saw her stumble, then pick herself up and continue a little unsteadily. Then Johnny Dubois' second bullet hit her, this time squarely between the shoulderblades, sending her headlong. There was the sound of more automatic fire, some from Dubois' direction, some from the helicopter that was landing nearby. I was almost safe behind the cover of the Range-Rover when I glimpsed Tony, lying ominously still on the ground close to Anna. And there was Johnny and his companion — whose name and function I never got to know — disappearing back along the path that led to the beach. Then I ducked out of sight.

I hid beneath the Range-Rover, cowering there, my head between my knees, listening to the beat of the helicopter blades, feeling the artificial windstorm as it landed. I heard orders being shouted, another familiar voice. But it wasn't until the engines had gone silent and there had been no gunfire for some time that I gingerly stuck my head out and saw several men occupying the clearing that a few minutes earlier had threatened to become my grave-site.

The man who had addressed us through the loud-hailer was standing closest to me. He was the same Chief Inspector Valence Dubois who had met Tony and me at the airport. I tensed, but then I recognised another face, belonging to a man in shorts, polo-shirt, and a Panama hat, whose white, not to say pasty skin, marked him out as a recent arrival from England. He turned just as

I was looking at him, and my eyes met his. Allardyce.

But then I heard a groan. Tony was still alive.

Before I realised what I was doing, I had squirmed out from under the Range-Rover and was making my way to his side. There was blood all over the front of his shirt. His eyes were shut, his mouth twisted in a grimace of terrible concentration. He clutched his hands over his belly, as if holding the life in. A horrible, waxen pallor was already draining the definition from his even-hewn features. I looked down at the man I had loved so much. Pity fought a brief struggle with loathing. Then, by some miracle, both gave way to a strange, distanced tenderness.

"Tony," I murmured with a sigh. I crouched down, put my hands on his shoulders. "Tony . . ."

My husband's eyes fluttered open. A cough racked his chest, and a tiny trickle of blood emerged from the corner of his mouth. He struggled to speak.

"I . . . love you," he said thickly. "I — "

"Tony, do you know who I am?"

Another cough. Then he slowly shook his head.

"Tony," I repeated. "Who am I?"

No answer. He gave what I thought was a shrug, but it turned into a convulsion, and a moment later the trickle of blood became a small cascade. I looked away, felt his shoulders jerk beneath my hands, and when I looked back I knew the life had gone. My husband of a few days was dead. I glanced over at Anna's body, just a few feet away, her face half-turned towards me, unseeing eyes seeming to watch me. A widow and an orphan in an instant.

I rose slowly to my feet. There were tears pouring down my cheeks. I looked at Allardyce. He had seen everything.

"Why did Tony marry me?" I sobbed. "When he never intended — "

Allardyce just stood there, waiting. The next moment I threw myself into his arms, although I knew that my clothes were stained with Tony's blood.

And Allardyce was so patient. He stood there, holding me gently, and waiting.

Eventually I calmed down sufficiently to speak.

"Harry," I said, using his Christian name for the first time. "I thought you had deserted me. I really did."

But he was staring past me. I turned and followed his gaze to Valence Dubois. I looked back at Allardyce, allowed myself a small smile of relief. But he just gently disentangled himself, stepped back, and then nodded to Dubois.

"Anna Julia Freeling," the Saint Theresan said stiffly, with the halting diction of a man who has been rehearsing something for a while but still isn't sure he has it right. "I am taking you into custody at the request of the British authorities, who have reason to believe that you may have committed crimes warranting extradition to the United Kingdom . . ."

I think that's when I collapsed. I don't remember anything else for a very long time.

26

I WAS held in the prison at Port-Choiseul for six weeks while they processed the British extradition request.

I had a good-sized cell to myself, which was very important. My Saint Theresan lawyer was augmented by a solicitor from England, a man recommended by Paddy Mulcahy as one of the best extradition specialists in the country. And Maggie came, visited me, decided that I was who I said I was. Saskia. Once I had recovered from the shock of that day and its consequences, I regained enough optimism to keep going, to begin to fight — for my innocence and, just as importantly, my identity.

During those weeks I learned how difficult it is to prove, *really* prove, who you are when your physical characteristics alone are not the crucial element. Fingerprints, you'll say. No two sets are alike. Maybe. I brought that up.

But if you have no criminal convictions and neither Anna nor I had ever got into trouble with the law before then no prints are on file, so no, there's no way of checking whose is whose. Sample prints were collected, of course — Allardyce flew back to London to supervise all that. Which was when I realised how well the set-up had been organised, and understood how badly I was in trouble.

A coffee mug from my flat. The prints matched those taken from Anna's body. A case from one of my cameras — definitive proof, you would have thought — again, my twin's. Most other things, oddly clean. Wiped. Part of my conspiracy, the police said. And a check at Anna's place revealed only my prints. It didn't matter that I tried to explain how Tony and I had cleaned up the place after it was burgled, which meant that we had handled so many things. They found not a single print of Tony's, you see. And no one was taking me seriously by now.

The envoys of the British Crown exploited this fact to the full. I can see the little courtroom in Port-Choiseul now in my mind's eye, with its fluttering overhead fan keeping time to those dry, matter-of-fact legal voices. The British police representatives. Allardyce. Gwen Carver at his side, cool and unobtrusively sexy. A smattering of stringers for the British press, some agency reporters who scented a case that could run very well on the crime pages, maybe even be worth a colour spread. The lawyer acting on behalf of the British authorities. I'll never forget his plump features, his sharp, ironic eyes peering over half-moon glasses, first at me, then at Maggie.

Had not Anna and Saskia been very close? he rasped. So close that there was scarcely a detail of the other's life with which each twin sister would not be acquainted? And might not Anna have made it her business, if she planned to impersonate Saskia, to perfect such knowledge, even to the extent of acquiring information about the practice and business of photography?

That was the problem, you see. No one contested the fact that Saskia Freeling/Patterson had been duped, persecuted, deliberately driven half-mad. The police knew that Tony, while pretending to rewire the flat during my absence in Saint Theresa, had buried speakers in the wall of our bedroom that played Anna's voice at nights. They knew that with Tony's help the disks had been removed from the computer, then returned, just to convince me that I was becoming deranged. They knew that during my trip down to Cornwall, in a climax to the campaign, I had been called up on my mobile with Anna's voice, and that the 'policeman' who stopped me at the motorway service area was also a plant. Above all, they suspected the existence of bank accounts all over the world where Anna's percentage of the laundered money had been hidden — and as yet remained unrecovered.

No, the sufferings of Saskia were not the problem, although it might have helped me if just one of the supposed conspirators had been there to bear witness in court, to submit to cross-examination. Anna and Tony were dead. Johnny Dubois and his accomplice had simply disappeared.

Zena Dubois appeared for just an hour on the third day. She looked me sadly in the eye — I could tell she knew that I was Saskia, and that the whole thing was a set-up, but she denied having sent a note to me on that last day before Anna and Tony died. More crucially, because she was probably telling the truth about the note, she assured the court that my statement about her brother Johnny's presence at the deaths must be untrue. Just an hour before the killings, he had called her from Miami, where he was at a party with friends — who, naturally, could confirm his alibi. And then the court was asked that Zena be excused further attendance. In December she had suffered a nervous breakdown and was still on heavy medication. A government doctor, supplied by Zena's uncle, the Deputy Prime Minister, attested accordingly, and the judge — also appointed by the uncle — allowed her to be excused. Zena stumbled slightly as she left the court. A burly woman in a sensible dress appeared and ushered her out with a grip that clearly wasn't going to be relaxed in the foreseeable future.

But the really damaging material, which cancelled out even loyal Maggie, who swore I was the real Saskia, and my own performance in the box, which I know rang desperately true, came from none other than Inspector Allardyce.

He looked at me often as he answered questions. Those calm, gently ruthless blue eyes met mine without apparent malice or guile. He described in cold, killing detail, the scene in the clearing that final afternoon, as he had observed it from the police helicopter.

"Chief Inspector Dubois of the Saint Theresan police called out Saskia Patterson's name," he testified. "And it was the other identical twin — not the woman you see here — who responded." He turned and looked earnestly at the judge as he spoke. "In such a situation, in my experience, instinct takes over. The true Saskia Patterson, nee Freeling, attempted to escape in response to Inspector Dubois' urging, and was tragically murdered by unknown gangsters, along with the unfortunate Tony Patterson." He fixed me with those penetrating eyes again. He might as well have got to his feet and pointed a finger, like a medieval inquisitor. But that placid, cool certainty of his was even deadlier, even more damning. "The woman in the dock is Anna Freeling, personally responsible for laundering tens of millions in drugs money and directly or indirectly guilty of murder. I am sure of it."

At the time I was deeply perplexed. Why was he doing this, denying me so brutally and inexplicably? For all the surface irritation, I had liked him, even carried a little torch for him. I had tried to help, but I was frightened and confused and, after what had happened, genuinely a little crazy.

The court recommended that I be extradited to the United Kingdom the following week.

I could hear the bad word going round among the press people in court, and my own lawyers did little to gainsay it. The general opinion seemed to be that I was cooked. With evidence like this against me, once I got back to London my conviction was a racing certainty.

★ ★ ★

I spent the next four days alone in my cell, overwhelmed at first by stunned disbelief, then consumed by abject despair. Maggie came to visit me, but I could not speak to her. She left in tears.

Until on the afternoon of the fifth day, as I lay on my cot with my face to the wall, the wardress entered.

"Visitor for you," she announced.

I started to get to my feet. The visiting room was just along the hall. Then she shook her head.

"No need to get up. Is the police. They talk to you in here. They allowed."

I stayed where I was, sat up on my cot, staring at the door. It opened again, and in walked two men: Chief Inspector Valence Dubois and Detective Inspector Harry Allardyce. The Englishman was carrying a briefcase.

Dubois acknowledged me with his habitual politeness. He stayed by the door, arms folded. Allardyce came towards me, on his way picking up the little wooden chair on which I draped my clothes before I went to bed. He placed it in front of me, sat down and positioned his briefcase on the stone floor beside him. He was too big for the chair. The effect was comical. Or not. Depending on your mood, and mine was not humorous.

"Hello, Saskia," he said softly.

For a moment I was struck mute by his casual use of my name. Then, before I could begin to frame a rational response, rage overwhelmed me and I lashed out with my fists. Allardyce had been expecting something of the sort, in his usual knowing way. He grabbed both my wrists before I could make contact with his face. I struggled. Slowly, grimacing slightly with the effort, he forced my hands down and held them on my lap.

"Promise not to hit me," Allardyce said, still pressing down on my hands. He leaned over and his voice dropped to a whisper. "You see, I'm on your side."

I glanced towards Dubois. He was still standing with his arms folded, looking at a point slightly above my head. He had unbuttoned his gun-holster, but his expression was completely neutral, impassive.

Allardyce smiled, released his grip on my wrists. "Don't mind Valence. He's here as an observer. And to make sure no one's listening in."

"Why?" I murmured, finally finding my voice. I knew there was no point in trying to hit Allardyce again. I just wanted this encounter to be over.

"Because this is a private meeting. This is not official." Allardyce looked at me almost kindly. "I daresay you thought I'd gone back to the UK," he said. "Well, I go tomorrow, actually. And you follow two days after that. But . . . " he paused. "Well, I wanted a chat, and things here on Saint Theresa are a little bit more informal, aren't they? I mean, in England you'd have a lawyer present, and I'd have to explain my business and all, and it would be a real drag."

"Why did you lie about me?" I asked suddenly.

"Because it was necessary."

"Did you organise the blonde in the Suzuki on the way down to Cornwall?"

"Maybe."

"Gwen, was it?" No answer. "And the

fake cops?" I persisted. "Pity about the white Sierra. You of all people should have known."

"Ah yes. It was the only car we had available at short notice. We didn't think you'd notice. And you didn't at the time."

"No. Not until I did a little homework."

"Yes. Had us worried for a bit there."

"Stop fooling around, Inspector," I said with sudden passion. "I want to know why."

"I'm coming to that. Patience."

I shook my head, half-turned away. Allardyce had a sadistic streak. He was playing with me.

"What do you want?" I asked coldly.

"The build-up's been complicated, but from here on in the answers get straightforward," Allardyce said. He was still smiling, but his eyes were expressionless. "I want a deal."

"A deal? After everything that's happened? After what you did to my sister, to Tony, to me?"

"Let's be realistic, Saskia," Allardyce said. He seemed offended. Really. "You're up for life. Plus a stiff minimum recommendation, the way the climate is at the moment. Murder. Concealing the proceeds of money-laundering."

"But I don't know where the money is," I said. "I genuinely have no idea."

"Exactly."

Allardyce was pleased with himself. So very pleased. I wanted at that moment to kill him, but I wanted even more to survive.

"You used Anna and Tony and then threw them away," I said. "You and the big people, the untouchables with the government offices and the nice titles. Tony always said you were a user — I know that was his part of the act, making me distrust you so I'd trust him all the more, pretending to dissuade me from helping the investigation, though of course you all knew that ultimately I'd never be able to resist staying involved." I closed my eyes briefly, for a moment paralysed by the memory of those emotionally-charged conversations with Tony, the knowledge that every one of them had been based on unalloyed manipulation and lies. Then I forced myself to continue. "All the same, deep down I think that poor sap of a man knew the score, knew you were a dangerous ally."

Allardyce shrugged.

"Did Tony actually ring you that last afternoon?"

"It wasn't necessary. We knew where you'd be at the end. The whole thing was a set-up. You were meant to come to Eugénie Bay."

"But you weren't," I said. "Not so far as Tony and Anna knew. She was genuinely surprised to see you and that helicopter and your friend Chief Inspector Dubois. That's when she knew who her real enemy was!" I paused, took in Allardyce's faint little half-smile of confirmation, then added softly: "How did Johnny Dubois know which one of us to shoot?"

"He made it his business to notice those vital little differences. Such as, though probably you never realised it, Anna had a scar on her leg. She cut herself climbing aboard Johnny's boat all those weeks ago. Johnny dressed it for her."

"You bastard."

"Anna would happily have killed you, Saskia."

"I loved her!"

Allardyce looked at his watch, sighed. "Don't torment yourself, Saskia." He looked at me with his clear blue eyes and seemed almost genuinely sympathetic. "I didn't enjoy what happened. But it was necessary. Regrettable, but necessary."

"So cold," I said. "So efficient."

Allardyce didn't bother to answer. In fact, he was beginning to look slightly bored. Tony and Anna were both in the past. Dealt with. He reached for the briefcase, pulled out a substantial-looking document and put it on his lap.

"Now, this document here is a power of attorney," he said.

I reached out to pick it up, but Allardyce put his hands over it and made a warning face.

"Oh no, you don't need to read it. Really."

"So why show it to me?"

"You just need to sign it, Saskia, at the bottom of the final page."

"And what happens afterwards?"

"Certain doors will be unlocked. All

manner of things will become possible."

"For me?"

"Not at first, no. I'm talking — metaphorically — about gaining access to certain bank deposits."

"Anna's secret accounts?" I asked softly.

"Does it matter?" Allardyce looked at me very intently. This was his moment. "Saskia, the doors you want to open are the ones at the Old Bailey, aren't they? The doors that let you back on the street as a free woman." He paused, milking every ounce of effect. "You put your name on this document, and your wish will be granted."

"How?"

"Oh, evidence will change. The main police witness might decide you're not Anna Freeling after all, but really her innocent sister. My evidence was very effective at the extradition hearing. I could get you a life sentence at the Old Bailey. Easily."

I suddenly heard footsteps outside. Chief Inspector Dubois moved quickly; he opened the door and growled something commanding in patois. There was an apologetic female voice and the footsteps receded again.

"Well?" said Allardyce very quietly. "What's it to be?"

There was a very long silence.

Then I heard my own voice say, surprisingly firmly: "What name do you want me to sign?"

And Harry Allardyce replied: "Your married name. Patterson. Mrs S. Patterson. OK? Smashing."

I took the pen he offered, glanced at the document. It was covered in figures, codes, endless names of financial institutions in strange places, none of which I had time to note or memorise.

I understood completely now the one thing that had continued to mystify me about Tony's role in this conspiracy. Why he had insisted we get married, had hurried the wedding through. It was because the accounts he and Anna had been opening over the past year or two were in the name of 'Mrs S. Patterson'. Perfect. Police forces all over the world would be looking for money that was either lodged in or somehow originated from accounts held by Anna Freeling.

But the money never even went near any account bearing her name. Payments were made straight into the 'Mrs S. Patterson' accounts. The innocuous name Patterson wouldn't stand out to the police trying to trace the money. Even the forename wouldn't link up with Anna's.

"Australia," I said almost dreamily, Allardyce's pen still poised over the document. "Good place to cool off, redirect their lives and perfect their stories, out of the way of old friends who might have spotted little flaws in Anna's impersonation of me. That's why they wanted the Australian visa, with my signature on it." I paused. "But one problem remains," I said, astounded at how matter-of-fact I sounded. "Anna could put her photograph on a fake driving licence or even a passport in my name, but the fact is that my signature doesn't match hers. It couldn't possibly match the specimen signature she'll have given to these banks."

Allardyce was starting to look worried. "She copied your handwriting, Saskia," he said with an edge of impatience, "so everything would match, no matter what.

Anna was a brilliant forger. If she could put Jilly Mattheson's name on important documents, she could do yours with no trouble."

"No matter what, they won't be identical."

"They'll be close enough. And that's our problem, not yours."

I felt like a cynical visitor from another planet. Nothing would surprise me about the people I found here on this earth, nothing.

"How do you know that after I've signed this and got off, I won't take it all back and tell them the truth about you?" I asked.

"Just sign, Saskia," Allardyce coaxed. "Please?"

I looked at him, I looked at Valence Dubois, and with a little flourish I wrote my married name in the space Allardyce had indicated.

The policeman's relief was palpable. He quickly slid the power of attorney document back in his briefcase and snapped it shut, as if to ensure I couldn't snatch it back.

"Why don't you want to answer my

question? About why I shouldn't backtrack on this deal once I'm free," I said.

Allardyce got to his feet, all business now.

"Two reasons," he said. "One, because we'll keep our word to you and therefore expect you to respect your side of the bargain. Two . . . " he flashed me one of his unfathomable little half-smiles " . . . because our people can always find you and point a gun at your window. They chose to miss you last time," he concluded briskly. "Any problems, and next time they won't."

★ ★ ★

Allardyce was right. His evidence turned out to be crucial.

In fact, the case never even came to trial. A couple of months beforehand, when I had been in Holloway for long enough to suspect that Allardyce wasn't going to keep his word, I was suddenly freed. The authorities had dropped the case. Fingerprints that were now definitely identifiable as belonging to

Anna Freeling had come to light during a final search of her office, and they were not the same as mine. Bang. End of story.

Of course, it occurred to me afterwards that Allardyce had conned me back in Saint Theresa. Perhaps something would have happened to vindicate me, even if I hadn't given in to his threats. But how could I have been sure? Just before I was extradited, I was in a weakened, terrified state, where nothing seemed true any more, anything — no matter how unjust or terrible — seemed possible, and I was staring twenty years' prison in the face.

Anyway, in the period immediately after I was released I was too busy fighting off the tabloid press, protecting my privacy, and restoring my sanity to worry too much about all that.

I fled to Trerose. To Maggie, and to the few human beings I could really trust. The Williams family. All the people who knew me from my childhood. I scarcely went out for six months, and it was a year before I could manage even a brief trip back to London. I saw none of my 'glitterati friends', as Anna had always called them. All that had turned to dust. I put the flat on the market soon after, and took a knockdown price to get it off my hands. Too many memories.

It's now two years since Anna and Tony died. I've been with Maggie at Trerose all that time. She's been wonderful. Kind, shrewd, completely respectful of my pain and my dignity alike. The perfect nurse.

And I really am getting better. Maggie knows this. This winter she trusted the strength of my recovery enough to go off to Lanzarote again with her seventy-year-old painter boyfriend — a sweet man, just right for her.

I could have sued the police for wrongful arrest, but that would have meant subjecting us to a second ordeal by tabloid press. And it might also have meant stirring up secrets best left undisturbed. Not for a moment have I forgotten Allardyce's last words to me.

They chose to miss you last time. Any problems, and next time they won't.

And I know Allardyce is a lingering, ominous presence. I've stayed in touch with Paddy Mulcahy, even after paying a legal bill that bit very hard into my inheritance. With his contacts in the profession he's privy to a lot of gossip. Specifically, Paddy heard that Allardyce, promoted to Detective Superintendent after his exploits in the 'Anna Freeling Case', retired from the Metropolitan Police last spring and took up a consultancy job abroad. In the Caribbean — as Special Adviser to the government of Saint Theresa in the 'war against drugs'. I heard Gwen Carver also resigned, in order to remain as Allardyce's assistant in his new job. His — their — luxurious new life in the sun.

Yes, I could be bitter about everything. Perhaps I would be. If I hadn't started taking photographs again in a modest way, starting during a day out above the rocks at Black Head, shooting pictures of the Green Cormorants who nest there. And, walking back towards Coverack, fallen in with a quiet man, a little older than me, who had his arms full of strange-shaped driftwood he had gathered from some of the remote little coves in that stretch of coast. With his burden of gnarled logs and his faintly embarrassed expression, Nick Roper was a perfect subject for a quick portrait. He told me he was a landscape gardener by trade, a sculptor by inclination, and a loner by necessity. And we ended up having a pasty and a drink together at the pub down in the village.

That was a year ago, and we're still seeing each other. Nick's not flash. He's not even that good-looking, by the dangerously tempting standards of Tony Patterson and Harry Allardyce. But he's good fun, he's clever, he's wonderfully, tenderly loving, and I know he appreciates what I do, not for its glamour but for its worth. Above all, he's in no hurry to take control of me.

We stay over with each other several nights a week. There's been talk of him selling his little cottage and our buying a place together one of these days. Though I've explained that with Maggie getting on, I wouldn't want to desert her. He understands. Anything we do together will be thought through, and it will be strictly half and half.

Ah . . . speaking of which, Nick knows about Anna and Tony and the terrible things that happened.

"I should warn you," I tell him. "In a way you're getting only fifty per cent of me. I mean, there'll always be that shadow. Anna's shadow. Can you live with that?"

Nick says he thinks so, or at least he'll try. And he's sorry things couldn't have been different — that Anna couldn't have been different and that he'll never meet her.

And then, on the nights we're not staying together, he goes back to his place, and I return to Trerose.

It's usually on such nights that I lie quietly in my room under the eaves, marooned between waking and sleeping, and I think I hear a sound on the landing. Something like a laugh, or maybe a playful whisper.

I tell myself it's just the wind rattling Anna's bedroom door, eddying through the rafters.

But I can't fight the urge that makes me slide out of bed and tiptoe across the landing, to sneak in there and join

my other half just like I used to.
The Fiendish Freelings. Anna and Saskia against the world. Paradise Lost.

THE END

***Other titles in the
Ulverscroft Large Print Series:***

TO FIGHT THE WILD
Rod Ansell and Rachel Percy

Lost in uncharted Australian bush, Rod Ansell survived by hunting and trapping wild animals, improvising shelter and using all the bushman's skills he knew.

COROMANDEL
Pat Barr

India in the 1830s is a hot, uncomfortable place, where the East India Company still rules. Amelia and her new husband find themselves caught up in the animosities which seethe between the old order and the new.

THE SMALL PARTY
Lillian Beckwith

A frightening journey to safety begins for Ruth and her small party as their island is caught up in the dangers of armed insurrection.

THE WILDERNESS WALK
Sheila Bishop

Stifling unpleasant memories of a misbegotten romance in Cleave with Lord Francis Aubrey, Lavinia goes on holiday there with her sister. The two women are thrust into a romantic intrigue involving none other than Lord Francis.

THE RELUCTANT GUEST
Rosalind Brett

Ann Calvert went to spend a month on a South African farm with Theo Borland and his sister. They both proved to be different from her first idea of them, and there was Storr Peterson — the most disturbing man she had ever met.

ONE ENCHANTED SUMMER
Anne Tedlock Brooks

A tale of mystery and romance and a girl who found both during one enchanted summer.

CLOUD OVER MALVERTON
Nancy Buckingham

Dulcie soon realises that something is seriously wrong at Malverton, and when violence strikes she is horrified to find herself under suspicion of murder.

AFTER THOUGHTS
Max Bygraves

The Cockney entertainer tells stories of his East End childhood, of his RAF days, and his post-war showbusiness successes and friendships with fellow comedians.

MOONLIGHT AND MARCH ROSES
D. Y. Cameron

Lynn's search to trace a missing girl takes her to Spain, where she meets Clive Hendon. While untangling the situation, she untangles her emotions and decides on her own future.

NURSE ALICE IN LOVE
Theresa Charles

Accepting the post of nurse to little Fernie Sherrod, Alice Everton could not guess at the romance, suspense and danger which lay ahead at the Sherrod's isolated estate.

POIROT INVESTIGATES
Agatha Christie

Two things bind these eleven stories together — the brilliance and uncanny skill of the diminutive Belgian detective, and the stupidity of his Watson-like partner, Captain Hastings.

LET LOOSE THE TIGERS
Josephine Cox

Queenie promised to find the long-lost son of the frail, elderly murderess, Hannah Jason. But her enquiries threatened to unlock the cage where crucial secrets had long been held captive.

THE TWILIGHT MAN
Frank Gruber

Jim Rand lives alone in the California desert awaiting death. Into his hermit existence comes a teenage girl who blows both his past and his brief future wide open.

DOG IN THE DARK
Gerald Hammond

Jim Cunningham breeds and trains gun dogs, and his antagonism towards the devotees of show spaniels earns him many enemies. So when one of them is found murdered, the police are on his doorstep within hours.

THE RED KNIGHT
Geoffrey Moxon

When he finds himself a pawn on the chessboard of international espionage with his family in constant danger, Guy Trent becomes embroiled in moves and countermoves which may mean life or death for Western scientists.

TIGER TIGER
Frank Ryan

A young man involved in drugs is found murdered. This is the first event which will draw Detective Inspector Sandy Woodings into a whirlpool of murder and deceit.

CAROLINE MINUSCULE
Andrew Taylor

Caroline Minuscule, a medieval script, is the first clue to the whereabouts of a cache of diamonds. The search becomes a deadly kind of fairy story in which several murders have an other-worldly quality.

LONG CHAIN OF DEATH
Sarah Wolf

During the Second World War four American teenagers from the same town join the Army together. Forty-two years later, the son of one of the soldiers realises that someone is systematically wiping out the families of the four men.

THE LISTERDALE MYSTERY
Agatha Christie

Twelve short stories ranging from the light-hearted to the macabre, diverse mysteries ingeniously and plausibly contrived and convincingly unravelled.

TO BE LOVED
Lynne Collins

Andrew married the woman he had always loved despite the knowledge that Sarah married him for reasons of her own. So much heartache could have been avoided if only he had known how vital it was to be loved.

ACCUSED NURSE
Jane Converse

Paula found herself accused of a crime which could cost her her job, her nurse's reputation, and even the man she loved, unless the truth came to light.

CHATEAU OF FLOWERS
Margaret Rome

Alain, Comte de Treville needed a wife to look after him, and Fleur went into marriage on a business basis only, hoping that eventually he would come to trust and care for her.

CRISS-CROSS
Alan Scholefield

As her ex-husband had succeeded in kidnapping their young daughter once, Jane was determined to take her safely back to England. But all too soon Jane is caught up in a new web of intrigue.

DEAD BY MORNING
Dorothy Simpson

Leo Martindale's body was discovered outside the gates of his ancestral home. Is it, as Inspector Thanet begins to suspect, murder?

A GREAT DELIVERANCE
Elizabeth George

Into the web of old houses and secrets of Keldale Valley comes Scotland Yard Inspector Thomas Lynley and his assistant to solve a particularly savage murder.

'E' IS FOR EVIDENCE
Sue Grafton

Kinsey Millhone was bogged down on a warehouse fire claim. It came as something of a shock when she was accused of being on the take. She'd been set up. Now she had a new client — herself.

A FAMILY OUTING IN AFRICA
Charles Hampton and Janie Hampton

A tale of a young family's journey through Central Africa by bus, train, river boat, lorry, wooden bicycle and foot.

THE PLEASURES OF AGE
Robert Morley

The author, British stage and screen star, now eighty, is enjoying the pleasures of age. He has drawn on his experiences to write this witty, entertaining and informative book.

THE VINEGAR SEED
Maureen Peters

The first book in a trilogy which follows the exploits of two sisters who leave Ireland in 1861 to seek their fortune in England.

A VERY PAROCHIAL MURDER
John Wainwright

A mugging in the genteel seaside town turned to murder when the victim died. Then the body of a young tearaway is washed ashore and Detective Inspector Lyle is determined that a second killing will not go unpunished.

DEATH ON A HOT SUMMER NIGHT
Anne Infante

Micky Douglas is either accident-prone or someone is trying to kill him. He finds himself caught in a desperate race to save his ex-wife and others from a ruthless gang.

HOLD DOWN A SHADOW
Geoffrey Jenkins

Maluti Rider, with the help of four of the world's most wanted men, is determined to destroy the Katse Dam and release a killer flood.

THAT NICE MISS SMITH
Nigel Morland

A reconstruction and reassessment of the trial in 1857 of Madeleine Smith, who was acquitted by a verdict of Not Proven of poisoning her lover, Emile L'Angelier.

SEASONS OF MY LIFE
Hannah Hauxwell
and Barry Cockcroft

The story of Hannah Hauxwell's struggle to survive on a desolate farm in the Yorkshire Dales with little money, no electricity and no running water.

TAKING OVER
Shirley Lowe and Angela Ince

A witty insight into what happens when women take over in the boardroom and their husbands take over chores, children and chickenpox.

AFTER MIDNIGHT STORIES,
The Fourth Book Of

A collection of sixteen of the best of today's ghost stories, all different in style and approach but all combining to give the reader that special midnight shiver.